Tyler pushed back the sleeve of his denim jacket and looked at his watch, puzzled. 8:15 A.M. He'd left Tucson late last night and driven hard to get here. Where could they be? He noted the back door was ajar and pushed it open wider. "Kit?" No answer.

He heard a car and sprinted around the house just in time to see Kit step out of a taxi. His heart jolted at how tired and stressed she looked as she paid the driver.

"Kit!"

She turned, and her face lit up in a way that gratified his heart even as the weary shadows under her eyes dismayed him. "Tyler!"

They met in the middle of the front lawn, unmindful of wet grass underfoot or wind-whipped rain slapping their faces. There were kisses and hugs and flurries of breathless questions, until Tyler held her at arm's length and teased lightly, "What are the neighbors going to think about this wild display of affection so early in the morning?"

She smiled, but it was an uncharacteristically gaunt smile. "What the neighbors think is the least of my worries."

A PALISADES CONTEMPORARY ROMANCE

CANYON

Lorena McCourtney

PALISADES

PALISADES IS A DIVISION OF MULTNOMAH PUBLISHERS, INC.

CANYON
published by Palisades
a division of Multnomah Publishers, Inc.

© 1998 by Lorena McCourtney
International Standard Book Number: 1-57673-287-8

Cover illustration by Paul Bachem/ArtWorks, Inc,
Design by Brenda McGee

Scripture quotations are from:
The Holy Bible, New International Version
© 1973, 1984 by International Bible Society,
used by permission of Zondervan Publishing House

Palisades is a trademark of Multnomah Publishers, Inc.,
and is registered in the U.S. Patent and Trademark Office.

Printed in the United States of America

For information:
MULTNOMAH PUBLISHERS, INC.
POST OFFICE BOX 1720
SISTERS, OREGON 97759

98 99 00 01 02 03 04 — 10 9 8 7 6 5 4 3 2 1

With thanks from the author to the crew of Wilderness River Adventures for a fantastic raft trip through the Grand Canyon several years ago, and special thanks to June Sanderson, Mike Reyes, and Paul Jones at Wilderness River Adventures for their answers to the many questions I asked while doing research for this book. With the qualification that any errors of fact that may have slipped in are strictly the author's own.

Love is patient, love is kind...it keeps no record of wrongs.
1 CORINTHIANS 13:4–5

PART ONE

ONE

Kit veiled her face behind the froth of delicate white lace. "What do you think?" She fluttered the lace below her eyes. "Which one do you like best?"

Tyler groaned. "I think we ought to elope."

Kit lowered the lace and mugged a face at her fiancé. "Now you sound like my father. When we were home on spring break, that's exactly what he suggested. Said he'd furnish a ladder, a map to the nearest justice of the peace, and a big bribe. And it would *still* cost him less than this joining-of-the-dynasties extravaganza we have planned."

"You know the old saying. Father knows best. But we couldn't *really* elope, of course," Tyler added in hasty response to Kit's semiferocious scowl. "But, uh, just out of curiosity, did he say exactly how big a 'big bribe'?"

Kit laughed and swatted him with the butterfly-wisp of lace. "And you know neither of you means a word of all your grumbling. You're looking forward to seeing me walk down the aisle in a white gown every bit as much as Dad is looking forward to giving me away."

Tyler grinned. "Yeah, you're right," he admitted. He draped a length of patterned lace around her neck and used it to draw her into his arms. He kissed her on the tip of the nose, his blue eyes gleaming with love and anticipation. "You're going to be the most beautiful bride in the world. It's just that waiting another seven weeks for you to become Mrs. Tyler McCord sometimes seems like forever."

True, Kit agreed, smiling to herself as she noted his exact calculation of the countdown: not a generic couple of months to wait but a precise *seven weeks*. And even though she knew he wasn't serious about eloping, the idea held a certain tantalizing appeal. Forget the bouquet (orchids or roses?), the ring pillow (satin or velvet?), and candles (white or pale pink?). Forget endless decisions about length of veil and pattern of lace and who's in charge of the guest book. Just run off and get married and leap into the stardust-and-sunshine future waiting for them. But impossible, of course.

"Our mothers would be devastated if we eloped," Kit chuckled. "Mine would drown the wedding gown in tears. She'd bury her face in our four-tiered wedding cake and suffocate."

Tyler nodded. "Mine would use the tires of our elopement car for target practice. Then she'd make us eat some of her awful hot-dog and green bean casserole."

They looked into each other's eyes and laughed again. Their mothers were as different as Pavarotti and Garth Brooks, cherries jubilee and cherry Jell-O, four-poster bed and sleeping bag on the ground. Kit's mother, Andrea, had already designed and hand created the bridesmaids' dresses and was now working on the wedding gown. Rella, Tyler's mother, had restored the antique carriage in which Tyler and Kit would leave the church and was now breaking her saddle horse to harness to pull the carriage. But the two mothers were united in their anticipation of all the pomp and circumstance of this wedding.

"I love you," Tyler said huskily. His arms tightened around her, and he kissed her with all the depths of the passion they kept under taut control these last long weeks.

"I love you," Kit repeated, the words coming out more shaky than she expected, her eyes riveted on his. "Now and forever."

His arms briefly arched her body hard against his before giving her an almost hasty release. He glanced at his watch. "But right now I gotta run." He picked up his books where he'd dropped them on the arm of the sofa. "I have to see some guys about some, umm, lab notes and stuff."

Kit smiled as she went to the open window and watched Tyler emerge from the front door of this old, Victorian style house that had been converted into apartments for students. Lab notes and "stuff," indeed. Tyler was too open and honest to carry out even this minor deception successfully. He was getting together a birthday party surprise for her tomorrow night.

Her heart swelled with love and pride as she watched from the third-story window as he strode toward his battered pickup. Long-legged and lean and just a little disreputable looking in his baggy old khaki shorts and T-shirt, curly blond hair not quite unruly, but, as usual, right on the edge of it. All man, all *hers!*

She didn't remember until then that he hadn't chosen one of the three samples of lace her mother had sent. Probably just as well, she decided. The lace samples had no doubt all looked alike to him. Not that it mattered. Even if Tyler McCord couldn't tell burlap from satin, he'd always be the love of her life.

She watched the pickup pull away, Tyler's sinewy arm lifting from the window in a good-bye wave. She stood at the window a few minutes longer, savoring the blue dusk of the spring evening and lightly caressing the diamond ring on her left hand. A faint ripple of music floated across the housetops from the University of Arizona campus a few blocks away, and from another direction came the evening jangle of Tucson traffic. The day had been hot even by spring-in-the-desert standards, but with the sun below the horizon, the air now took on a delicious coolness.

Her roommates Kelli and Autumn would be home soon, filling the apartment with lights and chatter, but for a moment Kit closed her eyes and imagined next fall when just she and Tyler would be sharing the apartment as husband and wife. A wave of pure, almost giddy happiness engulfed her. She had it all. The love of the greatest guy in the world, a dreamy fantasy of a June wedding, a summer of fun and excitement piloting rafts on the river…and tomorrow she turned twenty-one!

She started to turn away from the window—she had a business law exam to study for on Monday—but stopped short when a familiar but completely unexpected figure stepped out of a car that pulled up to the curb. After a moment to be certain she wasn't mistaken, she flew out the apartment door and down the two flights of stairs to meet him on the old-fashioned front porch.

"Dad!"

"Princess!"

He wrapped her in his usual bear hug, picked her up, and swung her around as if she were still ten years old. Then he held her at arm's length, inspecting her short and curly, almost black hair and blue eyes and pixie face as if it had been months, rather than the short time since spring break when he'd last seen her. She expected him to say, as he always did with that husky, father-of-an-only-daughter pride in his voice, "Princess, you look more like your mother every day!" But this time he just gave her another hard hug. Even as they started up the stairs and she chattered about his having just missed Tyler, she felt a sudden, inexplicable stirring of uneasiness at this small change in routine. She stopped abruptly at the open door of the apartment.

"Dad, is something wrong? How come you're here?" The river-running season was just getting started; he should be on the Colorado right now, herding a bunch of greenhorn rafters through the rapids and grandeur of the Grand Canyon. "You flew down? And Mom didn't come?"

"Right."

That figured. Andrea didn't mind flying in big commercial planes, but she'd always been apprehensive about the single engine, four-seater Cessna that Ben used for both business and pleasure. But for adventure-loving Ben, the fun of flying came second only to river-running. Tyler's father used to laugh and say that Ben would fly from home to the grocery store if he could.

"Let's go inside." Ben Holloway closed the apartment door behind them, a man who still moved swiftly and lightly in spite of the silver frost in his hair and a few pounds added around the midsection of his muscular body.

Kit still felt inexplicably uneasy. "Mom's okay, isn't she?" Andrea's health wasn't fragile, but she had food allergies that occasionally gave her problems.

"Andrea's fine," Ben assured her.

Kit's momentary apprehension vanished in sudden delight. She wrapped her arms around him and pressed her cheek against his big chest. "Then I know why you're here. You came to surprise me for my birthday!"

"Your birthday. Sure, your birthday!"

She switched on the light in the dusk-dim apartment just in

time to see the guilt flood his face and realize he hadn't even remembered her birthday, much less come in honor of it. She felt a larger ripple of alarm.

"I'm sorry, Princess, I didn't have time to get you a nice present, but—" He dug a fifty-dollar bill out of his billfold and thrust it at her. "Buy yourself something pretty and frivolous."

She looked at the wrinkled bill in dismay. Her Dad, who always knew exactly the right gift to give her, from a new barrel-racing saddle on her thirteenth birthday to a second-hand Jeep Cherokee for Christmas the year after she turned sixteen, her wonderful Dad offering her cold, impersonal *cash*? He added a second fifty-dollar bill as if thinking, from her unmoving reaction, that the first one must not be enough.

"I guess you didn't come for my birthday after all, did you?" Even to her own ears her voice sounded little-girl sulky, and she guiltily replaced it with something more cheerfully mature. "But since you're here, can you stay for the weekend? I think Tyler is planning a surprise birthday party for tomorrow night."

"Well, uh, no, I can't stay. We have a river trip taking off Sunday morning." Ben dropped the two bills on the kitchen table and returned the wallet to his pants pocket. "I have to talk to you about something."

Next he was going to say, "Let's sit down," she realized, and she felt a rough surge of panic. People always said, "Let's sit down" when there was something terrible to talk about. She saw him glance at the sofa, but he didn't move in that direction. He just stood there, one hand raking through his thick hair. His throat moved in a convulsive swallow.

"This is hard, Princess. Really hard."

Financial problems? Cancer? Her throat closed in sudden fear. The possibility of a deadly heart attack like the one that had killed Tyler's father three years ago? Never in a lifetime would she have guessed his next words.

"Your mother and I have separated. I saw a lawyer and started divorce proceedings yesterday."

"Divorce?" She repeated the word in an incredulous gasp, then

15

a choked whisper. "*Divorce?*" She couldn't remember her parents ever even having a fight.

"I'm sorry, Princess. I know it's a shock. But you're all grown up now, and you and Tyler are getting married in June, so it isn't as if it will really affect you."

Kit felt a stirring of mingled anger and humiliation. Did he really think she was so immature and self-centered that she'd think only of *herself* at a time like this? The meaning of his earlier words also stabbed through her. *He* had seen a lawyer about divorce proceedings. *He* was doing this!

"What about Mom?" she cried. "Don't you think it's going to have an effect on *Mom?* Why are you doing this?" In sudden frustration she slammed her fist against the table. The fifty-dollar bills jumped and fluttered to the floor. She didn't pick them up.

"Kit, even you must have noticed over the years how different your mother and I are." Ben's voice held an uncharacteristic note of pleading. "She hates the river. The few times she went along, she was miserable every inch of the way. I love running the river. It's my life."

Sure, Kit knew that difference. She loved running the wild rapids of the Colorado River through the Grand Canyon too. She and Tyler would become full partners in the river-guide business called Canyon Cowboys when they graduated from college next year. They were already thinking how they might expand the business into offering high-adventure rafting expeditions in South America or Alaska. She'd sometimes even been impatient with her mother's aversion to the river and her objections to Kit's taking the National Parks Service test to progress from being a "swamper" trainee to full-fledged lead pilot the summer after she turned eighteen. But that had nothing to do with this! These were her parents. They *belonged* together.

"You can't break up just because Mom doesn't like rafting the river!" she argued wildly. "My roommate Kelli's father is a plumber, and her mother doesn't go along handing him wrenches!"

"It's more than that, Princess. Much more." His voice sounded heavy, weighted. "Please, try to understand."

"I don't know what there is to understand! What will you do?

What will Mom do?" She determinedly did not let that immature little girl inside her wail in self-centered pain, *What will I do? What's this going to do to our wedding?*

"I'll go right on with Canyon Cowboys, of course. You and Tyler will earn most of what you need for college next year working for us on the river this summer, and I'll help out if you come up short. And I've already talked to my lawyer about paying alimony to Andrea for a year or two, until she…"

"Until she what?" Kit challenged as his confident plan faltered and stumbled. Never had her mother worked outside the home.

"There are training programs for women who need to find a career later in life."

Kit couldn't believe what she was hearing. He was abandoning his wife to a *training program?* "Maybe she won't give you a divorce!"

"It doesn't work that way these days, Princess. One partner in a marriage can delay and complicate things, but the other person *can* get a divorce."

Kit shook her head helplessly. "I just can't believe it." The room around her felt vaguely unreal, as if it were dissolving into an insubstantial mist. The overhead light shimmered in a strange fog.

"Andrea may want to leave Page, of course—"

Kit blinked in the peculiar misty light. "Why would she want to do that?" The suggestion sounded like another plank ripping from a leaky lifeboat already sinking beneath her feet. The little town of Page in northern Arizona had always been their home. She had been born there. It was where she and Tyler would make their home.

"You know Andrea came from the city originally. She's never complained, but I know she's missed some of the advantages of city life that aren't available in Page. Looking back, I can see it was a mistake to drag her out here."

"I don't think you 'dragged' her!"

Kit knew the story of how her parents had met. Andrea, raised by a stern great-aunt after her parents were killed in a car accident, had grown up in a genteel poverty of faded wealth. She was living at home while attending a small Philadelphia college on scholarship when Ben roared into her sheltered life. He'd gone back east to visit his old boyhood friend and rodeo buddy, Frank McCord, who'd married and moved to Philadelphia to work in his brother-in-law's car repair shop. Andrea brought her great-aunt's old Buick in for carburetor work while Ben was hanging around the shop, and it was a love-at-first-sight courtship that blossomed into marriage only three weeks later. So far as Kit knew, her mother had never regretted the decision that had changed her life so instantly and totally.

Not so, apparently, for Ben. But, with sudden, nerve-gnawing intuition, Kit knew that there was more to this than he was telling her.

"You're hiding something! What is it you aren't telling me?"

"I'm not hiding anything, Princess. I'm getting to the rest of it. But I know you're going to find what else I have to tell you even more upsetting and difficult to understand." He braced himself with a deep breath and dropped the bombshell that exploded Kit's world. "As soon as the divorce is final, Rella and I will be married."

Kit couldn't move, couldn't breathe. Her chest compressed around her lungs, her mind was numb. "You are going to marry *Tyler's mother?*" Stunned disbelief blocked all other emotion.

"Stepmother."

Kit barely heard the murmured correction. She'd always known Rella was actually Tyler's stepmother, of course, but Rella had been his mother since before Kit and Tyler met in third grade, and what did it matter anyway? Did her father think this fact somehow made a difference in the appalling specter of what he was telling her? She rephrased the question, as if different wording could perhaps change the outcome. "You're abandoning Mom to marry *Rella?*"

The answer was defensive but not indecisive. "If you want to put it that way, yes."

"How *could* you? How *can* you?" Kit's stomach churned on the verge of outraged revolt. She leaned one hand against the table for support and pressed the other hard against her abdomen. "I don't understand! When we were home on spring break, everything was fine—"

"No, everything wasn't fine. Rella and I just hadn't decided yet we couldn't go on the way we were, that we had to do this."

Kit let go of the table and backed away, hot fury now blazing through her shocked disbelief as she realized what this meant. This wasn't some sudden, misguided attraction between her father and Rella; this was a long-term, ongoing *affair*. Visions of Ben and Rella working together all those years, sneaking away from a crowd of river rafters to be alone together, surreptitiously meeting at the ranch house outside Page...

"How long has this been going on? Ever since Tyler's father died? Or maybe before, maybe that's what gave him his heart attack, finding out you and his wife were carrying on behind his back!"

"Kit, no! I swear! It's only been since Frank died. We tried hard to fight it. But we love each other."

"*Love!*" Kit scornfully spat out the word. "Why don't you call it what it is? Cheating. Unfaithfulness. *Adultery!*"

Ben's sun-weathered face paled, but he didn't deny her searing accusations. "Kit, you're not a baby anymore. You know these things happen between men and women." He gave her a surprisingly speculative appraisal. "You and Tyler—"

"Tyler and I have *never* done what you and Rella have obviously been doing all along," Kit flared fiercely. It hadn't been easy for her and Tyler, and sometimes they had almost weakened. Their relationship was close and of long standing, both their physical and emotional feelings were deep and powerful. But she and Tyler were both committed to the biblical principles of the sanctity of sex within marriage and had controlled their desires. And her father should have been just as strong!

Ben momentarily looked as if he might offer more arguments or rationalizations about his relationship with Rella, but he didn't. He simply leaned against the kitchen counter and folded his arms across his chest. "Rella and I love each other. We're getting married as soon as we can. That's it." His tone added an unspoken challenge: take it or leave it.

"Does Tyler know anything about this?"

"Rella is telling him. I dropped her off at his apartment while I came here."

"Does Mom know about you and Rella?"

Ben's cowboy-booted feet shuffled uncomfortably, but his voice was unyielding when he said, "Yes. I told her yesterday."

Kit's heart suddenly ached for the pain and bewilderment her mother must be feeling. Pain that Ben was ruthlessly ignoring! "Have you moved out yet?"

"I've already taken most of my things to Rella's place."

"You're going to live together before you get married?"

"Yes."

In spite of her horrified question, his answer didn't really surprise Kit; in the back of her mind she'd already guessed it. Yet it added another shock wave to those that had already almost flattened her. Ben Holloway, trusted husband, pillar of Page society, everybody's friend. Ben Holloway, her *father*, the solid rock of her life, the man she'd always subconsciously acknowledged was the model for the man she'd choose to marry someday. *Ben Holloway, walking out on his wife and moving in with the widow of his dead business partner.*

And Rella, oh, Rella! Kit's heart twisted with fresh anguish. Rella, her friend and role model and sometimes counselor. Rella, who'd trained Kit and her horse to a local barrel-racing championship. Rella, who'd held her and told her to be patient, that Tyler would get over his hurt and anger the time she'd foolishly broken up with him to date another guy in high school and then realized what a mistake it was. Instantly she fiercely rejected the unacceptable jolt of pain. That wasn't the real Rella! This woman she'd never known, this woman who'd ruthlessly stolen another woman's husband, this was the *real* Rella.

"And you're telling me Mom is fine with all this, that she's giving you her blessing?" Kit challenged.

"She's upset, of course." Ben's feet shuffled again, the sole of one boot squeaking on the floor, his eyes not meeting hers. "But she was working on your wedding gown when I was moving my stuff out. And this won't have any effect on the wedding, of course. Things are a little awkward right now, but everything will be settled down by then."

"No, nothing will be 'settled down' by then," Kit contradicted with fierce certainty. In her mind she saw her mother, huddled alone on one end of a pew in the church, Ben and Rella snuggled together at the other end, people gossiping in whispers, faces curious. An ugly circus, a travesty of love. "Don't come to my wedding. Not you, not Rella. Don't come anywhere near the church. I don't want you there."

Ben straightened, and his arms dropped from their folded position across his chest to hang at his sides. He looked stunned, as if he had never considered this possibility. "But I'm going to walk you down the aisle—"

Kit held back the explosion building within her, the feeling that if it once started it would turn into a chain reaction that wouldn't stop. The fury, the outrage, the *scorn* that he'd thought he could do this, and everything would smooth over like water covering a pebble dropped in a lake. She simply said, with fists clenched so hard her fingernails bit into her palms, "No, you're not."

He raked callused fingers through his hair. Looked at his watch. "Look, I know you're upset now, and I understand. But I'll call you in a few days, and we'll talk."

He patted her shoulder with uncharacteristic helplessness and retreated to the door. Kit just stood there, numb and motionless, as his boot steps lightly trod the stairs.

A stray breeze drifted through the open window, and the fallen bills fluttered, gently mocking her with their indifferent presence.

TWO

Tyler's heart plummeted as it hadn't since the first time he tumbled from a bucking raft into a roaring rapids when he was only twelve years old. He stared at his mother's face—stepmother's face, he thought vaguely, as he seldom did—seeing the familiar high cheekbones, streaky blond hair in a ponytail with the inevitable escape of loose strands, eyes the same sky blue as his own, tanned and faintly freckled complexion devoid of makeup. A pioneer face, he'd always secretly thought admiringly, strong and beautiful. Yet now she was telling him...

He shook his head in disbelief. "You can't be serious!"

Beyond the door of the bedroom one of his roommates howled in outrage as the wrong team scored on the TV game. In here, Tyler felt as if he'd just found out the world wasn't round after all.

"It isn't a decision we made lightly, Ty." Rella's competent hands gripped the rail at the foot of his old metal bedstead, her white knuckles showing the strain in spite of her composed face. "I know you find it shocking, but..."

"I find it more than shocking. I find it *wrong!*" he exploded. "How can you do this to Kit's mother? You've been friends for years."

"Ty, we tried not to let it happen, but we *love* each other!"

"Then you didn't try hard enough, because love doesn't turn wrong into right!"

Color flared in her cheeks, but she didn't back down in the face of his accusing anger. She was almost as tall as he, athletic, fearless on the river, their coloring so similar that no one would guess they weren't mother and son by blood. Her gaze flashed to the open Bible on his nightstand. "You think right and wrong are so easy to separate, don't you, Ty? You stand on your Ten Commandments and righteously decide it's all black and white, no shades of gray. But it isn't that way in real life! When two people

22

love each other the way Ben and I do…"

Tyler didn't repeat the stand he'd already taken against that argument. He put his hands on Rella's shoulders, his voice softening. "Mom, I know how devastated you were when Dad died. I know how difficult it's been for you. But you jumped in and took Dad's place in Canyon Cowboys, and you've done a fantastic job of both helping run the business and guiding on the river. I know how lonely you've been…"

She threw up her arms, brushing his aside, blue eyes sparking. "Don't patronize me, Ty. This isn't about loneliness. It's about *love*."

Tyler's patience evaporated in a fresh blaze of anger. "*Love!* Listen to yourself! You sound like some teenager with a starry-eyed infatuation, or an overwrought character in a sleazy soap opera. Think about other people, not just yourself and this great *love*. You're breaking up almost a quarter century of Ben and Andrea's marriage!"

"You're saying this is all my doing? My fault?"

No. As the old saying went, it took two to tango. Rella and Ben put in long hours working together, both on the river and off. Rella was a vital and attractive woman, and Ben wasn't blind. He'd probably made the first move. But that didn't change the fact that it took only one to stop the dance, and she obviously hadn't done it. "I'm saying if you want a husband, find one of your own! Don't steal someone else's!"

The flushed color drained from Rella's face as Tyler's harsh words thundered between them.

The phone by the bed rang, the incongruous sound of a quacking duck that one of Tyler's roommates had rigged on it. He saw a shadow of troubled guilt tremble across Rella's face.

"That's probably Kit," Rella said, her voice hoarse and strained. "Ben went over there while I came here."

"She's going to take this hard…" Tyler broke off. How was Kit going to take it? She adored Ben. He doubted Ben had ever done anything wrong in her eyes. Tyler had sometimes found it intimidating to realize that she undoubtedly expected him to live up to Ben's example. What would it do to her when her father-hero crashed from his pedestal?

Rella came to him and swiftly kissed his cheek. "I'm sorry, Ty. I know I've disappointed you. Perhaps we should have waited until after you and Kit were married, but we just couldn't continue the deception any longer. I hope you and Kit won't hate us."

She slipped out the door, and Tyler picked up the quacking phone.

"Tyler, Dad was just here..." Kit broke off, her voice anguished and lost, like a little girl wandering alone in some desolate wilderness.

He didn't waste time on the phone. "I'll be right over. I love you," he added roughly even as he wondered if that was enough at a time such as this.

Tyler parked across the street from the apartment, jumping out almost before the pickup stopped rolling. Light flared from the third-floor window, with laughter and the warble of Whitney Houston singing into the spring evening from Kelli's CD player. Kit wasn't there, he knew, not with everything in the apartment so normal.

He found her huddled in her Cherokee parked in the driveway. He slid in beside her and took her in his arms. She wasn't crying, and he had the feeling that was very bad. Kit was an open, emotional person, easy to laugh, easy to cry, and now she was hiding here as if everything had drained out of her.

"I can't believe it," she whispered. "I just can't believe it."

He stroked her hair and kissed her forehead. "Have you talked to your mom yet?"

"I tried to call her, but the line was busy."

"She's probably talking to a friend from church or her arts-and-crafts club." He massaged her bare arm comfortingly. A fresh blare of rap music from a lower-story window suddenly jangled his already taut nerves. "Let's take a drive so we can talk."

Kit didn't agree, but she didn't object when he turned on the ignition. Her body was close against his, her cheek soft against his shoulder. Usually she did snuggle close, but now she simply sagged limply against him, and he had to reach around her to put the stick shift into reverse. He drove out of town, heading for an old dirt road down a gulch that he remembered from a geology field trip.

The moon hadn't risen yet, but starlight bathed the desert saguaro and ocotillo in soft silver by the time he parked in the faint shadow of a lacy palo verde tree. At some other time he'd have taken time to appreciate the glory of God's night, but now he just turned in the seat and put his arms around Kit.

"Hey, let's talk about this, okay?" he urged softly.

"I don't know what there is to talk about." Her face dipped, her voice barely a whisper. "It's all just so…awful. They had an *affair!* What are we going to do?"

"I don't know that there's anything we can do," Tyler admitted reluctantly. "Except pray that they realize how wrong this is and stop before it's too late."

"Prayer doesn't matter to them," Kit said bitterly. "They're not believers."

"Prayer doesn't affect just believers."

But the statement about Ben and Rella not being believers was true, of course. Rella was a wonderful woman in so many ways. No-nonsense as a stepmother, but also cheerful and loving and generous. But Christmas at the McCord household when Tyler was a kid meant Santa Claus and Rudolph the red-nosed reindeer, not Christ's birth, and Easter was bunnies and colored eggs, not resurrection. And Ben? Once, camped on a sandy beach by the river, Tyler had heard him say, in his big, jovial voice, "How could anyone look up at all those stars and not think there's a God?" And Ben's face wasn't totally unfamiliar around church. He got there a few times a year on special occasions, such as back in high school when the Christian youth group Tyler and Kit were in put on a skit or special music. But he more often spent Sunday mornings glued to a football or baseball game on TV. Andrea never nagged at him, although she was active in the church, devoted to missions and Sunday school activities.

Kit stirred in his arms. "I've already done one thing." Her voice held a note of bitter satisfaction.

"What?"

"I told my father that he isn't walking me down the aisle and giving me away. That I don't want him or Rella at the wedding."

Tyler hesitated, not certain of his own stand here. "Will they be married by then?"

"I don't know. I don't know how long a divorce takes. Maybe it would be even worse if they are married. I won't have them there ruining everything for Mom!"

Tyler thought of the long hours of work Rella had put into restoring that antique carriage so he and Kit could make a memorable exit from the church. Which didn't make up for what she and Ben were doing, of course, but…

"Maybe you ought to see how your mother feels about this," he suggested cautiously. "Maybe it's what she wants, too."

How well, he wondered, did any child really know his parents? He'd never have believed Rella could do this. Maybe Andrea *was* eager to get out of the marriage. Yet he couldn't really swallow that. Andrea wasn't insipid or unintelligent; she was a warm and wonderful homemaker and mother. She must have baked a million cookies for school doings, sewed clothes for herself and Kit that looked as if they came from the most expensive boutique in Phoenix; she cheerfully accepted Kit's love of horses and rafting that was so foreign to her own home-centered interests. But she looked to Ben for even the smallest decisions. Tyler remembered his surprise one time when he was at the Holloway house and a distressed Andrea came in to tell Ben the coffeemaker wouldn't work and what should she do? At his house, Rella would never have done such a thing. She'd simply have bought a new appliance, or else taken the old one apart and fixed it herself. How could Andrea get along without Ben?

"I've got to talk to her." Kit straightened, sliding out of his arms, her petite body suddenly tense. "Something's wrong, and I've got to talk to her *now!*"

Tyler wheeled the car in the ruts of the road, swirling a cloud of dust that blotted the stars, and headed back toward town. He thought Kit meant she wanted to get to the apartment and call Andrea as soon as possible, but it turned out that what she meant was *now*.

"There, that phone booth by the laundromat, stop there," she commanded. She sounded on the edge of snapping, like a frayed rope down to its final taut strand.

He stopped the Cherokee, and she jumped out and dashed to the booth. He watched as she tried half a dozen times to get the call through before giving up and returning to the vehicle.

"The line is still busy. I can't get through."

"I'm sure it's good for her to be talking with someone instead of…"

"I didn't know you'd taken Psych 101!" Kit snapped. Then she rubbed a hand across her forehead. "I'm sorry."

Tyler drew her into his arms again. "What we can't do is let all this cause trouble between *us*." Maybe it would be better if they did elope, he added silently to himself. It might save a lot of awkwardness and hard feelings.

"It's just that I feel something is terribly wrong. Mom doesn't talk on the phone for hours at a time."

Back at the apartment, over his protests, Kit sent Tyler home. There was nothing he could do here, she said, and he had to be up early for his weekend job helping an early-bird professor with a research project on desert lizards.

Kit tried to call her mother at ten-minute intervals until midnight. Always that same relentless busy signal. Then she reluctantly dialed Ron Roderick's number. She really didn't know him well because he'd been pastor of their church in Page only since last fall, but she didn't know who else to call at this time of night. As she listened to the phone ringing in that distant house, another jolt of anger and loss ripped through her. Twenty-four hours ago, it would have been Rella she'd call in an emergency—calm, resourceful Rella she'd turn to for help. How could Rella have done this? *How?*

Pastor Ron was out of town, but his wife Elyse unhesitatingly offered to run over and check on Andrea. Kit didn't give her all the ugly details, just that there was a family problem and she was extremely worried about not being able to reach Andrea by phone all evening.

Kit hoped to hear directly from her mother, but after an endless half hour, it was Elyse Roderick who called back.

Elyse sounded guarded. "I just wanted to let you know I'm here with your mother now."

"What's wrong? Is she okay? Is she crying?" The frantic questions tumbled out of Kit. "Why was the phone line busy so long?"

"She's in the kitchen," Elyse soothed. "I'm fixing her a cup of tea."

Kit struggled to stay polite. "May I talk to her, please?"

A few rustles as Elyse carried the phone to the kitchen, then her mother's voice, unnaturally shaky, saying, "Hi, sweetie. How wonderful to hear from you." Andrea spoke as if there was nothing unusual about her daughter calling in the middle of the night.

"Are you okay, Mom? I've been trying for hours to call you, and the line was always busy. Dad was here and told me everything, and I've been so worried about you."

"I'm fine, hon. You and Tyler are okay, aren't you?"

The statement was what Kit wanted to hear, but the synthetic brightness and unnatural shallowness of the banal, I'm-fine-how-are-you conversation instantly ratcheted Kit's already taut nerves a notch tighter. Then Kit realized what her mother was doing.

"Mom, you don't have to try to spare me," she said fiercely. "You don't have to pretend Dad is the great guy I always thought he was. It's out in the open now what kind of man he really is. And what kind of woman Rella is! I've already told him that I don't want either of them at the wedding."

Silence, silence so total that Kit could hear the faint tick-pause-tick of the hands moving on the blue ceramic owl clock in her mother's kitchen. Then Andrea said brightly, "Oh, that reminds me. Did you get those lace samples I sent down?"

Kit stared at the phone in dismay. Her mother was acting as if Ben's desertion and Rella's betrayal simply hadn't happened. In disbelief she heard Andrea chattering on about the merits of the various samples of lace.

Kit finally interrupted. "Mom, may I talk to Elyse again, please?"

"Of course. Oh, here she is now, with some nice, hot tea for me."

More rustles, as if Elyse was carrying the phone out of Andrea's hearing.

"What's going on?" Kit asked frantically. "She's acting as if none of it happened!"

"Kit, what did happen?" Elyse sounded baffled. "When I first arrived she acted so strangely that I almost called an ambulance. The house was dark and I thought she must be in bed, but I tried the door and found it unlocked. That didn't seem right so I let myself in, and she was just sitting in the living room with the lights off and the phone fallen on the floor. Not actually ill, but disoriented. Dazed. Ben is on a river trip, I suppose? Do you know when he'll be back?"

"She hasn't told you anything?"

"I've been scurrying around turning up the heat and getting her into warm clothes."

Disoriented. Dazed. Sitting there alone in the dark and cold. And Ben out living it up with Rella! Kit realized she had the phone cord twisted so tightly around her hand that her fingers were turning numb. No point in trying to hide the ugly truth, she decided grimly. Everyone was going to know it in a day or two.

"Dad has left her. He's filed for divorce. He was down here just a few hours ago to tell me."

"Oh, Kit! I'm so sorry to hear that!"

"He's moved in with Rella, Tyler's mother. They're going to get married as soon as the divorce is final."

Stunned silence. "Oh, Kit... I don't know what to say. I'll get hold of Ron as soon as I can. And I'll stay with Andrea tonight. I don't think she should be alone."

"I don't either. And I'd appreciate it very much if you would stay with her."

"I'll get her to the emergency room immediately if it looks as if she needs medical attention. Pray for her, Kit," Elyse added with sudden urgency. "She's going to need all our prayers to help her through this."

Prayer was what had held Kit together during those agonizing ten-minute intervals between merciless busy signals on the phone, what she was doing with one frightened part of her mind even now.

She tapped her fingers on the phone after she hung up, not trying to decide *what* to do, but how to do it.

THREE

F ly? There were no direct flights from Tucson to Page, so going by plane would mean flying into Phoenix first, then waiting to catch a flight to Page. It might be midday or later before she got there. She could cover the four hundred miles faster than that on her own.

She started to call Tyler to tell him her plans but hung up without dialing. He'd try to talk her out of driving all night or insist on coming with her. And she wasn't certain, given his close relationship to Rella, how his presence might affect her mother right now. She'd just call him later from Page. She scribbled a note telling her roommates she was going home for a few days and anchored it to the refrigerator.

She didn't pack, just grabbed a jacket and was on her way within ten minutes after another brief call to Elyse. Her last act was to retrieve those fifty-dollar bills from the floor. She didn't like touching them. They felt tainted. She'd never buy herself something "pretty and frivolous" with them. But everything was different now; she might need this money.

Traffic wasn't heavy on the freeway, and between headlights she caught glimpses of the desert under glow of moonlight. Saguaro standing sentinel, cholla haloed with deceptively innocent silvery fuzz, mountains ringing the horizon with dark silhouettes. She couldn't enjoy the beauty of the night, but she felt less frustrated now that she was actually doing something rather than uselessly pacing the apartment.

She was too edgy with anger and hurt and worry to fear falling asleep at the wheel as the hours passed. She stopped only for gas and the rest room, not even taking time to eat.

Elyse Roderick met her at the door of the brick house in Page. Under different circumstances Kit probably wouldn't have noticed the drooping gutter over the door and the unpruned shrubbery under a window, but now these blemishes blared her father's neglect as he chose to spend his time sneaking around with Rella.

"How is she?" Kit stepped inside, her voice automatically dropping to a whisper.

"We were up most of the night, but I think she's sleeping now." Sleepless weariness made puffy circles under Elyse's friendly hazel eyes, but her smile was compassionate and warm. She was midgeneration between Kit and Andrea but without children. "I just made fresh coffee. You look as if you could use a cup."

Kit followed Elyse to the kitchen, absentmindedly noting her mother's handiwork along the way. The handwoven wall hanging over the sofa, the fragile porcelain-faced doll with a bead-encrusted Victorian costume on a corner stand, the hand-caned seat of an antique rocking chair. On the window shelves of the cheerful kitchen, pots of African violets bloomed with delicate exuberance. Kit thought of all the violet plants her mother had given Tyler's mother over the years, until Rella had finally laughed and said, "No more. I'm tired of being a plant murderer. They're too delicate for me," and turned to putting pots of sturdy cactus in her windowsills.

Yet Kit was also painfully aware of what she was *not* seeing. Her father's old leather work jacket, with his sweat-stained cowboy hat draped over it, no longer hung from a hook by the back door. His bronc-riding buckles and trophies were gone from the shelf in the dining room, along with the framed cover of a national magazine showing Ben and Tyler's father taking a raft through the wild rapids of Lava Falls.

Kit gratefully accepted a cup of the steaming coffee. She didn't add her usual cream and sugar; she needed it black and strong. "Did Mom talk about what happened?"

Elyse shook her head no. "I had the impression that she felt, if she didn't talk about it, it wouldn't be true." Kit nodded at Elyse's perceptive insight. "But we prayed together."

"Mom prayed?" Kit interjected, relieved that Andrea had perhaps revealed her inner feelings to the Lord, if not to Elyse.

"Well, I prayed," Elyse amended wryly. "Ron will be over this evening. How long can you stay?"

Kit hadn't even thought about that. She had that important

business law exam on Monday, but she could probably make it up. More critical were the philosophy lectures she'd miss. Philosophy was not her strong point and could definitely lower her GPA.

But none of that was as important as helping her mother through this crisis.

"I'll be here as long as Mom needs me," Kit said resolutely.

Elyse hugged her. "You're a wonderful blessing to her." They shared a brief prayer, hands clasped, and then Elyse said, "I'm supposed to be at the day care center today, so I'll run along, unless...?"

"I can manage," Kit assured her. "And thanks again for your help."

Kit tiptoed into the bedroom after Elyse left. It was a softly feminine room, the peach drapes lending a faint blush to the morning light filtering around them. Andrea's petite body looked almost childlike curled under the unrumpled bedspread, the white and gold corner posts of the elegant antique bed looming over her. With sudden intuition, Kit knew her mother's motionless silence didn't necessarily indicate sleep.

Kit knelt by the bed and touched Andrea's shoulder lightly. "Mom?"

Kit didn't know what response she expected. Flood of tears? Hug of gratitude for coming? Maybe even her mother comforting her for this awful thing he had done to them? What she got was that dazed, vaguely disoriented manner Elyse had mentioned. And a terrified feeling that her mother didn't recognize her.

"Hey, Mom, it's me," Kit said softly. She felt momentarily disoriented too, as if some flip in time and reality had made her the mother and Andrea the child.

Andrea slowly sat up and pushed the dark hair out of her eyes. "Oh, Kit, sweetie, how wonderful to see you." She smiled but her voice was unnaturally vague, and she didn't ask what Kit was doing here.

Kit was simply grateful that Andrea had recognized her. "I just thought it would be good if we spent the next few days together."

"Why, yes, that's wonderful. We can decide which lace to use for the sleeves of the wedding gown."

Andrea was acting just as she had on the phone, Kit realized, as if nothing had happened. She fought a panicky burst of help-lessness and uncertainty. What was she going to do? How could she cope with this? She was no nurse, no wise counselor, no psy-chiatrist!

Hot anger with Rella flooded through her. Rella, who could skillfully pilot a raft through the wildest rapids, keep a group of rafters from panicking when a raft hung up on a rock, comfort Kit when her horse was injured in a fence and had to be destroyed; Rella would know what to do here! But she couldn't call on Rella, not now, not ever. *She* had to cope with this. She was all Andrea had now.

Oh, Lord, she cried silently, *help me, help me, help me!*

With cheerfulness snatched out of thin air Kit said, "Have you had anything to eat? How about some nice scrambled eggs and raisin-bread toast?" That was what Andrea had always made for her when she was a child and feeling droopy.

"Oh, I don't think so, dear. I think I'll just rest a bit longer."

Andrea's head slumped back to the pillow. Her eyes fluttered shut, and Kit, not knowing what else to do, helplessly retreated from the room. Maybe she should have let Tyler come along after all.

She dashed to the phone and dialed his apartment number. But he'd be at the professor's lab now, of course, she realized as the answering machine picked up with Tyler's roommate doing his drawly imitation of John Wayne telling the caller to, "Say yer piece, Pil-grim, and we'll git back to yuh." A trio of Christian guys they were, deadly serious they were not. Usually she was amused by the ever changing messages on the machine, but now she wanted to pound the phone in frustration.

"Tyler, this is Kit," she finally said hurriedly. "I'm at home in Page. Call me as soon as you can."

She called Andrea's doctor immediately, thinking a first step was to make certain her mother was physically okay, but the answering service said the office was closed until Monday. They gave her the name of another doctor taking his calls over the weekend. Kit tiptoed back into her mother's bedroom, but this time she was asleep, and Kit decided sleep might do her more good than a trip to a strange doctor.

On the way out of the room, her feet tangled in something lying on the floor. An old red-plaid, flannel shirt of her dad. A memory surged back of a time when she'd gotten sick at grade school, and Ben had come and wrapped his jacket around her and carried her to the car. She'd buried her head under the jacket, feeling so wonderfully secure in the warmth and comforting Daddy-scent of it. Almost unaware of what she was doing, she rubbed the soft flannel against her cheek, reaching for that old feeling of security.

Her gaze lifted to the closet on the far side of the room, the louvered doors open. Andrea's clothes still hung on one side, blouses, skirts, pants, dresses, all neat and orderly, but the other half of the closet gaped empty, an open hole. Only a few abandoned clothes hangers dangled where Ben's clothes had once hung.

What must Andrea have felt as he roamed through the house, carrying away everything of himself, changing *ours* to the irrevocable split of yours and mine, ruthlessly slashing the union of their marriage? He and Rella would be back in Page by now, out at the warehouse on the McCord ranch getting equipment and supplies ready for tomorrow's launch on the river. Thinking only of themselves, uncaring that Andrea lay here alone, lost and hurting and confused. How could they? *How could they?*

He'd dropped the shirt as he was moving out, she realized, and here she was, clinging to it as if it were some precious treasure. With an anguished cry, she threw the shirt to the floor and fled the room.

In the kitchen, she steadied herself with another cup of coffee and spent most of the next hour deep in prayer. Andrea dozed all afternoon. When Tyler called, they came close to an instant battle on the phone.

"Kit, it was an irresponsible thing to do! You could have been carjacked or fallen asleep on the road or..."

"If you want to launch an attack on irresponsibility, go jump on my father and Rella!" Kit lashed back. She needed Tyler's strength and support, not a long-distance lecture! "Look, we can fight about this later if you want. But right now helping Mom is all that matters."

Brief silence, then Tyler gruffly agreed. "Yeah, you're right. I'm sorry I jumped on you. I was just worried. What's going on?"

Kit explained about Elyse Roderick coming to the house, the phone off the hook, Andrea's strange, dazed behavior and peculiar refusal to acknowledge what Ben and Rella had done.

"She's just so...out of it, Tyler! I'm frightened. It's as if she's crawled off into some place in her mind where none of this happened, and she isn't coming out until it all goes away. I don't know what to do!"

"I'll be there by morning." Tyler's take-control, authoritative tone and words slowed the panic roaring through her like a storm wind out of the north. "Keep her calm and quiet. Is she eating?"

"No."

"Keep trying to get something down her. Don't push her to talk, but encourage her if she does want to. She probably just needs time to work this through. I have to make a few arrangements, but I can leave here..."

"No, Tyler, wait."

She desperately wanted him here. Wanted to bury her face against his chest and feel the strength and security of his arms around her, wanted his protection against something ominous that seemed to lurk just outside identification by her senses. Wanted him here because she loved him! But now the panic didn't feel quite so much like a predator waiting to swallow her alive.

Logically she knew he hadn't told her anything she didn't already know about taking care of her mother; it wasn't high-tech advice, just common sense. But just hearing his sensible, practical attitude steadied and reassured her.

"You don't need to come. Pastor Ron should be here before long."

"I want to be there to help you."

His very willingness to drop everything and rush to her revitalized her own strength. "I know. And I'd rather you were here. But she'll surely snap out of this in a few days, and I can manage until then. But there is something you can do."

"Just name it."

"Tell whoever you invited to my surprise birthday party that I can't be there after all."

Tyler groaned. "I was so worried I forgot all about the party. Okay, I'll cancel my order for a carload of pizzas. Though it's probably too late to cancel the cake. Hey, how'd you know about this? It was supposed to be a surprise."

"Because I know *you,* Tyler McCord," she said, the love overflowing like a fountain within her. "And I'm sure you and the guys can figure out something to do with the cake." The eating capacities of Tyler and his roommates made bottomless pits look shallow. "I'm going to get Mom up and try to get some soup down her now, and we'll talk again tomorrow night, okay?"

"Kit, I know this isn't an appropriate moment to say happy birthday, because it's a long way from a happy day. So I'll just say *I love you,*" Tyler said softly.

"That's more important than any birthday." Twenty-one had once loomed as such a momentous milestone in her life. Now she knew she had passed a much more meaningful milestone: she wasn't Daddy's little princess anymore. "I love you, too."

"Do you want to know what your birthday present is?"

Kit thought of past birthdays when her father had teased her for days with mysterious clues about a present. And what had he given her this year? The announcement that he was destroying their family. She swallowed the lump of pain in her throat.

"No, surprise me later," she whispered. She desperately needed a sweet surprise somewhere out there in the future to look forward to.

She got Andrea up, maneuvered her into the shower, helped her dress, and coaxed her to swallow a few spoonfuls of chicken noodle soup. Andrea wasn't uncooperative; she was, in fact, agreeably pliable. But the words Kit had used to describe her to Tyler were all too accurate: *out of it.*

Pastor Ron arrived about seven. Andrea acted cool and remote toward him, but, ever the good hostess even in this strange, disconnected state, she politely offered him coffee and lemon pie. Ron said no, he'd eaten, and they sat in the family room, Ron in Ben's old recliner, Kit and her mother on the sofa. On a shallow level, Andrea could pass for normal, even initiating a stilted conversation about a special musical program coming up at the church.

But several times she lost focus in the middle of a sentence, and over and over, with mechanical precision, she pleated and repleated a fold in the leg of her tailored pants. It was a nervous, fussy gesture totally unlike her usual composure. Kit could see Pastor Ron observing her closely, and finally he suggested, "May I have a few minutes alone with your mother, Kit?"

Kit caught his meaning instantly. Perhaps Andrea would discuss with him subjects she didn't think suitable for discussion with her daughter. "Yes, of course! I'll just run out to my old room and…" Do what? Cry? Rage? Beat the walls? "…and check on some things," she finished lamely.

In her old bedroom she absentmindedly cuddled a tattered doll Andrea had made for her years ago. Tommy the Teddy-Cat Kit had named him, because he was built like a teddy bear, soft and huggable, but his little embroidered face was much too sly and smugly catlike to be a teddy *bear*. He leaked stuffing now, and half his embroidered smile was gone, but there was something comforting about holding him close.

She had slept in the room just a few weeks ago, over spring break, and then it had felt snug and familiar, but now she saw it with newly disillusioned eyes.

Andrea had always wanted her to make the room more girlish, more pink and ruffled, but Kit had clung to a hodgepodge, tomboyish style. Patchwork denim curtains, windowsill lined with chunks of petrified wood she and Tyler had found, her old spurs draped over a barrel-racing trophy, walls decorated with blowups of photos taken on river trips.

Tyler had taken most of the photos. Dramatic shots of soaring cliffs, colors ranging from delicate pastels of sunrise to vivid blaze of sunset. Bits of rock and driftwood arranged by the river into a composition of poetic harmony on the sand; whitewater caught in a split moment of explosion against a rock, the drops like a crown of glory. Tyler's eye for the artistic angle or composition never failed to surprise Kit because, without camera in hand, artistic he was not. His projects in shop were utilitarian and practical; he never noticed a picture hanging crooked on a wall or a jarring clash of colors; a flower arrangement to Tyler meant a fistful of wildflowers in a Mason jar, not some dramatic floral-shop creation. She smiled with a sudden rush of love and tenderness.

Other photos were of Tyler, not by him. One of Tyler and her, each riding the pointed front ends of the inflated pontoons attached to the sides of a river raft, a daredevil caper known as "riding the horn." The raft tilted at a perilous angle in the rapids raging around them and white water sprayed their carefree, laughing faces. Another photo of Tyler and her in dark silhouette against the curved opening of Redwall Cavern. One of Tyler and Ben and Rella frolicking in the Little Colorado, a tributary of the main river, the waters a fantastic milky turquoise color.

In sudden fury, she tore that photo off the wall and ripped it to shreds, picking one up and ripping it again when Rella's face still smiled at her.

A realization that had so far totally escaped her attention suddenly crashed down on her. She wouldn't be guiding on the river as part of the Canyon Cowboys crew this summer. She couldn't, not with Ben and Rella there not just as co-owners and coworkers but as...lovers!...their union brazenly proclaiming their disdain of the moral codes of marriage and friendship.

Her gaze bounced wildly around the room. The bedspread, decorated with copies of cattle brands—Rella had given her that! She yanked it off the bed and dumped it on the floor. The seashell lamp, a present from her father, bought when the Holloways and McCords had taken a trip to Hawaii together one winter. Was her father sneaking around with Rella even then? She tossed the lamp on the bedspread, heard it shatter when she threw the spurs—another gift from Rella!—on top.

Earlier she had sagged with weariness from a night and day without sleep, but in a burst of raw energy she carried everything out the back way to the trash can. She ran back to her mother's bedroom, snatched up the fallen shirt, and slammed it, too, into the trash.

Then she sat on the back steps and cried.

Pastor Ron came to her there. He sat beside her, comforting her with his silent presence rather than words while her shoulders shook with sobs. Kit liked and respected him, but at the moment she desperately wished Pastor Ed, who had been with the church when she first gave her heart to the Lord, was there. Pastor Ron handed her a big handkerchief when the tears finally turned to harsh sniffles.

"I'm sorry," she muttered finally. "Bawling doesn't help anything."

"The Lord knew what he was doing when he made tears," Pastor Ron said gently. "We needn't be afraid to use them."

Kit jumped up, suddenly aware that they had been out here long minutes while her mother was inside alone. "I have to get back to Mom."

He glanced toward the window of the family room. "I can see her from here. She hasn't moved."

Yes, the angle of a mirror in the room reflected Andrea's profile. She still sat motionless on the sofa. Kit had the peculiar feeling that if no one intervened, that was exactly where Andrea would be at midnight tonight, just as she had been last night.

"Did she talk to you about what happened?" Kit asked.

Pastor Ron shook his head. "No. All she'd talk about was you and the wedding. I don't think it's a good idea at this early point to try to *force* her to talk about what's happened with Ben and Tyler's mother. Let her come to it in her own time."

"Do you know her?" Kit asked. "Tyler's mother, I mean."

"No, I don't think we've ever met."

Not surprising, of course. Even when Tyler and Kit were in high school, Rella would only laugh and make some joke about what an "ol' sinner" she was when they tried to get her to go to church with them. She undoubtedly had even less reason to go after Tyler and Kit were away at college, and she was sneaking around with another woman's husband.

Now Kit shook her head helplessly. "What they've done just seems so incredible, so totally incomprehensible." It was the same thought that had been running around her mind like a train trapped on a circular track ever since Ben had told her. "Dad. And Tyler's mother. Cheating on Mom. I don't know what it's going to do to her. I want to help her, I *have* to help her, but…"

"Don't try to take all the burden on yourself, Kit. Lay it on the Lord. Day or night, he's always on call."

Kit nodded. Then she remembered something Pastor Ron had to know because he was officiating at the wedding. "There's been a change in the wedding plans."

"This isn't coming between you and Tyler!" He sounded alarmed.

"Oh, no! He's as appalled as I am. It's just that Dad won't be walking me down the aisle now."

"I see. Will someone else take his place?"

She hesitated briefly before answering firmly, "No."

She'd walk alone. She didn't need Ben Holloway. Not for her wedding. Not for anything. And she'd crawl away from the church on her hands and knees before she put one foot in that carriage Rella had restored.

FOUR

K it and Andrea didn't attend church on Sunday morning. Kit needed the peace of mind and reassurance that being in the house of the Lord always gave her, and she knew everyone there would be kind and tactful, but it was also obvious that Andrea wasn't up to public exposure yet. Tyler called again that afternoon, and they talked and prayed together for almost an hour.

"I guess I wish Mom would rant and rave and throw things," Kit confessed finally. She understood how all this had devastated her sweet, gentle mother, but at the same time she felt frustrated by Andrea's lethargy and remote attitude. And then felt guilty for feeling frustrated. "Sometimes it's what *I* feel like doing."

"Your Mom isn't a ranting, raving, throwing-things kind of person."

Kit smiled wryly, noting that Tyler wasn't saying *she* wasn't that kind of person. "I know. It's just that she's so zombielike about it all, so limp. As if someone could twist her into a pretzel shape and she'd just stay that way."

"Kit, she isn't…suicidal, is she?"

Kit had asked herself the same disturbing question. It was one of the reasons she'd slept on a cot in her mother's bedroom last night and would do so again tonight. "I don't think so. But I'll get her in to see the doctor tomorrow." Even if she had to climb over half a dozen other patients to do it, she vowed.

"Is she saying anything about the breakup yet?"

"No. I guess I can understand why she might not want to discuss Dad and Rella's relationship with me. But when she won't even talk to Pastor Ron about it." She paused, puzzled by something she had sensed even though she couldn't quite pin it down. "Actually, she seems to feel almost hostile toward him."

"It's going to take time," Tyler said, as he had before, a phrase that Kit unexpectedly found more grating than soothing. "I've heard it said that the death of a marriage isn't all that much differ-ent from the physical death of one of the partners. It takes time."

"And someone else's husband for comfort?" Kit suggested bit-terly, thinking that was how Rella had coped with the loss of her husband.

"Castigating them isn't going to help your mom."

"So what am I supposed to do? Run out to the ranch and offer congratulations? Say, 'Never mind that you've broken my mother's heart and turned her life upside down, isn't it wonderful that you're so madly in love'?"

Tyler didn't respond to the remark, instead said, "I think I should come up there."

"You can't miss classes or exams and risk lowering your grades. And you shouldn't miss any of your hours working on Dr. Jorgenson's research project. A strong recommendation from him may be especially important now." Much as she'd like to have Tyler here, she'd thought this through. Guiding on the river with Canyon Cowboys this summer was no longer possible. And join-ing Ben and Rella in a full-time business partnership after gradua-tion was totally unthinkable. It would be fraternizing with the enemy, heaping further betrayal on Andrea. "Everything is changed now. Our whole lives are going to be different."

"You don't know yet when you're coming back?"

"No. But not for a couple of weeks, at least." She'd already lengthened the time from the original few days she'd thought it would take. She heard a small noise from the living room. "I think Mom may be waking up, so I have to hang up now. I'm still trying to get a decent meal down her."

"Okay. Talk to you tomorrow. I love you, Kit. Your mom is a wonderful woman, and the Lord will help her through this."

She could, at least, cook a decent meal, Kit thought with a cer-tain grim satisfaction as she prepared a nicely browned omelet. She'd learned to cook from her mother, who could turn stray vege-tables and leftover pasta into a fantastic dish, or whip up a fairy-tale dessert from a few kitchen staples. As opposed to Rella, who could expertly dress out a deer carcass or barbecue half a beef in an outdoor pit, but whose kitchen meals were as unimaginative as an army cook's. And if Ben had never happened to notice Rella's shortcomings in the kitchen, Kit thought with a sour satisfaction, he could be in for some unhappy surprises.

Kit got her mother in to see Dr. Simonson the following afternoon. He was new in town, having replaced old Dr. Taylor with whom Kit had grown up. Doubting that Andrea would tell the doctor anything about her situation, Kit insisted on a brief conference with him first. After the exam, he reported he found nothing wrong with Andrea physically, prescribed a common antidepressant, and offered a referral to a therapist. Kit said they'd consider the referral, but she was disappointed with the doctor's hurried, impersonal attitude. His big concern appeared to be the status of Andrea's health insurance now that she and Ben were divorcing.

Pastor Ron came by again that evening. There were also calls from concerned friends because word about this local scandal was getting around, and two women from church brought casseroles. Andrea, pleading weariness, avoided seeing or speaking to anyone, leaving Kit to cope with their shocked astonishment and tactful attempts at bewildered sympathy.

Kit and Tyler talked every evening, and her roommate Kelli also called. Kelli offered to send Kit's books and get copies of lecture notes from her classes, but Kit told her not to bother for now. She missed the busy hubbub of college classes and activities, the sparkle and laughter of her roommates, the nights of sitting around in serious discussion or silly chatter. She felt lonely and left out. She desperately missed Tyler and guiltily wished she were there with him instead of here struggling with problems that seemed beyond her. But at the same time, college began to feel oddly distant, almost a frivolous memory from her past, totally irrelevant to the real-life problems of *now*. She was also beginning to feel panicky about the wedding. She knew there must be a million things left to do, but she had no idea what they were, and Andrea, of course, was in no condition to do anything.

She also wondered about the future. She and Tyler had never made alternate plans; Canyon Cowboys and the river had always been their future. Tyler's studies were related to his concerns about what human activities were doing to the river and canyon; Kit had planned to use what she learned as a business administration major to improve the financial management of Canyon Cowboys, an area of the business both Ben and Frank McCord had usually treated with good-natured neglect. What would she and Tyler do now?

A little over two weeks after Kit returned home, Andrea finally made a jump toward improvement. Kit, waking from a leaden sleep on the cot in her mother's bedroom, smelled fresh coffee and realized Andrea was in the kitchen making breakfast. Hastily she dressed in leggings and a faded sweatshirt, her clothes these days coming from the supply of semicastoffs in her old bedroom closet, and dashed out to the kitchen.

"Hi, sweetie." Andrea smiled and flipped a perfectly browned slice of French toast in the skillet. She put a pitcher of maple syrup in the microwave to warm.

Kit hugged her mother with gratitude and relief. "Mom, it's so wonderful to see you feeling better!"

"It finally occurred to me that I really must get your gown finished. And the wedding is only five weeks away, and the invitations haven't even gone out yet!" Andrea chattered on about other wedding details as she poured orange juice and set the table.

A dizzying array of tasks had yet to be done, Kit realized. The photographer and caterer had been scheduled, but menu details were yet to be worked out, as well as flowers, music, wedding favors, and the rehearsal dinner. Kit uneasily realized her mother had bounced too far in the opposite direction from her lethargy, but she was too grateful for *any* change to try to slow the burst of vivacious energy. After breakfast, Kit hand-addressed invitation envelopes while Andrea ordered the lace they had chosen and sewed slithery panels of satin together. After lunch Kit suggested a trip to the grocery store before they returned to work.

"We're out of milk and fresh fruit, and it's such a gorgeous spring day," Kit coaxed. Although a more important reason in her own mind was that neither of them had been out of the house since Kit got home.

"Oh, I don't know, hon…"

Kit suspected she knew why her mother hesitated. Andrea didn't want to see anyone she knew. She wasn't ready yet for the curiosity or even the sympathy that was out there. Which was, in a way, a relief; it meant that even if she wouldn't talk about the situation, Andrea was at least acknowledging to herself that it had happened.

"I know!" Kit said. "We'll drive over to Kanab!"

"For *groceries?* Hon, it's more than eighty miles over there."

"Who cares? We'll make a real getaway afternoon of it. Do our shopping, get something to eat. It'll be fun!"

Andrea peered out the window, something she hadn't done in days. "It is a beautiful day for a drive…"

In the first attention she'd shown to her appearance, Andrea put on makeup and a spring dress, and they were on their way in twenty minutes. Over the bridge near massive Glen Canyon dam that created the many-armed shape of the blue waters of Lake Powell backed up behind it, past the Vermilion Cliffs whose spectacular red walls rose abruptly from the desert floor. The scent of sage spiced the spring air, and Andrea smiled delightedly when Kit found a radio station playing the soaring strains of Vivaldi. Country and western music made Andrea shudder; Rella yawned at classical music. But Kit, raised on both, could happily enjoy both the majestic crescendos of the Philharmonic or the cowboy twang of a guitar.

Suddenly Andrea clasped Kit's arm. "Your birthday! Oh, hon, I'm so sorry!"

"No big deal," Kit assured her.

"I didn't send your present down to Tucson because I was afraid it would break. But I planned to call and tell you about it. And then…"

And then Ben and Rella shattered everything.

"You can show me when we get home, okay?" The birthday had lost importance for Kit, but she was glad her mother had remembered because this was the caring, loving mother Kit had always known. Gaily she added, "And today, as a late birthday celebration, you can treat me to some enormous, million-calorie, hot-fudge thing. With a cherry on top!"

"You got it," Andrea agreed with a rare touch of slangy casualness, plus a smile that lifted Kit's spirits.

In Kanab they window-shopped for spring clothes and shoes, browsed a tourist-oriented antique shop, and loaded up on groceries. In a garden store Andrea bought special fertilizer for her African violets and a new houseplant in a miniature windmill pot. Just a few doors away Kit paused by an ice-cream shop, where colored posters of gooey goodies plastered the windows.

"Ummm, maybe I'll change my mind and have that banana split with three kinds of syrup, or maybe the…"

Kit stopped in midsentence as the door to the shop opened with the musical tinkle of a bell. They hadn't seen anyone they knew all day. Andrea had been smiling and cheerful. And now…

They were laughing, holding hands, sharing an oversized ice cream cone. Two tall, handsome, carefree people in love.

With a small cry Andrea dropped the box holding her new plant. It crashed to the sidewalk, bits of shattered windmill flying, fragile plant crumpling among the shards.

"What are you doing here?" Kit gasped.

The laughter stopped. Rella lowered the ice cream cone from Ben's mouth. He swiped the back of his hand across his lips. "We flew over to see about having some new brochures for Canyon Cowboys printed here…" Then, in typical Ben Holloway fashion, he jumped from defense to attack. "What are *you* doing here? Why aren't you down at college?"

"What am I doing here?" Kit repeated. She turned her gaze to Andrea, whose normally alabaster skin had turned sickly pale, her hands still rigid in front of her as if she didn't realize the little plant had fallen from them. Kit's voice jumped to an angry level she barely recognized. "What do you *think* I'm doing here?"

Andrea swayed, and Rella reached out to steady her, but Kit lunged between them and shoved Rella's hand away. "Don't touch her," Kit warned fiercely. She wrapped a protective arm around her mother's shoulders. "Don't you put so much as a finger on her."

Rella looked at Ben, their gazes meeting on a level above Kit and Andrea's heads. "I'll meet you over at the printers," Rella murmured. She ducked away without letting her eyes meet Kit's.

Ben's gaze darted from Rella to Andrea. Seeing her through Ben's eyes, the change in her from just a few weeks ago was shocking: thinner in face and body, bleak shadows under her eyes showing through the makeup. She looked desperately fragile, ready to crumple and break like the fallen plant on the sidewalk. Yet Ben appeared not so much concerned, Kit thought angrily, as simply uncomfortable.

"I didn't know..." he muttered. "I mean..." His gaze slithered away to follow Rella, as if he'd like to flee after her.

"What did you think? That she was out partying every night? Scouting around to steal someone else's husband to replace the one who cheated and abandoned her? This is the first day she's even been out of the house, the first day she's seemed close to normal, and now you did this to her!"

Kit's grip around her mother's shoulders tightened. Andrea's skin felt cold to Kit's touch, as if all the heat had drained out of it. Carefully Kit turned and propelled her mother toward the Cherokee parked in the next block. She didn't realize Ben was following until his hand reached around her to open the car door. Kit, ignoring him, helped her mother inside and started to march around to the driver's side. His rough grip on her arm stopped her.

"How long have you been home?"

"Since the morning after you came to see me in Tucson."

"Kit, you can't miss this much school! You should..." With a jerky glance at Andrea sitting rigidly in the car, he broke off as if uncertain where to go in his argument that Kit should be in Tucson.

"You think I should just run off and leave her like this?" Kit challenged. "Abandon her the way you did?"

"Kit, thousands of couples divorce every year. People have to face up to reality and get on with their lives. Andrea has to accept that. And you should be down there with Tyler, at school." He sounded impatient now, almost accusing, as if she and Andrea were at fault rather than Rella and himself.

"Mom needs me more than I need college. It's a matter of loyalty and responsibility." It was a deliberate jab at *his* lack of loyalty, and Kit knew it got to him. He'd always been one to say proudly that his handshake was his word. Again Kit asked the question that echoed endlessly in her mind. "How could you do it, Dad, how could you and Rella *do* this?"

"Love can't be explained, Princess."

"But when it hits, you just grab and run with it, like a kid with a new toy, right?" Kit asked bitterly. "No matter if it makes a mockery of every standard of decency and every marriage vow you made."

"Things change…"

"Right and wrong don't change! Aren't parents supposed to be an example to their children? What kind of example are you and Rella? How will you feel if Tyler does to me what you've done to Mom?"

He paled at the question, and she knew it was something he'd never considered. "That's different. You and Tyler have built your relationship over years together. He loves you."

"You've always acted as if you loved Mom! And you've been together for years. I thought words like *unfaithful* and *adulterer* applied to other people, not my father!"

"Kit, there isn't any point calling names or arguing this over and over. It's settled. It's *done*. And I want you to reconsider the wedding. You're still my daughter. I want to be there. So does Rella."

"I'm not changing my mind. It's settled. It's done," she added in contemptuous repetition of his own words.

"I don't think you're being fair…"

"Fair?" Kit almost choked over the word. "Where do you get off talking to me about *fair* after what you've done? And speaking of *fair*, the only money I can find that you left Mom is what's in the household checking account. You call that fair?"

Kit had written checks to pay utility and insurance bills and knew how skimpy the account was. Before, Ben had always taken care of all the family finances and bill paying.

"My lawyer is working on a property settlement and appropriate alimony." He sounded stiff, coached, as if the lawyer had warned him not to get into any private discussion about money. The trio of weathered lines between his heavy eyebrows deepened into a frown. "Kit, I'm not *unconcerned* about Andrea…"

"You have a strange way of showing it!"

"Look, the lawyer will probably chew me out for it, but I'll bring a check over before we leave on our next river trip day after tomorrow."

The grudging way he said it, as if he were being so brave and generous circumventing the lawyer, infuriated Kit. She wished she could shout, "We don't need your tainted money! We don't need anything from you!" She couldn't do that. Not now. But someday she would, she vowed fiercely.

For now, there was something else she could do.

"Yes, you make out a check. But send it, don't come to the house. We don't want to see or talk to you again."

He nodded without argument, as if he were relieved not to have to come to the house. Yet, with his next words, Kit realized he'd missed the bottom-line meaning of her statement.

"We need to get together and talk before you go back to Tucson, Princess. I know you're angry and confused, but if we can just sit down and discuss this calmly, I think you'll understand."

She tilted her head back to look him defiantly in the eyes. "There is no way I will *ever* understand what you and Rella have done to Mom. It's despicable, cruel, self-centered…"

"Kit, I've had about enough of this self-righteous, holier-than-thou attitude of yours! If what you're saying…"

"What I'm saying," Kit spelled out said with deadly softness, "is that you're out of my life. I don't want to talk to you. I don't want to see you. Not in a few days, not in a few weeks, not in a few years. Not *ever.* I am not your daughter anymore."

FIVE

Y ou've completely cut your Dad out of your life?" Tyler
repeated Kit's words to make certain he understood the
full extent of what she had just told him. He rubbed the
towel over the rowdy tangle of his blond hair. The phone had
quacked just as he was putting his pants on after a shower.

"Yes. And I assume he understood the same went for Rella."

Tyler toweled his chest dry. "How did Ben react?"

"He said I was acting like a spoiled brat, and he wasn't going
to let me come between him and Rella. Then he turned and
stalked off. Mom was sitting there just *shattered* by running into
them like that, and he never even looked back. And Rella ducked
out like someone dodging a bill collector. It's as if they've turned
into two different people! As if they feel they can do anything,
hurt anyone, and it's all justified because they exist on this higher
plane of *love*, far above the rest of us. And Mom doesn't matter at
all."

That was the attitude Tyler had detected in Rella, too, that
nothing could or should stand in the way of this precious jewel of
"true love." Yet underneath it all, he was almost certain that guilt
gnawed at her heart and mind. It wasn't like Rella to run like
someone dodging a bill collector. But obviously neither she nor
Ben were going to let crosscurrents of guilt affect what they were
doing.

"Have you talked to Rella since she came to see you?" Kit
asked.

"No."

Tyler draped the towel around his neck. He'd thought about
calling Rella, but he knew she'd hang up on him if he sermonized.
But he couldn't say that even though he strongly disapproved, he
understood. Because he didn't understand! The Rella who had
raised him, even though she had no Christian beliefs, had always
set an example of honesty and strong principles and dependability.

How could she abandon all that for a stolen love?

"You don't think I was wrong, do you?" Kit asked.

Tyler hesitated. He didn't disagree with what Kit said about the wrongness of what Ben and Rella had done. It was immoral, heartless, and selfish. It made him want to grab them both and shake some sense into them! And yet.... "Cutting him out of your life is a rather drastic step."

"Anything less would be condoning what they're doing! *You* don't condone it, do you?" she challenged.

"No, of course not. I'm as appalled as you are." But could he, after all Rella had done for both him and his father in the past, ruthlessly cut her out of his life as Kit had done with Ben? "Have you prayed about this, Kit? Are you sure it's what the Lord wants?"

"I know my Bible well enough to remember Paul's harsh rebuke of the Corinthians for letting an immoral man remain among them! He told them in no uncertain terms to 'expel the wicked man from among you.' And that's what I've done, expelled him."

Tyler again hesitated. "There's also some biblical space devoted to not passing judgment on others. Jesus' own words from Matthew say, 'Do not judge, or you too will be judged.'"

"Yes, and a verse in Luke says, 'If your brother sins, rebuke him, and if he repents, forgive him.' But I don't see anything about forgiving if he doesn't repent, if he just keeps wallowing in the sin, as Ben and Rella are doing!"

Kit always was faster than he with a Bible verse, Tyler thought ruefully. In sword drill she could beat him almost every time.

"Are you telling me you *aren't* going to cut them out of your life?" she demanded. "That you're going to go on as if everything they've done is just fine?"

"I want to conduct myself toward them as the Lord would have me do," Tyler said, phrasing his words carefully. "I want to do what he wants me to do."

Sharp silence ensued as Kit considered that. Then she abruptly changed the subject. "Mom was sick to her stomach by the time we got home from Kanab. She may have gotten hold of something she's allergic to when we ate a pizza sample in the grocery store.

Or maybe it's nerves. She took a pill and went to bed, but if she isn't better by morning, I'll take her to the doctor again. And I have to find a plumber. The drain in the kitchen sink is plugged up."

Kit sighed dispiritedly, and Tyler decided on the spot that he was going up there this weekend. This time he wouldn't discuss it with her; he'd just show up at the door.

They talked a few minutes longer. Kit said she was going to consult a lawyer immediately, that she didn't trust Ben to treat Andrea fairly in the divorce. Tyler didn't ask when she thought she could return to Tucson; with these new setbacks he could see the date silently receding.

He went back to his computer and a paper on managing wetlands that was due at the end of the week, but the question he'd asked himself earlier circled like a predatory bird. Finally he realized he was staring at it on the computer screen, that he'd typed it out in blunt words: *Can I cut Rella completely out of my life?* Kit expected it; perhaps it was what he should do. But he owed Rella so much.

He could still remember the very first day Rella had come into his life. He was nine years old, and he and his dad were camped on the back side of some ramshackle rodeo grounds in the middle of nowhere. His mother had died about a year earlier, a mysterious puzzle to him at the time, although he knew now that it was a vicious, fast-acting type of leukemia that had killed her. Her dying had left him bewildered and sad, scared when he went to school every morning that maybe his dad and his big dog, Bear, would disappear, too.

A couple months after she died his dad had quit the mechanic's shop, or maybe he'd been fired, because Tyler had hazy memories of him sitting at the kitchen table with a bottle night after night and then sleeping most of the next day. They drifted west, and Frank went back to rodeoing, something he'd done before Tyler was born. Tyler thought his dad was the best bronc and bull rider in the world, and he did win now and then when he was sober, but mostly he wasn't sober. Tyler pretty much took care of himself and Bear. He'd sneak into a grocery store and snitch canned dog food and crackers and bologna when his dad forgot about mealtimes.

Sometimes, when they ran out of money, Frank would get a job for a few weeks. Then Tyler might have to go to school, and he hated it because he was always far behind and the other kids made fun of him. Sometimes he vowed he'd just never go back to school again.

Then something really bad happened. It was at a little rodeo in Texas, and somehow a couple of the Brahma bulls got loose as they were being unloaded. Tyler was sitting on a corral fence watching, and one of the big, humped bulls crashed right into it. Tyler went down in a tangle of shattered boards and flying hooves and wicked horns, and he knew right then he was going to get trampled and killed, just like he'd seen happen to a cowboy in a rodeo arena. But Bear was there, grabbing on to that big ol' bull's nose, hanging on like gum stuck under a table. Tyler scrambled away and looked back just in time to see the bull slam Bear into a fence. The big dog died a few minutes later, with Tyler's tears wetting his shaggy coat and holding him tight.

And Tyler got another harsh lesson in how much loving could *hurt*. That night he thought about how his dad, when he was sad or angry, went to that bottle he kept rolled up in his sleeping bag, and Tyler went there, too. The liquid fire in the bottle didn't make him feel better, just sick, but that was okay too because while he was sick he wasn't hurting inside so much. After that, he nipped on the bottle every now and then, and after a while it didn't make him sick anymore, and he liked the comfortable little glow it gave him.

Bear had been gone about two months on this particular morning. Tyler woke up just as the sun was peeking over some runty mountains to the east. He didn't have to dress before he crawled out of his sleeping bag because, like usual, he'd slept in his jeans and T-shirt. His dad was just a curled-up lump in the other sleeping bag, not even the top of his head showing. The air smelled of fresh hay and dust and horses, plus a heady scent of bacon frying at the stand where some town group was putting on a rodeo breakfast. The smell made his stomach feel flat and empty as a licked-clean Popsicle stick. While he was just sitting there a woman walked by leading a flashy sorrel horse to the watering trough. She was tall and slim in her faded jeans, her streaky blond hair tied back with a piece of rawhide. He remembered seeing the horse in the barrel race the day before, and that long hair, too, flying out from under this woman's cowboy hat as they ripped around the barrels.

"Hi," she said.

"Hi." He was wary of strange women. Sometimes they were what his dad scornfully called "do-gooders," from welfare or church or someplace, always suspicious of how his dad was raising him.

"You all alone?" she asked. She had a husky voice, not masculine, but not soft and gentle like he vaguely remembered his mom's being. She didn't sound like someone you'd want to give any back talk to.

"Nah. My dad's over there." He jerked his head toward the other sleeping bag that looked like an old thrown-away horse blanket. He busied himself putting on his boots, and she went on without saying anything more.

Tyler filled his empty stomach with water from a faucet, went to the portable restrooms, and wandered around the rodeo grounds, once in a while going back to check on his dad. It was maybe midmorning when the woman came by riding her horse. She reined him to a stop and eyed the unmoving lump in the sleeping bag.

"Your dad still asleep?"

"I guess."

"What'd he do, party all night?"

That was exactly what Frank had done, but Tyler wasn't about to tell some busybody woman so. He just shrugged. "I dunno."

"You had any breakfast?"

He thought carefully before answering. What he finally figured was maybe she had in mind feeding him. So he said, "I could eat somethin'."

But instead of offering to get him breakfast, she dismounted and handed him the reins. Then she walked over and kicked the lump in the sleeping bag. And kept right on kicking until his dad stuck his head out and looked up at her all bleary-eyed. "Hey, what the..."

"Get up, you lazy buzzard." Another kick, even though he was awake by then. "What d'you mean, leaving your kid out here alone and hungry?"

"Get away from me," Frank muttered. He sat up and held his head in his hands. "Tyler can look out for himself."

"If you're not out of there in exactly sixty seconds, I'm going to set fire to that sleeping bag."

One part of Tyler thought maybe he ought to go over and protect his dad, but another part was just openmouthed astonished and curious about whether she'd really do it.

Evidently his dad figured she would because even as he was grumbling, "Lady, you got a kick like a mule," he was crawling out of the sleeping bag.

She stood right there looking mean while Frank stuck his head under a nearby faucet, dried off with his shirttail, and muttered to Tyler, "C'mon, let's go get something to eat."

Then, astonishing Tyler still further, the woman gave him a jaunty little wink and took back the reins.

They saw her at rodeos often after that. Her name was Rella, and her horse was Teton Joe. Sometimes she let Tyler cool Teton out after a hard barrel-racing run. He heard his dad ask somebody about her once, and the cowboy said her husband had been killed when his horse got tangled in a rope in the steer roping and fell on him. She'd been rodeoing, barrel racing, by herself since then.

Once, waking up in the middle of the night, Tyler had wandered over to where a rodeo dance was going on and saw his dad and Rella dancing together. His dad looked happy then, but he stumbled into the sleeping bag drunk along toward daylight. Which must have made Rella mad, because she looked right through him at the next rodeo. His dad acted like he didn't care, but Tyler was pretty sure he cared a lot. Then they made up and got all lovey-dovey, but he overheard Rella tell his dad that this wasn't going anywhere unless he changed his ways.

Tyler wasn't sure how he felt about all this stuff that went on between grown-ups. He liked Rella okay, but he didn't figure his dad was going to change his ways. Which meant Rella was probably going to get mad and take off for good sometime, so there wasn't much point in liking her too much.

Tyler was right about his dad not changing his ways. He kept right on drinking and running out of money, and then he started getting sick a lot, too. He was in the hospital a couple times, and Rella kind of looked after Tyler, though he sure didn't let her think she could boss him around. The third time his dad was in the hospital really scared Tyler because this was getting to be like before his mom died. So while Rella was at the hospital with his dad, Tyler sneaked into the bottle that was always in the sleeping bag. He maybe got too much that time because when Rella came back, he felt all giggly and light-headed, and she took one look at him and apparently knew exactly what he'd done. And she was *mad*.

She threw her big leather purse clear across the pickup seat, got in, and stomped on the gas, and he thought she was just going to dump him somewhere. Instead she made him swallow some yukky medicine and stuck him in a motel bed to sleep off his little-kid drunk.

But if she wasn't mad at him, which he finally figured out she wasn't, she was sure enough mad at his dad. Frank looked limp and glassy-eyed as a dead fish when he got out of the hospital, but she tore into him about raising Tyler to be another drunken bum just like himself. Then she moved all their stuff out of their battered old pickup, which by then had two flat tires anyway, into hers, fastened Frank and Tyler in with seat belts, and started driving.

She took them to some dinky little campground that she said was in Nevada but was more *nowhere* than anyplace Tyler had ever seen. Just two scrawny old trees surrounded by sagebrush with a herd of messy cows that wandered in for water every morning. She went through Frank's stuff and smashed bottles Tyler didn't even know he had. And that was where they stayed, Teton Joe running loose with the cattle. His dad groaned and moaned and said he was gonna die if he didn't get a drink. Rella told him go ahead and die, but he wasn't going to do it before he married her, so that after he was dead, she'd have some claim on Tyler. So they drove into a grubby little town with a big, gloomy-looking building that had the word *Courthouse* carved into it and got married.

In later years, Tyler somehow doubted Rella's method was an accepted treatment for someone in his dad's alcohol-steeped condition, but it apparently worked. After a while longer at the campground, he stopped grumbling about getting a drink and kind of perked up. Rella told him he wasn't going back to rodeoing so he better decide on something else. He hemmed and hawed and finally said he had this buddy he used to rodeo with who was a river guide now. So Rella called Ben Holloway, sold Teton to a rancher for gas and food money, and that was how they wound up in Page, Arizona.

Frank took to running the river "as if he'd been born on a raft," as his buddy Ben proudly liked to say. Frank himself said it was more fun than drinking ever was. But if that solved one problem for Rella, Tyler loomed as another big one.

He turned *bad.*

Rella made him go to school, where he was put in third grade rather than fourth, where he should have been, because he was so far behind. He had to take baths, brush his teeth, wear clean clothes, go to bed at regular times, and study at night. With stubborn defiance he fought her every step of the way. He skipped school, started fights in the cafeteria, and got suspended for cussing out the teacher. He was sullen and uncooperative at home, snitched stuff from the store even though he no longer needed it, deliberately muddied and ripped his clothes going through fences, and yelled at Rella that she wasn't his real mom so he didn't have to do what she said.

Looking back from adulthood at that chaotic time, he could see what he was doing. He was still scared Rella might pick up and leave, and he was determined not to love her. He was also testing her to see if she really loved him.

And through it all, unlovable as he made himself, Rella loved him anyway. She didn't baby him; she could hand out stiff discipline. But when he yelled at her that she wasn't his real mom, she'd calmly say, "I may not be your real mom, but I'm your mom now. And you're my son, and that's that." She got him a dog and somehow even managed to go buy Teton back. By then the horse had hurt his leg and couldn't barrel race anymore, and maybe it was her loyalty to the broken-down horse that finally proved to his small-boy mind that he could trust her, that you didn't have to be perfect for her to love you, and she wasn't going to walk out on them.

So somehow, in spite of their strange beginning, the three of them became a real family filled with love and laughter. Rella was the world's worst cookie maker, so she didn't do much of that kind of stuff, but she was always right there with him in other ways, never missing a school event or meeting. By the time he was in junior high, Frank and Ben had formed their own guide outfit, Canyon Cowboys.

What would have become of his dad and him if Rella hadn't come into their lives? He might well have become a juvenile alcoholic, homeless and uneducated. His father would surely have died years earlier than he did. But Rella, dogged and determined, had turned their lives around.

His only regret about their family life had been, after he and Kit found the Lord, that he had never been able to lead Rella and his father to the same commitment. Yet he also remembered that Rella had never tried to come between him and the Lord, never argued or tried to discourage him.

Now Rella had done this terrible wrong. But could he completely turn his back on her because of it? And how would Kit feel if he *didn't* do it?

SIX

Tyler rang the doorbell again. No answer. Odd. Kit's Cherokee stood in the driveway, and classical music flowed from a radio or CD somewhere inside the house. With a blustery spring rain falling it seemed unlikely that Kit and Andrea were in the backyard, but he circled the house to look for them.

Backyard empty, wet grass in need of mowing, wind whipping the budding trees. Tyler pushed back the sleeve of his denim jacket and looked at his watch, puzzled. 8:15 A.M. He'd left Tucson late last night and driven hard to get here. Where could they be? He noted the door was ajar and pushed it open wider. "Kit?" No answer.

He heard a car and sprinted around the house just in time to see Kit step out of a taxi. His heart jolted at how tired and stressed she looked as she paid the driver.

"Kit!"

She turned, and her face lit up in a way that gratified his heart even as the weary shadows under her eyes dismayed him. "Tyler!"

They met in the middle of the front lawn, unmindful of wet grass underfoot or wind-whipped rain slapping their faces. There were kisses and hugs and flurries of breathless questions, until Tyler held her at arm's length and teased lightly, "What are the neighbors going to think about this wild display of affection so early in the morning?"

She smiled, but it was an uncharacteristically gaunt smile. "What the neighbors think is the least of my worries." She held up her arm to check the time, sheltering her watch from the rain with her sleeve. "I have to get back to the hospital…"

"Hospital! Your mother's allergies are worse?"

"No. Come inside. I guess we have time for a cup of coffee."

"And scrambled eggs? I'm starved."

"I guess I am, too," Kit admitted, as if food were something that often slipped her mind lately.

In the kitchen, Kit made coffee and Tyler set a Teflon pan on the burner. "Okay, now tell me what happened," he commanded as he cracked eggs into the pan with a one-handed flourish.

"I heard Mom get up, but it was barely light and I thought she was going to the bathroom. Then something woke me again later, and her bed was empty. I found her in the sewing room. She must have stumbled or tripped. She and the sewing machine were on the floor, she had a gash on her head, and her arm was twisted under her." She swiped a knuckle across her eyes, swallowed, and went on. "The doctor at the hospital says it isn't anything awful. Just a compression fracture above her right wrist, and the gash isn't nearly as bad as all the blood made it look. But coming on top of everything else…"

Tyler wrapped his arms around her and pressed his cheek against the soft fringe of her dark hair. "What can I do to help?"

"You are helping," Kit said fervently. The strength in her petite build and slim arms always surprised him, and she held him now as if he were an island of safety in rapids threatening to sweep her away.

"How come you were in a taxi?"

"I rode to the hospital in the ambulance with Mom, and I never thought about needing a car after I got there. She's supposed to be released later today, provided they don't find anything else wrong. Oh, Tyler, so *many* miserable little things have been going wrong!"

She listed them while the coffee perked, and he scrambled the eggs and made toast. The sink drain, still plugged because she hadn't yet been able to get a plumber to come and fix it. The appointment with the lawyer, which she had to go to alone because Andrea said she wasn't up to it. Papers to sign and complicated information the lawyer wanted about family finances. A problem with the phone bill. Unexpected bills. Andrea's refusal to see the therapist more than a couple of times. A bridesmaid calling to say she couldn't participate after all, plus dozens of other details still up in the air about the wedding.

"I guess I'm discovering I've lived a much more sheltered life than I ever realized," she finally said ruefully. "There are all these gritty little details of everyday life that I never had to deal with before."

"Now we know why grown-ups were sometimes grumpy when we were kids, right?"

After breakfast, they discovered one more disaster. In the sewing room, where a raw scent of blood hung in the air, blood also soaked the wedding gown, lurid scarlet against the pristine white satin.

Even Tyler could see that no miracle of stain removal or dry cleaning could salvage the gown. "It's not the only wedding gown in the world," he soothed as Kit just stared at the garish mess. "Stores have wedding gowns."

He knew Kit was about to burst into tears, and he instantly chastised himself for the insensitive suggestion that a store-bought gown could replace this one handmade by her mother. But she stifled the sob in her throat and cut off tears with a hard rush of blinking eyes.

"Mom doesn't need to know about this right away, okay? She's upset and depressed enough without adding this to her worries."

He was so proud of her at that moment, unselfishly thinking of her mother's feelings rather than her own harsh disappointment. He nodded. "Good idea."

Andrea was lying in a cubbyhole off the emergency room when they reached the hospital, a bandage around her head, a plastic brace held in place with an elastic bandage around her right wrist. Kit hugged her, and so did Tyler. He realized now what Kit meant about Andrea's vagueness; her gaze didn't quite focus on him. Although at the moment that could be because she was groggy on painkillers.

Andrea tried to sit up, clutching the rail with her one good hand, then dizzily lay back down. "The wedding gown! I didn't tear it when I fell, did I?" Her tone was fearful.

Kit truthfully answered, "No, it didn't tear."

"I really must talk to the caterers again…"

"There's plenty of time," Kit soothed, a statement that Tyler knew was not so truthful. "You just rest now, okay?"

"What did I do to my arm?" Andrea's thin left hand fretted with the rigid brace. She wiggled the fingers on her right hand, but the gesture was feeble, like a puppet manipulated by worn-out strings.

"The doctor calls it a compression fracture. You'll have to wear that brace for several weeks, which will be awkward, of course, but it's nothing serious. You must have put your arm out to break your fall, and the impact kind of scrunched the bone together. And you do have a smidgen of a cut on your head, too."

Something of an understatement, Tyler thought, as Andrea's hand wandered shakily to the bandage.

"So, no handstands or cartwheels for you for the next few days." Kit playfully shook a finger at her mother, and Tyler knew she was desperately trying to treat this lightly. But Andrea wasn't buying it.

"God does seem to have it in for us, doesn't he? I wonder what unpleasant surprise he'll throw at us next."

There was nothing vague about those cynical words, so unlike the sweet-natured Andrea that Tyler had always known. He stepped forward to say something, but a nurse bustled in to wheel her off for X rays on her back.

The X rays showed no spinal damage, and the doctor released Andrea just before noon. She refused lunch when they got home. What she wanted was to work on the wedding gown again, but Kit gently detoured her to the bedroom. Tyler stretched out on the sofa, planning to shut his eyes for just a few minutes before tackling the plugged-up drain, but he woke to find he'd slept for almost three hours. Kit set her Bible on the arm of the chair where she'd been reading by the window and smiled. She knelt beside the sofa and kissed him.

"Hey, do you know you're a fantastic sleeper?" she said softly. "You make all these fascinating little twitches and jerks, but never an obnoxious snore." She tousled his hair and kissed him again. "I could marry a man like that."

"I should hope so."

"But I've been sitting here thinking…"

He sat up. "About *not* marrying me?"

"No. I'm marrying you. You can't escape now," she answered with teasing certainty. "It's just that I think maybe we should postpone the ceremony. The gown is ruined. There are a million things left to do for the wedding, and I don't see any way we can get everything pulled together now. Mom's going to need even more help now, and with the hassle of the divorce, it's all just too much."

Tyler could see that. He'd always been relieved that organizing a big wedding was not the bridegroom's responsibility. "But we could still have a small, private ceremony." He could pull that together.

She hesitated. He knew how much she'd looked forward to the big ceremony and reception they had planned. Because it meant so much to her he'd also wanted it, but all he really cared about was making her Mrs. Tyler McCord. As soon as possible.

"We'll think about it, okay?" she said finally. "Although we may have to put even that off until fall."

He felt an unfamiliar sinking sensation inside, a powerful urge to grab her and drag her off to a preacher *now*, because every minute they delayed opened a wider crack for something unknown and threatening to slip between them. He instantly rejected the panic as unmanly and foolish. A few more weeks or months, though possibly endangering the water supply because of an increasing need for long, cold showers, couldn't really matter. And yet...

He dodged the inexplicably ominous feeling with a question on a different subject. "What about school?"

"I can't come back this spring. I was doubtful even before Mom got hurt, and now there's no way. I'll just have to take an extra heavy class load next year to make up the credits I'll lose." She hesitated, and Tyler knew what she was thinking. Next year was no longer the secure rung on the ladder of their long-range plans that it had once been.

"What about you?" Kit asked. "Any chance you can work full-time for your professor this summer? Or do you have something else in mind?"

64

It was a question tied to his ongoing prayers and Bible scrutiny about the situation, which so far had only left him dangling in a state of confusion. Although Kit had no idea he was still struggling, of course; for her everything was clear as a fresh-washed windowpane.

"I guess I'll just have to see what's available," he now said noncommittally. He also gave her the birthday presents he'd been saving for her: a big box of her favorite chocolate-covered macadamia nuts, a book of inspirational quotations, and an enlargement of a photo he'd taken. It was of a big dog and a tiny duck curled up together, the duck sheltered under the dog's floppy ear, as if the fuzzy yellow creature were whispering to the dog. He'd attached a whimsical caption that read, "We may have our differences, but I really wuv you."

Kit smiled and clasped the framed photo to her heart. "You'll talk baby talk to our kids, won't you?" she accused with loving teasingly.

Tyler grinned. "Yeah, I probably will."

"That's okay. Because I wuv you, too."

While Kit helped Andrea shower and dress, Tyler, after borrowing a wrench from a neighbor since Ben had apparently appropriated every tool in the house, cleaned out the plugged-up drain. He offered the blessing at the dinner table. Kit murmured an amen, but Andrea didn't echo it, and a glance out of the corner of his eye showed her head unbowed, her gaze fixed on the centerpiece of candles and silk flowers.

Kit had to cut Andrea's chicken for her. The plastic brace was not as restricting and clumsy as a cast, but the fork kept slipping through her limp fingers, and she had to eat with her left hand. She was quiet throughout the meal, and Tyler uneasily thought perhaps she resented his presence. Then, as Kit refilled their coffee cups, Andrea unexpectedly put her good hand on his wrist.

"I'm sorry I'm such poor company tonight. But I want you to know I appreciate your being here. Kit needs you. I've been a real burden on her. I know I shouldn't let all this get to me the way it has." She shook her head, a quick glisten of tears in her vulnerable blue eyes.

"Let the Lord help you, Andrea," he urged. "Lean on him."

She ignored the plea. "And it was so terribly *clumsy* of me to take that tumble in my sewing room."

"It wasn't clumsy," Kit cut in quickly. "Remember the time I pirouetted right off the stage when I was a dancing elf in that sixth-grade play? Now that was clumsy!"

Tyler immediately chimed in with a reminder of one of his own disasters. "And how about that time I was going to put the star on the top of your Christmas tree, and the star and the tree and I all wound up on the floor, with most of the decorations on *me*."

Andrea laughed, for the first time sounding almost like her old self. "Yes, covered with so much tinsel and snow foam that we had to vacuum you off. Then Ben came in and…" Her words broke off as if a guillotine had slammed down on them, and there was a moment of silence before she stood up so quickly that he had to reach out and steady her.

"Well, I really must get back to the wedding gown, or Kit will be standing at the altar in her borrowed blue garter and not much else." The quip was bright, but the laughter was shallow.

"Actually," Kit said carefully, "there's no rush. We've decided to postpone the wedding."

Andrea dropped back into the chair, a stricken expression on her thin face. "Because of me? I did do something to the wedding gown when I fell, didn't I!"

Kit glanced at him as if appealing for some acceptable detour, but at this point there seemed no avoiding the truth. In a studiously neutral tone she said, "There are a few bloodstains."

"If it's just one or two panels I can replace them."

Kit apparently decided to take a chance on jumping in with both feet rather than tiptoeing delicately. Almost cheerfully she said, "It was the whole dress, Mom. Blood everywhere. Actually, it looked like the scene of one of those gory chain-saw murders in the movies."

Tyler momentarily thought the reckless approach was a mistake, but unexpectedly, after a moment of horrified shock, Andrea smiled wryly. "I guess we'd best hope your father doesn't inexplicably turn up missing now, hadn't we?"

The slightly macabre comment startled Tyler, but a moment later Andrea's fluctuating emotions dipped again. She slumped in the chair and shook her bandaged head. "I'm so sorry about ruining the gown, sorry about ruining the wedding, sorry about everything."

"Mom, if we're going to assign blame, let's put it where it belongs," Kit said fiercely. "On Dad and Rella."

"The wedding isn't ruined, just postponed," Tyler added, aiming for diplomacy rather than accusations.

Andrea studied her injured arm as if it belonged to someone else. "I want to be strong and sensible and practical. I want to be one of those capable women people admiringly call a survivor, not a burden."

"You're not a burden!" Kit said, her voice still fierce.

"It's just that life doesn't seem quite *real* without Ben. I love him. It seems as if I've always loved him. And a wife is all I've ever been. What does a wife do after she's lost her job?" Andrea's gaze wavered between them, hurt and vulnerable and bewildered.

"We'll find you an even better job," Kit assured her, although her quick side glance at Tyler reflected his own doubts.

"And I also feel so incredibly naïve and foolish. I had no idea anything was going on, not a clue. How could I have been so blind?"

"You were a good, trusting wife, and they were clever traitors. And we can all get along just fine without them, can't we, Tyler?"

The sharply targeted question caught Tyler by surprise, but he nodded slowly. Yes, he could get along without Rella. He wasn't a child with basic survival needs anymore. But was cutting her out of his life what the Lord wanted him to do?

Andrea sighed. "Sometimes it seems as if the worst part will be living right here in the same town with them. Knowing people are gossiping, feeling the curiosity and pity. Running into them, the way we did in Kanab." She looked around the familiar rooms, where a powerful echo of Ben's strong personality lingered even though he'd removed all physical evidence of himself. "Living here among all the memories…"

"You want to leave the house? Leave Page?" Kit sounded dismayed, and Tyler couldn't blame her. The decisions and logistics involved in getting rid of this house and finding and setting up Andrea somewhere else looked as daunting as making a vertical climb up Glen Canyon Dam.

Andrea shrugged and patted her daughter's hand. "Oh, it's just a passing thought. I can't imagine where I'd go." She smiled ruefully. "Actually, I'm having trouble visualizing *any* future alone, which is the real problem, I suppose."

"Well, we don't need to decide anything tonight." Kit jumped up almost too energetically and began clearing the table. "Why don't we just do something fun this evening? I know! Kelli showed us this crazy card game a few weeks ago."

After the dishes were in the dishwasher, Kit located a deck of cards and explained the game. It combined a lot of fast-action card slapping with a gleeful cry of the name of the game, "Bottoms Up!" whenever a particular sequence of cards appeared. Tyler suspected it was a bit rambunctious for ladylike Andrea, but she gamely entered into the fun. Afterward they snacked on the unlikely combination of cappuccino and s'mores made under the broiler.

Kit directed him to the guest bedroom while she changed Andrea's bandage and helped her get ready for bed. He hung his jacket in the closet, careful not to touch the frothy bridesmaids dresses hanging there, then took his Bible out to the living room. Kit joined him a few minutes later, and they spent an hour in study and prayer. One of the matters Kit brought up in prayer was the desire her mother had expressed about leaving Page. Then she broadsided him with something else.

"Somehow I get the feeling you aren't necessarily as committed as I am to cutting Ben and Rella out of our lives."

"It's an ugly situation." He hesitated. "But I'm not positive turning our backs on them and cutting them out of our lives is the way to handle it."

"I don't see how you can consider anything else! Look."

She grabbed her Bible and flipped from page to page as she pointed out various passages to him, like a lawyer assembling the applicable statutes from a lawbook. She had obviously already given this a good deal of prayer and thought and study, and she had strong ammunition.

She started with the passage in 1 Corinthians that she had mentioned before, the one in which Paul admonished the Corinthians to put out of their fellowship a man involved in a particular sin. "Paul specifically says here in verse 9 not to associate with sexually immoral people!" She went on to 2 Thessalonians 3:14, which counseled not to associate with wrongdoers, so that those wrongdoers might feel ashamed. "And if anyone should be ashamed, it's Dad and Rella!" She showed him the list of people and their sins in the third chapter of 2 Timothy, which ended with the stern admonition of verse 5, "Have nothing to do with them."

She closed the Bible and set it on his lap, as if now inviting him to see for himself. "And there are all the places in Deuteronomy that say, 'purge the evil from among you.' Sometimes the Old Testament gets a little heavy-handed, but it's plain enough that we're to get rid of an evil, not embrace it."

"There's the passage in John about Jesus and the adulterous woman," Tyler began. "Jesus said, 'If any one of you is without sin, let him be the first to throw a stone at her,' and then he says that he doesn't condemn her. We're not without sin, Kit, so we probably shouldn't load up on stones. God still loves Ben and Mom, even if they've done wrong." He hesitated a moment, examining his own feelings. "I do, too."

"I also recall how that passage in John ends," she retorted instantly. "It's with Jesus telling the woman, 'Go now and leave your life of sin.' He doesn't say, 'I don't condemn you, so feel free to go right on sinning.' Are Ben and Rella leaving their life of sin? We both know the answer to that question!"

In the guest room, he showered, brushed his teeth, and reflected on the evening. Knowing that it would be much longer than he'd anticipated before he and Kit would be married and not going their separate ways at bedtime was frustrating and disappointing. But maybe the wait wouldn't be too long. Andrea's moods were skittish, but she was at least talking about the situation with Ben and Rella, something she apparently hadn't done before. She'd eaten a reasonably hearty dinner and accepted the demise of the wedding gown without falling to pieces. She didn't want to go to church in the morning. "And have everyone see me looking like a candidate for some disease-of-the-week show on TV?" she'd said lightly, but Kit thought she could be left alone while the two of them went. He and Kit weren't totally in sync about how to treat Ben and Rella, but they'd discussed the situation calmly, not jumped into some bitter argument about it.

All in all, a reasonably encouraging situation.

So why, when he glanced at the pastel gowns in the closet just before he turned out the light, did he feel a disturbing slap of apprehension?

They were full skirted, delicately lovely gowns, two lavender, two pale yellow. No, Kit had called them something more flowery than that...orchid and jonquil, that's what they were. And there was surely nothing threatening about two orchid and two jonquil dresses hanging quietly in a guest-room closet.

Yet there *was* something chilling about the way they floated there like nostalgic mementos from the past, souvenirs of an event that had never taken place. Pastel skeletons.

Foolish, he chided himself firmly as he switched off the lamp and slid into bed. Morbid and foolish. The wedding might be postponed, but it certainly was not *off*. Nothing was going to come between Kit and him at this late date.

Except that a predatory bird of a question wouldn't stop circling endlessly in his mind. What happened if he and Kit couldn't come to an agreement about Ben and Rella?

SEVEN

H e knew the Lord could work fast, but sometimes his speed astonished even Tyler.

They stopped at the grocery store for a carton of milk after church the following morning. A well-dressed man stepped into the checkout line behind them. A younger couple pushed a cart loaded with kids and groceries in behind him.

"I'm glad I ran into you," the first man said enthusiastically to the couple. "We got a call from our Phoenix office yesterday. They have a client who's transferring to a job here and would like to trade his home in Phoenix for a house in Page. Any chance you'd be interested?"

Kit and Tyler exchanged glances. Someone interested in trading a house in Phoenix for one here? But the clerk handed Kit her change, and they couldn't just stand there snooping on someone else's conversation. They also had no idea who any of these people were, so even though this was an intriguing bit of information, it was a dead end.

Except that as they were leaving the parking lot they saw the first man getting into a vehicle with R. J. Andrews Realty on the side.

"Is God hitting us over the head with this, or what?" Kit murmured with a quizzical look at Tyler.

She tried to call the real estate office when they got back to the house, but there was no answer on a Sunday afternoon. Tyler had hoped to talk to Andrea about her troubling comment that God had it "in" for them, but he didn't see her again. Andrea's head and arm were hurting, and she was also having another of her allergic stomach upsets and didn't come out of the bedroom before he had to leave for Tucson.

The long drive gave him plenty of time to think. About the postponed wedding. About the problem of his relationship with Rella and Ben. About the possibility of Kit helping her mother start a new life somewhere away from Page.

A house trade for a home in Phoenix could be a wonderfully neat solution. Overhearing the conversation the very day after praying about a move suggested the Lord's helping hand. Yet Tyler was also aware that not every incident in life was an opening from God; accepting every little event or coincidence as divine guidance could deteriorate into a kind of *un*godly superstition leading to pitfalls and errors.

Yet, from the way the situation flowed over the next few days, like the healing oil and wine the Samaritan poured on the injured man's wounds, the Lord appeared to be providing some healing oil of his own.

Kit called the real estate office on Monday. Yes, the agent said, their Phoenix office had a client interested in a trade. He laughed when she admitted the unlikely source of her information. He gave her details about the Phoenix house and inspected their house that afternoon. The young couple she'd overheard him talking to weren't in the picture at all, which relieved Kit's mind about barging in on someone else's deal; they planned to move to Texas and had no interest in a Phoenix house.

Kit threw herself into the details of postponing the wedding, and two days later the Phoenix homeowner flew to Page. After looking at the house, he expressed definite interest. Kit contacted Andrea's lawyer, who contacted Ben's lawyer, who conferred with him between river trips. Kit was surprised when he agreed to sign the house over to Andrea immediately, making that a part of the property settlement. Although, on second cynical thought, she decided she shouldn't have been surprised. He was undoubtedly delighted to get his soon-to-be-ex-wife out of town so easily. He even agreed, as a further part of the settlement, to pay the real estate commission on the exchange. Oh, yes, he was *eager.*

Kit made a rush trip to Phoenix to look at the house. Andrea didn't want to go and said she'd trust Kit's judgment, which once again reminded Kit that she wasn't Daddy's little princess now. She had mature responsibilities and important decisions to make. One decision she made was to use some of their limited funds to hire an acquaintance from church to accompany her, a retired builder who could give her an expert opinion on the house's structural soundness and electrical, plumbing, and heating and cooling systems.

She liked the house as soon as she saw it. Smaller than the Page place, but still with a comfortable three bedrooms and two baths. Plus an easy-upkeep yard, attractive red-tile roof, and a nice view of Camelback Mountain. Jerry Rawling's only negative comment was that the heat pump was an older model, not as efficient as newer ones, but it was in good shape and should give satisfactory service.

Then it was down-to-decisions time. Did Andrea really want to do this, leave familiar church and friends and home? For two evenings they talked about it long and earnestly. Kit prayed about it, too, although she suspected she was alone in that. Andrea never wavered. She wanted out of Page.

They made the deal, including most of the heavy furniture in each house. Neither home was encumbered with a mortgage, and the real estate agent pronounced it one of the swiftest, cleanest deals he'd ever handled.

Kit woke before daybreak on moving day. A peek around the drapes showed a sky still dark overhead, only a faint blush of pink in the eastern sky. She tiptoed back to the cot, past a sleeping Andrea. She couldn't pick up the rental moving van until nine o'clock; Tyler wouldn't arrive until midmorning to help with the move. College was out for the summer now, and he was bringing the last of her belongings with him. Within a few days he was also starting a desk job with a seed-testing laboratory, transferring information from an old computer system to a new one, a ho-hum job he was not thrilled about. Everything was as packed and ready as she could make it. The new owners were already in town, spending the night at a motel, poised to unload their moving van as soon as the house was vacated. She should just go back to bed and get as much rest as possible. It was going to be a hectic day.

But she was wide awake, too restless to sleep. She padded

barefoot to the kitchen, noting the faint pale squares marking where pictures had hung in the hallway. The glass window shelves in the kitchen were bare of plants, the ceramic owl clock gone from the wall. She knew she'd probably never be in this house again after this day, this home that had cradled the secure and loving family life of her growing-up years. Tears gathered, painful ones, but she resolutely blocked the flow.

It was, after all, just a *house*, a man-built structure of brick and wood. And the memories it held were bittersweet now.

She was also losing something more important than a house.

Swiftly and silently she returned to the bedroom and dressed. She left a note for Andrea and quietly slipped out to the Cherokee.

Her destination, in cross-country distance, was not far, but by road it was some forty miles, the highway sweeping across the lonely, high-desert plateau, making a sharp switchback at the turnoff to the canyon. Finally she crossed the high span known as the Navajo Bridge, parked, and walked back to the center of it. A gold rim of sunlight gleamed in the east now, but below her the canyon walls were still in blue shadow, the Colorado river a dark ribbon over four hundred feet below. Lee's Ferry, the launching point for all the river trips, was just a few miles upstream.

Here the river flowed serenely, quietly, no hint of the wild rapids downstream. How many times had she rafted the cold, green water beneath this bridge, never dreaming that one day she'd be standing here, looking down, and saying good-bye?

Because it was good-bye. Oh, this wasn't so far from Phoenix that she couldn't make an impulsive jaunt up here. Or she could go to the South Rim and peer into the canyon as so many thousands of awestruck tourists did each year.

But she was parting company with the life on the river she'd always expected would be hers and Tyler's. This was good-bye to the nights sleeping under moon and stars on the sandy beaches, the laughter and tall tales, the glorious sunlight slipping down one side of the canyon walls in the morning, the dark line of shadow rising on the other side in the evening. Good-bye to the thrill of crashing through those thundering giants of the river, Crystal

Rapid and Lava Falls. Good-bye to Vasey's Paradise, where water gushed from a barren cliff and created a garden of lush green below and sometimes made her wonder if a bit of the Garden of Eden hadn't somehow been preserved in this spot. Good-bye to Elves Chasm, a place of whispering waterfalls and sleek rock sculptured with swirls and hollows, which indeed felt as if elves might magically appear any moment...and where Tyler had kissed her the very first time. Good-bye.

Tyler filled the gas tank in Flagstaff and checked the ropes on the tarp over the load of Kit's belongings. Kelli and Autumn had already moved out of the apartment, and he'd simply loaded up everything remaining. Not, he suspected ruefully, packing as carefully as Kit would have done. But his mind had been on other things. It still was.

Rella had called him two days ago. It was the first time he'd spoken with her since the evening she had given him her shocking news. The only contact between them since that time had been the note he'd sent to tell her he'd be working in the seed laboratory this summer.

The conversation had started on a strained note, with overpolite how-have-you-beens, references to the weather, and Rella awkwardly saying she was sorry about the postponement of the wedding. He didn't ask how she'd heard, just challenged brusquely, "That's why you called?"

"No. I called because we're in a real bind, and I didn't know what else to do."

One of their lead pilots had been injured rescuing a guest who had decided to try out his amateur cliff-climbing skills in the canyon. Another man had unexpectedly quit to take a job in Alaska, and a love-smitten third had followed a girlfriend who'd moved back east. "We've promoted one of the swampers to second pilot and hired a new swamper, but that still leaves us short a lead pilot. Everything's just hit us all at once." She paused and then added with a lightness that sounded forced, "A situation that might be interpreted as God's vengeance for our misdeeds, I suppose."

He doubted she really believed that, but he'd never before heard her express even any joking concern about God's opinions. "Could be," he murmured noncommittally.

"I know you'll think that, under the circumstances, it takes a lot of nerve for me to ask this," Rella said, "but I'm going to ask anyway. Would you consider working for us this summer after all?"

"As I told you, I have another job lined up."

"Not a job where you get to sleep under the stars, eat the best steaks money can buy, run the rapids, and earn some nice tips." He heard the strained playfulness in Rella's voice as she listed the rewards with which he was already familiar.

He shot back a list of some of the less desirable aspects of the job. "As well as set up the portable toilets and haul out the products thereof, *cook* that fantastic food and clean up afterwards, plus risk my neck if some idiot decides to pull some showy stunt such as cliff-climbing to impress his girlfriend."

Rella dropped the bantering. "We need you, Ty. You know how it is at this time of the season. There isn't a dependable lead pilot available anywhere. They're all already on the river working for someone else. You wouldn't have to associate much with Ben and me, if that worries you. You'll be in charge on the trips we aren't on. Trips we may have to cancel if you won't come because we can't run them without an experienced lead pilot." She paused, and he heard her swallow. "Please, Ty? We're desperate. It's really important."

He thought of sarcastic retorts. *As desperate as you were when you stole another woman's husband? This is important, but what you did to Andrea wasn't? And how about the fact that Ben betrayed not only his marriage and his wife but his daughter's trust in him, too?*

Why should he do anything for Rella and Ben, ever?

Yet he also thought of the alternate life he might have lived if Rella hadn't rescued him. And of the salvation she didn't have. What he finally did was mutter, "I'll think it over and call you back."

So he had thought about it, and prayed and studied the Lord's Word. Studied it *hard,* harder than he'd ever studied for any exam, continually asking the Lord to open his eyes and show him the path he should take.

Kit had already lugged much of the stuff from house to van by the time he arrived in Page. Most of what remained required the hands and muscle of two people, and, as usual, the muscular strength in Kit's petite body surprised him. He was glad, however, that Kit and the other owners had agreed on an exchange of most of the heavy furniture. Andrea's dining room table and four-poster bed were struggle enough.

They left Page about midafternoon, Tyler driving the moving van, Kit and her mother following in the Cherokee. Andrea's car was temporarily stored at a neighbor's, and Tyler would retrieve his pickup when he returned the moving van.

Driving the loaded van was not a speedy proposition, and a flat tire didn't help. It was close to midnight by the time they finally parked in the driveway of the Phoenix house. By then they were too tired to do more than collapse, so Andrea and Kit slept on the guest-room twin beds that were part of the house exchange, and Tyler got the hide-a-bed in the living room.

In the morning, after a take-out breakfast from a fast-food place a mile away, they unloaded the van. They wrestled Andrea's four-poster bed into the master bedroom and her treasured claw-footed oak table into the dining room, but most of the boxes and cartons were simply dumped in the living room for later disposi-tion. Andrea tried to help, but she looked so tired and fragile that Kit shooed her off to the bedroom for a nap while they finished up.

"There, it's done," Kit finally proclaimed triumphantly as she carried in a last box that had received special treatment, the set of delicately gold-trimmed dishes Andrea had given her for her birthday.

"With only one casualty." Tyler rattled the broken lamp he'd tossed into a box after accidentally tromping on it.

Kit grimaced. "Only one casualty, unless you count my back." She arched her back and pounded the small of it with her fist. "Let's not make a career out of being household movers, okay?"

Tyler smiled. "Suits me." He glanced at his watch "Well, I'd better get started back."

"You're not leaving right now, are you?" Kit protested. "Your job doesn't start until Monday. I thought you'd stay until tomorrow."

"So you could rope me into lugging all these cartons from one room to another while you decide where they belong?" he teased lightly.

She draped her arms around his neck. "Maybe so I could tell you how much I appreciate your doing this. And how much I love you."

"I love you, too, Kit." The familiar statement came out differently than he intended, perhaps even a little defensive, and she leaned back against his encircling arms to look up at him quizzically.

"Do I hear a *but* in there?"

"No *buts*. I love you. But I have to talk to you about something." Uneasily he noted that there was a *but* after all. "Mom called me a couple of days ago."

"Oh?" With the wary word came a slight stiffening of her slim body.

"Canyon Cowboys is having guide problems." He explained the situation as Rella had told it to him. "She asked me to work for them this summer after all."

Her arms flew from around his neck, and she jumped a step backward. "You're not considering doing it!"

He couldn't dodge the issue any longer. "I called her back last night and told her I would." He looked at his watch again, which he guiltily knew was a ploy to avoid facing Kit's blazing eyes. "I have to be there for a launch tomorrow morning."

"Don't you think we should have discussed this?"

"I took it to the Lord, and this is what I've decided to do."

"I can't believe this!" Her glance darted to the closed bedroom door down the hallway. "After what they did to Mom? And me, too? I had to drop out of college because of them. We're here right now, in a strange house in a strange city, with an unknown future, because of them! And all you're thinking about are *their* problems?"

"No, I'm not thinking just about their problems. Although Rella did enough for me in the past when I had big problems that

I certainly owe her something. It's also a good job, Kit. You know that. A job I love. Something I'd ten times rather do than sit in front of a computer all summer. I can also make more money for college next fall...."

"Money? You'll do this for *money?*" she gasped. "What's your price, Tyler? Thirty pieces of silver?"

"You're being melodramatic, Kit. And I also don't think you're being fair."

"Not being *fair?* Those are the exact words my father used that day in Kanab! Maybe they're also saying something rather significant about the similarity of your thinking. You call betraying my mother *fair?*"

"I don't think I'm betraying your mother."

"You call consorting with the enemy, cozying up to Dad and Rella and playing their ain't-love-grand game *fair?*"

"I know that on the surface it may look like the wrong thing to do," he agreed doggedly. "But I also know I've prayed about it. I've asked for the Lord's guidance and studied his Word...."

"And you found Scripture telling you that what my father and Rella did was okay after all?" she challenged. "Words that say that love turns wrong into right?"

"No. What they did isn't 'okay.' But the Lord led me to the admonition 'Do not judge,' in both Matthew and Luke, with the addition of 'Do not condemn' in Luke. He showed me the story in John about Jesus meeting the woman at the well. Jesus didn't simply condemn her for her five husbands and drop it there. He told her about the living waters of eternal life."

"We're getting into reruns of the same old question, Tyler! Are Dad and Rella sorry for their wrongdoing? Are they leaving their life of sin? And the answer is always the same. No! They aren't sorry for what they've done. They aren't asking for forgiveness. Not ours, not Mom's, certainly not the Lord's! They're just blithely going their own immoral way. Didn't you also find the admonition in 1 Corinthians that we're not even to *eat* with people like that, let alone be a part of their business? What about the fifth chapter of Ephesians, where Paul plainly says of people guilty of sexual immorality and greed, 'Do not be partners with them'? And don't forget the warning that is also in Corinthians that we're not to be yoked together with unbelievers."

Kit had obviously done her homework on this subject. He never had been able to memorize with her speed and ease, a fact that had often mildly frustrated him. But the hours he'd spent with his Bible wrestling with this particular problem had burned a few lines into his own brain.

"There's also Ephesians 4. 'Be kind and compassionate to one another, forgiving each other, just as in Christ God forgave you.' And John 3:17: 'For God did not send his Son into the world to condemn the world, but to save the world through him.' In Romans I see, 'Do not be overcome by evil, but overcome evil with good.' And in Romans 5:8: 'God demonstrates his own love for us in this: While we were still sinners, Christ died for us.' And that's a message I want to bring to Ben and Mom. I don't want to see them lost for eternity."

"Now you're trying to make some noble cause out of this to justify what you're doing?" Kit gasped, her voice almost a jeer. "Tyler, we've been trying to get this message across to them for years, and they've never shown a spitwad's worth of interest!"

"It's also a message I'll never get a chance to repeat to them if I cut them out of my life."

"And the opposite side of the message, that there are punishments for wrongdoing, that repentance for sin matters because there is punishment, may get through to them better if we do both cut them off! Then they can see and feel on-the-spot consequences of wrongdoing. We need to show them that what they've done is totally unacceptable, that love doesn't turn wrong into right. If we don't do that, what are they going to think? Well, good ol' Tyler is a staunch Christian and he's sticking by us. So if he doesn't think what we did was some big sin, it probably wasn't so bad after all."

"I'm not saying I don't think what they did was wrong."

"Then if you believe it's wrong, why don't you *act* as if it's wrong!" she demanded passionately. "Aren't we supposed to put our words and beliefs into *actions*?"

"Because this action would be like abandoning someone who

is drowning. Without Christ, they *are* drowning."

"Or maybe you don't really think what they did is all that wrong," she challenged suddenly, her eyes widening with shock, as if internal eyes had also just been opened. "You're thinking that sometimes there are—what's that helpful term?—mitigating circumstances. You're thinking, well, if Ben and Rella are really happy, really in love, maybe it's okay after all. Andrea will get over it eventually."

"Kit, stop thinking you can read my mind. And stop putting words in my mouth!" he exploded. "All I'm saying is that I think kicking Mom and Ben out of our lives like a couple of untouchable lepers isn't the best way to handle the situation."

"And I'm thinking, how can I trust a man who doesn't wholeheartedly believe cheating on a wife is wrong, that under some circumstances, if there's this great *love* involved, maybe it's even acceptable! I'm also thinking that if you're so willing to take their job and mingle with my mother's betrayers—if you can actually *do* this!—that you must be a different man than I always thought you were. And if we're so far apart on this, maybe we'd better change our plans to postpone the wedding. Maybe we'd better just cancel it!"

They stared at each other across the canyon widening between them, like some geological event of the ages compressing into a few earth-shattering moments. He saw her waiting for him to change his mind and capitulate to her views. He saw himself waiting for her to apologize for her accusation that he might follow in Ben's footsteps as an unfaithful husband.

Neither happened. All that happened was the words gritting through his own stiff lips. "I think maybe you're right."

Her lips parted, as if she had expected argument, not agreement. Then she yanked at the ring on her left hand, twisting it savagely to get it past the obstructing joint, and thrust it at him. He hesitated for a fraction of a second—no, he didn't want this! Then, head held as stiffly as hers, he grabbed the ring and stalked to the door.

EIGHT

A month later, Kit still hadn't told her mother about the breakup with Tyler. Nor had she told Andrea that he was working for Ben and Rella. Her mother had asked about him, but Kit had sidestepped direct answers, and Andrea, though her smooth forehead creased in worry lines, didn't pry.

By now they were unpacked and comfortably settled in the house. At first, after Kit flew to Page to retrieve the car, Andrea had been nervous about driving in Phoenix traffic, but she was gradually gaining confidence. She was seeing a new doctor, and she no longer had to wear the brace on her wrist. Her problems with her stomach had also disappeared, leading Kit to suspect that they had been caused more by nerves than true allergies. Here Andrea no longer had to fear some chance encounter with Ben and Rella; here no one knew the small-town-scandal details of the breakup of her marriage.

Kit had tried a couple of churches but hadn't yet settled on one. Andrea hadn't shown any interest, but Kit hoped her mother would accompany her after she did find a church home. Although a voice inside warned, *Don't hold your breath.* Since the breakup with Ben, Andrea seemed to have closed the door on her spiritual life. Which seemed strange to Kit, because Ben had never been part of that life anyway.

The divorce was proceeding on schedule. The alimony issue hadn't yet been settled, but a check from Ben, routed through the two lawyers, arrived. Skimpy, Kit thought, but enough to get by on until they figured out what to do. She was working part-time at the reception desk of a health club and had found a displaced homemakers program for Andrea. It was supposed to teach her about living on her own and help her with education or training for a job, although Andrea had so far shown little interest in the future. She spent much of her spare time working on another of the delicate dolls in fancy Victorian costume, a project that looked boring and tedious to Kit but which her mother apparently found satisfying. And she was, slowly but surely, improving.

Kit carefully hid her own heartbreak, not wanting to undercut her mother's tenuous equanimity. She joked with clients at the health club. As a perk of the job she had free use of the equipment and regularly worked out an hour a day. Sweat therapy, she privately called it wryly. She hammered at the thought that she was glad all this had happened before she and Tyler made the mistake of marriage.

Yet beneath the assurances she gave herself, beneath the careful act played out in her mother's presence, she ached. Sometimes, when something specific reminded her of Tyler—a glimpse of a lanky, blond guy who turned out not to be him, a letter with handwriting that momentarily looked like his—the pain of loss hit her head-on, like a blinding flash of headlights before a crash. Sometimes the pain sneaked up from inside, a sweet memory billowing out of nowhere to club her like a hammer blow inside the head. And there was the grinding, heart-deep pain that was simply always there. She woke with it in the morning; it shadowed her through the day; it gnawed as she waited for sleep at night; it haunted her when she woke in midnight darkness.

Sometimes, when she wakened like that and padded silently to her bedroom window, she thought of another time, another window. A window back in Tucson, when she was still a carefree college girl. She remembered that moment of pure joy when she exulted in the thought that she had it all: Tyler's love, glorious wedding plans, a future of fun and excitement on the river. Now what did she have? A bare ring finger, a broken heart, a muddy future.

She missed him, she missed him so much. In spite of her anger and dismay and disappointment in him, she'd catch herself thinking, *Oh, I'll have to tell Tyler that* about some little thing, then a great yawning emptiness would fall away inside her because there was no Tyler to tell. She missed laughing with him, exploring the mysteries of their faith together, building their plans for the future. She missed his hugs and kisses, sweet and tender, yet with promise of the man/woman passion that awaited after they were husband and wife.

Sometimes she toyed with the thought of writing him and suggesting that they get together. Yet what would that accomplish? Talk wouldn't change anything. They were rooted to opposite sides of that canyon between them, a canyon wider and deeper than any chasm cut in earth and rock. A canyon of opposing loyalties to people they loved, a canyon of differences in opposing beliefs about what path of action was right with the Lord.

None of which canceled out *love*. It would be easier, she sometimes thought with a resentment targeted at love in general, if it did.

Sometimes she also thought about that last photo Tyler had given her, of the big dog and fuzzy duck. The caption about differences between them that had once seemed sweetly whimsical now emerged as an ominous prophecy of troubles to come. Troubles that not even "wuv" could conquer.

On this day, about midafternoon, Kit and Andrea returned home from different directions, scurrying from air-conditioned vehicles to air-conditioned house. Inside, the first thing Kit did was flip through the mail. Bills. Advertisements. Junk. She tossed it aside unopened.

She kicked off her shoes and flopped on the sofa. "Well, how'd it go today?" she inquired, trying to sound more cheery than she felt.

"Oh, fine. Although my counselor seems to think that old adage about cleanliness is out of date, that it's really computer proficiency that is next to godliness." Andrea rolled her blue eyes in mild exasperation. "And you know how I feel about computers."

"You can learn to be computer proficient if you want, Mom," Kit assured her. "You're divorced, you know, not *dumb.*"

Andrea smiled her thanks for that offbeat vote of confidence. "I know. I suppose I could also learn to eat parsnips. But that doesn't mean I could ever *like* them."

The answering machine glowed with a message signal, and Kit flicked it on. A female voice breathlessly told them they'd just won a fantastic prize, and all they had to do…she cut the message off in midsentence.

"We aren't even listed in the phone book yet," she grumbled. "How do they track us down?"

Andrea nodded wisely, as if this confirmed her suspicions. "Computers. Electronic predators. Cyberspace bloodhounds." She checked the mail, too, going a step further and junking most of it in a wastebasket. She gave Kit a sideways glance. "Were you expecting something from Tyler?"

"Not really."

Andrea lifted an eyebrow and waited for an explanation of that listless answer. When none came she asked in a troubled voice, "Hon, am I imagining things, or is it a fact that you *aren't* hearing from Tyler?"

Several times Kit had almost broken down and spilled everything. Sometimes it throbbed like a great, pulsing logjam trapped between her head and heart. But she'd wanted to protect Andrea's fragile steps toward recovery from sabotage by this latest disaster. She also didn't want to reinforce her mother's earlier accusation that the Lord somehow had it "in" for them.

"Kit, is there a problem between you and Tyler?" Andrea prodded. "I've tried to ask before, but you always give me this clever runaround…."

"Like you do when I try to talk to you about anything spiritual?" Kit retorted lightly.

Andrea ignored the small challenge. She sat beside Kit on the sofa and wrapped her hands around Kit's. "Hon, I know I always seem to be leaning on you lately, but I want to help if you have problems. Is Tyler upset because of the wedding postponement?"

Kit had intended, when she finally got around to telling her mother about the breakup, to do it calmly and unemotionally. But her mother's sweet tenderness, her earnest desire to help even in her own wounded condition, crumbled Kit's defenses. She buried her face in her hands.

"It isn't a postponement. There isn't going to be any wedding. We broke up." The words filtered through choking sobs, muffled by her fingers.

"I can't believe…I knew you weren't hearing from him, but… not you and Tyler!"

Kit heard an echo of the shock and incredulity she'd felt when she first heard about the breakup of her parents' marriage.

"Oh, hon, why didn't you tell me?" Then, without even a pause, Andrea half-angrily answered the question herself. "Because you wanted to spare me further worry. Oh, Kit, I'm so sorry!"

Andrea wrapped her arms around her daughter and rocked her back and forth as the whole story tumbled out, all the held-back tears bursting through the gates of self-control. Tyler's decision to go ahead and work for Ben and Rella, the argument, the return of the ring. Each word brought a fresh slash of pain for Kit, a fresh explosion of anger.

"He's acting as if what they did is okay, that it doesn't matter that they care only about their own feelings, that it doesn't matter that they betrayed you, that it doesn't matter what they've done is *wrong!* And I just can't do that!"

"Kit, if you're doing this for me, don't! Don't tear up your life just because mine is torn up. I won't hate you if you don't cut Ben and Rella out of your life!"

Kit shook her head. "I couldn't do it even if I tried. That day in Kanab, the two of them together, knowing they'd been together behind your back for months…"

"Oh, Kit…"

"I suppose it's better that Tyler and I found out all this about each other before we married. He thinks I'm harsh and judgmental. I think he's condoning what Ben and Rella did when he doesn't stand firm against it." She shook her head helplessly. "But one of the hardest things to understand is how he and I can be so far apart on this! We're both believers, we both prayed and went to our Bibles searching for answers, wanting to do the right Christian thing, and yet we came up with totally different paths to follow."

"Paths that took you in opposite directions." Andrea went to stand at the window, her arms crossed at her slim waist, her mouth uncharacteristically thin and hard. "I wondered what unpleasant surprise God had in store for us next. Now I know."

The bitterness in her mother's words and voice shocked Kit. "Mom, this didn't happen because God had it 'in' for us, because he's somehow picking on us!"

"No?"

"No!"

"Through all of this, your faith has never wavered, has it?" Andrea's voice held a strange blend of doubt and wonder and despair. She shook her head. "Maybe if I'd had your faith…"

"You were the one who helped me find my faith, Mom. You always took me to Sunday school, read me Bible stories…"

"And I was a fraud, Kit. A busy churchgoer masquerading as a believer. All those years of faithful church attendance, working on missionary committees, making things for church boutiques and bake sales, singing in the choir. But when the chips were down, there was nothing there." Andrea again shook her head, light from the window turning her dark hair into a glossy halo. "I suppose I even defrauded myself, because it wasn't until this crisis came along that I realized there *wasn't* anything there. And that's when I encountered the real me."

"The real you?" Kit repeated, puzzled.

"Oh, I know how it looked. A big part of me was so hurt and depressed and bewildered that I just wanted to curl up in bed and never come out. But deep inside was the real me, the furious me, the me who wanted the Lord to jump in and lash out at these people who had wronged me. The real me who wanted God to strike them down with lightning bolts of vengeance. The me who was angry and furious with the Lord and the church and even innocent Pastor Ron because nothing was happening. I saw myself as this good, virtuous, upstanding woman, and Ben and Rella as immoral sinners. This man cheated on me, this woman stole my husband! And the Lord wasn't *doing* anything about it. Ben and Rella weren't being struck down. They were happily going their way, and I was the one suffering."

"I had no idea," Kit said in honest astonishment that all this had been rampaging inside her quiet mother. "Do you still feel that way?"

Andrea smiled wryly. "I think I'm beyond the stage of hoping for avenging thunderbolts. But I still don't understand the Lord's workings or why any of these things happened."

"But that doesn't make you a fraud! I don't always understand the Lord's workings either, especially in all that's happened lately, but I still believe the Lord is *there*, that he loves me, that I can always count on him. Don't you believe that?"

Andrea smiled sadly, and Kit knew that, no, her mother didn't believe any of that. Then a stricken look crossed Andrea's face, and she rushed back to the sofa. "Kit, here we are talking about me and my problems again! I'm sorry. I didn't mean to get into any of this. What can I do to help *you?*"

Kit started to beg her mother to come to church with her on Sunday, but with sudden illumination she realized this wasn't necessarily what Andrea needed. Andrea had already been the route of busy church attendance and activities, and what she needed was real one-on-one with the Lord, real contact with the One who was above all, who was always there to lean on.

She swiped the back of her hand across her cheek, where the skin felt stiff and tight from the flash flood of drying tears. She inspected her mother's face thoughtfully. "Actually," she said, "there is something you can do for me."

NINE

J ust tell me, sweetie," Andrea said. "Anything. I'm ashamed that I was so wrapped up in my problems that I left you to cope with yours alone."

"Pray with me, Mom. Right now."

"I was thinking more along the lines of acting as a go-between for you and Tyler." Andrea's frown changed to a rueful smile. "But I walked right into this one, didn't I, saying I'd do 'anything'?"

"Yes, you did, Mom. And this is what I want."

Andrea held to her promise, and they knelt by the sofa together, Kit asking that the Lord open her mother's heart to his love, that he guide them both, that he help them cope with the problems in their lives. She waited hopefully for Andrea to follow with prayer of her own. None was forthcoming, but there was, finally, a small, grudging *amen*. It wasn't much, but it was a tiny first step.

The following Sunday Kit didn't pursue her search for a church home. Instead she placed her Bible on the coffee table and invited her mother to join her.

"Is this more of that rash promise I made about doing 'anything'?" Andrea grumbled lightly.

Kit nodded firmly. "Yes."

Andrea gave an exaggerated sigh of being put-upon, but she planted herself on the sofa beside Kit. Kit had thought about this for several days, and she now offered another quick appeal for guidance. Then, with brisk matter-of-factness, she said, "What I got out of our talk the other day is that you feel abandoned by God, that he doesn't love you."

"Not necessarily just me. Injustice and suffering are everywhere. Much of it worse than my problems, of course. But yes, basically, I don't see much evidence of God's love in what's happened to me. Or you. Ben and Rella do wrong and live happily ever after. You and I…don't."

"Mom, is there anyone you love enough that you'd deliberately send *me* out to die for them?"

Andrea drew back, shocked. "You, Kit? Of course not. I could never..." She broke off as if suddenly aware where this was going and not liking the path.

"But that's what God did, didn't he?" Kit pursued. "He sent his Son here to die. For you. For me. Because he *loves* us."

"I've heard that a thousand times in church. But I've never thought about it on such a personal basis before." She looked at Kit with troubled eyes, creases between her dark brows, as if really envisioning what it would take to send her own daughter out to suffer and die.

"I can't explain all the suffering and injustice in the world," Kit said. "But I do know God loves us."

Kit led her mother through the words of 1 John 4:9: "This is how God showed his love among us: He sent his one and only Son into the world that we might live through him." She took her into Jesus' own promise in Matthew 28:20: "I am with you always, to the very end of the age." And on to the glorious proclamation of John 3:16.

She knew none of this was truly new to her mother, but she also knew Andrea was seeing it from a new perspective. Yet when Kit finally closed her Bible and offered a prayer, Andrea didn't eagerly jump to accept it all. She simply tapped her fingertips together in an absentminded way and said quietly, "I'll have to think about this."

They followed this routine of Bible study and prayer for several Sundays. During that time Andrea found a job at an arts-and-crafts store. "No computers involved!" she told Kit happily. Kit's job expanded to full-time. Ben offered a reasonable property settlement and alimony, and Andrea signed the papers. She had already let contacts with friends in Page drift, preferring, Kit suspected, not to be filled in on local gossip. Kit agreed. The more ties they cut with the past, the better.

The hot summer and fall crawled along. Kit donated the

bridesmaids dresses to Goodwill and put the birthday dishes in the storage room. She went out on dates with a couple of guys she met at the health club. Returning to college no longer seemed a viable possibility. But she did occasionally hear from her former roommate Kelli, who, because of financial problems, also hadn't returned to college and was working in a lawyer's office. Ben, Rella, and Tyler may as well have been on another planet, for all the news she and Andrea heard of them.

Life wasn't terrible. Andrea didn't hate her job; neither did Kit. But, if she were painting her life, Kit dispiritedly knew she'd color it *drab*.

Then something happened that made *drab* look not so bad after all, infinitely preferable to the black hole that suddenly opened and swallowed her.

It was a letter from Kelli, who had kept in touch with their former roommate Autumn at college. Kit was pleased when she saw the envelope. Kelli could make cheerful, amusing stories out of the most mundane of happenings. Kit got a 7-Up from the fridge, kicked off her shoes, and settled on the sofa to enjoy the letter. As expected, Kelli had a funny story about a recent date. Then the tone of the letter changed.

"I don't know if I should pass this along to you," Kelli wrote in script on her computer. *"Maybe you already know. Maybe you aren't interested. Maybe you'd rather not know. But then I thought, if I were you, I'd want to know. So, after all that hemming and hawing, here goes. I just heard through Autumn that Tyler is dating a girl named Ronnie Willoughby, and she's claiming they're 'practically engaged.'"*

Kit swallowed, blinked, read the line three more times, each time more slowly than the last, feeling as if her brain were helplessly chugging to a halt. Tyler. Almost engaged. To a girl named Ronnie Willoughby.

In sudden denial, she crumpled the letter and slammed it in the wastebasket. Even in her anger over Tyler's betrayal, even in the depths of her despair over the breakup, some small nucleus of hope had remained. It was a secret place of comfort to which she sometimes guiltily retreated. Yes, there was this canyon between them now, but they *loved* each other.

So this simply could not be true. It was just cruel or frivolous gossip. Everyone knew how gossip got distorted as it passed from person to person! She grabbed that thought and made a fifty-yard dash with it. After a few spins through the gossip mill, a chance encounter, and a friendly cup of coffee could expand to a passionate affair.

Yet it almost had to be based on some scrap of concrete evidence.

Okay, she granted, putting her hand on her chest and forcing herself to take a deep breath, maybe he'd dated someone a few times. She'd done that. It didn't mean anything. She'd thought about Tyler almost the whole time she was out on those other dates. She reluctantly retrieved the crumpled letter, straightened it, and read on.

Autumn had told Kelli that she didn't know much about the girl. Ronnie Willoughby reputedly came from a wealthy east-coast family with money older than Arizona, maybe enough to buy Arizona. She'd transferred from some eastern university to the U. of A., belonged to a sorority, and was a music or drama major. She was tall and willowy, with an aura of cool poise (*read that "snob,"* Kelli had inserted), long blond hair, green eyes, and fingernails always manicured to perfection.

Actually, Kit thought as she looked down at her own unadorned fingernails, that was quite a lot to know about Ronnie Willoughby. Enough to know that she was as different from Kit as Phoenix heat was from Arctic ice. Which was exactly the kind of change her father had made when he abandoned Andrea for her opposite in Rella.

She didn't burst into tears as this bleak impact sank into her heart. She just sat cross-legged on the sofa, not even aware of the leaking tears until they soaked the paper and smudged the print.

Over. It really was over now. Irrevocably and forever. Now she understood why Elyse Roderick had found Andrea sitting in the dark, numb and blank, that night months ago. Kit was just sitting there in the evening dusk when her mother got home from working late an hour later. She took one look at Kit and rushed to kneel beside her daughter.

"Hon, what is it?"

Silently Kit handed her the tear-damp letter. Then they held each other and cried together, encouraged and comforted each other, and cried some more. They said insulting things about men in general, and finally they managed to laugh through the tears at the sheer outrageousness of the things they were saying. They even shared scrambled eggs and raisin-bread toast, and Kit knew that one of the many things for which she could still be grateful was this wonderful closeness with her mother.

A bright spot came along later that fall. No, Kit thought when it happened, this spot went far beyond bright. This spot shimmered, sparkled, and danced.

It happened on Thanksgiving Day. They had been invited several places for dinner, but by mutual agreement they were eating at home, just the two of them. It seemed preferable to trying to create an imitation of the Holloway-McCord family celebrations of former years. A roast turkey breast instead of the big turkey they'd always had, scaled down trimmings, a "lite" version of the usual rich pumpkin pie.

Kit offered the prayer before they ate. Andrea still wasn't going to church with her, but Kit knew that she often read her Bible late into the night before turning out the bedroom light. Now, as usual these days, her mother added a few generic words of gratitude to the prayer. When she stopped abruptly, Kit thought the prayer was over and opened her eyes. But the prayer wasn't over. Her mother's eyes were tightly closed, her face turned upward. And real words of thanks suddenly poured out of her, as if a plug had been pulled on some held-back torrent.

"Thank you for my wonderful daughter, Lord. Thank you for all the blessings of our lives. We aren't hungry or homeless—we have each other! Thank you for bringing me through the painful time even when I was angry with you, when I failed to trust you, when I failed to believe you were even there. Thank you for loving me, for sending your Son to die for us. Forgive me for my poisonous feelings toward Ben and Rella."

When Andrea finally opened her eyes, they glowed with both peace and exhilaration. With a surprised wonderment, she said, "Finally, it all got through to me." And with a radiant smile she added, "And you know what? I'm not a fraud anymore!"

Which, as far as Kit was concerned, made it the best Thanksgiving ever.

The following evening, comfortably full of Thanksgiving leftovers, Kit sat on the sofa turning the pages of a dental supply catalog that had arrived in the mail that day. Idly she wondered what crazed computer had mistakenly put them on this particular mailing list.

Andrea put down the Victorian doll costume she was working on and flexed her fingers. "Ellouise wants me to bring something for the Christmas arts-and-crafts show at the mall, but I can't possibly get this done in time."

Kit turned another page of the catalog, wincing at the display of sharp, wickedly shiny instruments. Casually, with no idea of the future impact of what she was saying, she suggested, "Why don't you make up a couple of those teddy-cat dolls like you made for me years ago?"

PART TWO

TEN

Tyler slouched comfortably in the kitchen chair, cup of coffee in hand. This wasn't home now, but it felt good to be here. The Christmas tree spilled a woodsy scent from the darkened living room, and the colorful strand of lights glowed cheerfully over the faint flicker of the TV. All he could see of Ben was his legs, feet comfortably turned outward on the footrest of the recliner. Ben and Rella had been married since a couple of weeks after the divorce was final. He and Ben got along okay, but not like in earlier times; now there was always an undercurrent of awkwardness and tension between them.

"I'm glad you could make it here for Christmas this year." Rella set a piece of lemon pie in front of him. He forked a bite to his mouth and nodded approvingly. She still didn't go in for fancy frills with food, but, after all these years, her cooking had definitely improved. He suspected complaints from Ben may have had something to do with the change. "It wasn't the same without you last year."

He'd been on the Bio-Bio River in Chile at this time last year. And still had the scar on his knee to prove it, he thought wryly.

"I cut this out of the Phoenix newspaper a few days ago." Rella handed him a folded clipping. "I thought you might like to see it."

Her tone was so casual that he had no suspicion of what was coming until he unfolded the page. The front legs of the chair slammed into the floor hard when he saw the face he hadn't seen for more than two and a half years smiling up at him from the newspaper photo.

Her dark hair was longer now, curving smooth and sleek against her cheek. She'd always been pretty, but time had brought out her cheekbones and emphasized her eyes, transforming her pixie good looks into sculpted beauty. She wore a dark business suit, no-nonsense but feminine, and her figure was as sleek as her hair. It was difficult to believe that this sophisticated young woman with the polished smile was the same breathless, giggling, barefoot girl in cut-off jeans that he'd long ago kissed for the first time at Elves Chasm.

He was concentrating so intensely on Kit that for a moment he didn't even notice the other figure in the photo. Andrea, of course, her short, dark hair and gentle smile exactly as he remembered her, no scars of her emotional problems after the breakup now visible. She wore a loose-fitting smock and held an armload of floppy dolls that looked vaguely familiar.

He dragged his eyes from the photo to skim the article below.

Some years back it was Cabbage Patch dolls. More recently Tickle Me Elmo and Sing & Snore Ernie and Barney have held the spotlight. This year, the toy every child must have, the toy for which parents will battle like hockey players, is a Teddi-Cat. Or, better yet, a whole family of Teddi-Cats.

There's Teddi-Cat Dad and Mom, the teenage twins Kevin and Krissi, adorable Baby Boo, right on through an extended family that includes aproned Aunt Thelma, Cousin Danna, the glamorous model in sunglasses and purple jumpsuit, and various other quirky members. The family even has its own pets, Teddi-Cat Kitty and Teddi-Cat Pup. The dolls can be purchased singly, but the aim of every child is to acquire the entire family, of course, and the toys have proven surprisingly popular as collector items among adults also.

Teddi-Cats are the product of the creative imagination of Andrea Holloway, affectionately known to friends and coworkers as Andy...

Tyler stopped short. Andy? He couldn't quite imagine Andrea as Andy; yet when he glanced at the photo again, he did see an aura of happy confidence he didn't remember from the past. He continued reading where he'd stopped in midsentence.

...with shrewd business acumen supplied by her daughter, Kit Holloway. Together they head up Andkit, Inc., the hottest new entry on the national toy scene.

Tyler read on, how the Teddi-Cats had begun when Andrea made a couple of the toys described as a "fun cross between a teddy bear, a stuffed cat, and a doll" for a Phoenix arts-and-crafts show. They were purchased by a woman for her niece back east, a niece who just happened to be the daughter of the owner of a chain of department stores. The owner in turn was impressed with how wild his daughter and her friends were about the odd little cat-dolls with such endearing faces. He saw the possibilities and tracked down the creator.

Last Christmas, when Teddi-Cats were produced on a cottage-industry basis by a handful of women in the Phoenix area, the dolls had made a respectable entry into the market. This year, when an appropriate voice message was added to the internal construction of each doll, and the manufacturing process went professional, the Teddi-Cat craze exploded. Another small photo showed eager buyers lined up waiting for an expected delivery of the dolls at a store back east. Looking ahead, the article ended, the Andkit team wasn't resting on their laurels; they would be bringing out a much anticipated new line of dolls next year, although details were still under wraps.

Now he knew why the dolls Andrea was holding looked vaguely familiar. Kit had treasured a similar one her mother had made for her years ago. His gaze jumped back to Kit, as if his eyes were too hungry for sight of her to stay away for long.

"She looks good, doesn't she, Ty?"

"Very good."

"Do you have any contact with her at all?"

"No."

"Have you ever *tried* to have any contact with her?"

"No."

Rella rolled her eyes in semiexasperation. "It wouldn't hurt to give her a call, you know, or write her. Or just drop by and see her sometime when you're in Phoenix. Take a tour of their manufacturing facility, perhaps. Does she know what you're doing now?"

"I have no idea."

"Maybe she doesn't know that you never went into business with us. That might make a difference in her feelings."

"I keep in touch with you. I still come here occasionally."

"Which, from Kit's point of view, means you're still contaminated?" Rella deduced wryly.

Yes. Still mingling with her mother's betrayers, still consorting with the enemy.

"I'd really rather not talk about Kit." Suddenly half angry, he shoved the newspaper clipping back across the table. "Has Ben gotten that carburetor problem on the Cessna fixed yet?"

Rella didn't apologize for saving the clipping for him even if he now rejected it. "It came out of the repair shop last week. We'll probably make a checkout flight down to Kingman next week." Then, as if it were a perfectly logical extension of discussion about the Cessna, she added, "You're not seeing anyone else, are you?"

Tyler gave an exasperated roll of his own eyes. "I'm not a hermit. I go out once in a while."

"Why, yes, you do, don't you?" Rella's words agreed, but her teasing tone made fun of his claim. "I believe it wasn't more than six months ago that you mentioned having lunch with a woman who was working on the sound track for one of *The World of White Water* segments."

"Get off my back, Mom," he groused. "I don't meet all that many date prospects. I'm not exactly surrounded by eligible women in my line of work, you know. But I'll find someone when I'm ready."

"Someone like Ronnie Willoughby?"

Tyler groaned. "Don't even joke about that," he said reproachfully. "And you needn't bother to say 'I told you so.'"

"I've never said that," Rella protested with a show of motherly indignation.

"Only because you know I've said to myself enough times, 'Well, Mom was right after all.'"

Rella just smiled, letting silence say more than words. She freshened their coffee and sat down at the table with a piece of pie for herself. Always persistent, she returned to the original subject. "You probably wouldn't be all that interested even if you were surrounded by attractive women because you've never gotten over Kit. Because if you were over her, you wouldn't be so touchy just talking about her."

"Not being completely over her and wanting to revive the relationship are two very different things. And I *don't* want to revive it," he added firmly. With rigid self-control he kept his gaze from straying to the photo again. "We discovered big differences between us. You know that. Nonnegotiable then, nonnegotiable now."

Rella stopped eating and dabbed her fork at the pie. Her strong shoulders lifted in a sigh. "I've always regretted that Ben and I didn't wait until after you and Kit were married before we did what we did. Maybe things would have worked out better for you if we had."

Tyler noted that she didn't express regret for what they'd done, only the timing. He could still wish they had *never* done it, but the timing was one point on which he was certain. He shook his head. "The timing wouldn't have made any difference. If you'd waited, we'd probably have had a broken marriage, not just a broken engagement."

"I'm sorry, Ty. My happiness cost you yours."

He inspected her thoughtfully as she dawdled with the pie. She wasn't conventionally beautiful, never had been, but her weathered, pioneer face had a strong, timeless elegance little changed from her younger years. She was in her familiar slim jeans and a blue chambray shirt, streaky blond hair—were a few of those streaks gray now?—tied back with a leather thong. "Are you happy?" he asked impulsively.

"Mostly."

"Is Ben?"

She shrugged lightly and repeated the same ambiguous word. "Mostly. Although I wouldn't recommend guilt as a strong foundation for top-of-the-line happiness. And yes," she added, as if in answer to an unspoken question, "we haven't escaped feeling guilty. But Andrea seems to have come through everything in fine shape. When the original time period on the alimony ran out, Ben offered to extend it, but we were informed through her lawyer that they no longer needed financial assistance. Perhaps, as the old saying goes, success is the best revenge."

"Andrea was never a vengeful person." But he suspected that being able to tell her father what he could do with his money was a sweet triumph for Kit. Now he gave back the same suggestions Rella had made to him. "Maybe Ben ought to try making amends with Kit. He could call or write her."

"Ben is a stubborn man."

"Seems to run in the family."

He meant Kit went he said that, but Rella's gaze focused squarely on him as she gave him a knowing nod and reinterpreted the statement. "Oh yes. Stubbornness definitely runs in this family."

Tyler decided not to get into any further discussion along these lines and glanced at his watch. "I don't suppose I could interest you and Ben in coming to the Christmas Eve services at church with me tonight?" Over the years he'd talked to Ben and Rella many times about the faith to which he was committed, but, as Kit had once charged, they'd never shown much more than a "spitwad's worth of interest."

"Ben won't go. I mentioned it to him earlier today." That statement surprised Tyler, but her next words surprised him even more. "But I wouldn't mind tagging along."

"Great!"

Then, as if to make certain he didn't interpret what she'd said as some sudden interest in the spiritual side of Christmas, she added, "At least that way I get to spend a little more time with you."

For several days Tyler toyed with the idea of calling Kit or stopping in Phoenix to see her on his way back to southern California. Then he'd ask himself, why? As he'd told Rella, he wasn't about to plead for a rekindling of their relationship. What point was there in reopening old arguments, old wounds?

Yet, just as a friendly gesture, it wouldn't hurt to congratulate her on the success of the new business.

He narrowed the idea of contact down to a phone call. Better a phone slammed in his ear than a door slammed in his face, he figured. Then he narrowed it down still further. A phone call on New Year's Eve. Yes. If she was out somewhere on this night when couples were always together, he could assume she had a new love in her life. But if she was home alone...

He carefully did not stop to dissect motivation for finding out if she was involved with someone else. He got her home phone number from information. He debated a proper time. Late enough to find out if she was actually staying home, not so late as to make her think he was trying to kindle sentimental memories of past kisses at the stroke of midnight. He finally decided on a nicely neutral nine-thirty.

But two days before New Year's Eve, he received a phone call from Royce Morrison, his partner in the river-running series they were doing for release on PBS television.

"We're in, man!" Royce said excitedly. "At the last minute, they finally decided to grant us permission. Definitely not the ideal time of year, of course, but get your beat-up body down here, and let's go for it before they change their minds!"

They'd been trying for months to arrange this, equipment and supplies ready, everything *go* except for official authorization from a foot-dragging government. So, as it turned out, on New Year's Eve Tyler wasn't calling Kit after all. He was on a flight to China with Royce for a once-in-a-lifetime rafting expedition on the Yangtze River.

On impulse he did try to call Kit just before he left Page an hour after Royce's call. All he got was an answering machine and, after a long hesitation, he simply put the phone down without saying anything.

And when he finally did call her months later in August, it was for an entirely different and much more somber reason.

103

Kit checked the PBS listings in the TV guide as she did regularly after accidentally catching the last few minutes of a program called *The World of White Water* last winter. In astonishment she'd heard Tyler's voice giving part of the narration about a white-water rafting trip on the Zambezi River in Africa, and, gaze riveted to the TV screen, seen his name listed among the credits as a photographer. Later she'd seen another segment of the series, a full-hour program of an expedition on the Bio-Bio River in Chile, and that time she'd even gotten a good look at him when someone else operated the camera.

She'd barely noticed the roaring rapids smashing around tangled boulders, the bucking raft tilting to an almost vertical plunge before disappearing in an avalanche of white water. She saw only Tyler: unruly blond hair sticking out from under a protective helmet, arm muscles bulging as he dug the oar deep in treacherous water. A zoom-in close-up caught the tanned sun-crinkles around his eyes and a virile stubble of red-gold beard framing his reckless grin. She heard his familiar whoop of joy in the churning water, oar uplifted in victory as they shot out of the rapids.

Her emotions rocketed crazily as she watched him, physical reactions running just as wild. Somersaulting heartbeat, paralyzed breath, clenched hands. For a moment she was there beside him, whooping and laughing with him, loving him and the adventure.

Some momentary glitch on station or film momentarily blurred the scene into jagged black-and-white lines and dropped her back into not-there reality. Yes, he was living the adventures they'd one time planned to share, but he was doing it without her, carefree and happy. Or maybe by now he was married to someone else.

Autumn had dropped out of college shortly after passing along to Kelli the news that Tyler really was engaged. Later Kelli reported that she'd heard in a roundabout way that the engagement hadn't lasted, but it was such fifth-hand information that Kit couldn't put much stock in it. And, even if Tyler hadn't married Ronnie

Willoughby, he could be married to someone else by now.

She'd long ago acknowledged that any possibility of marriage between Tyler and herself was lost in the jagged depths of that canyon separating them, but the thought that he could be married to someone else still depressed her, still made her heart feel tattered and ragged. Yet now she also wondered what his new adventures meant in his relationship with Ben and Rella. Was he doing this during the winters, the off-season of Canyon Cowboys' trips through the Grand Canyon? Were Ben and Rella also involved in the expeditions?

Later she thought about dropping him a line, in care of Ben and Rella, to tell him what a terrific series *The World of White Water* was. The programs were certainly worthy of praise. Fantastic river-running sequences, but much more. There was skillfully worked-in information about the ecology of rivers, the people who lived near them, and what man was doing in sometimes saving, more often destroying, the world. But after writing the note, even addressing and stamping an envelope, she hadn't sent it. He might interpret it as a fishing expedition, she'd decided, a foolish attempt to revive something long dead between them.

The TV guide showed no segments of *The World of White Water* scheduled this week. She padded dispiritedly to the living-room window and stared at the climbing vine withering on the wires she'd strung to support it. August heat had blasted this well-named Valley of the Sun almost since dawn. She'd always loved the blazing heat of the river canyon, even the hot nights when each molecule of air felt stalled in breathless place, but this urban heat, accompanied by the endless false coolness of air-conditioning, somehow seemed to drain her energy.

She turned away from the window, restless as well as disheartened. Andrea was out for the evening, conducting a meeting of the divorce-recovery group she had helped start at the friendly church they'd joined. Maybe she should go to the health club and swim or work out for an hour. Or drive over to the mall and wander around.

Not even the inducement of promising herself an icy latte prodded her into action, and the briefcase of work waiting in the bedroom-turned-office nagged at her anyway. She had a sleek, modern office in Andkit's main manufacturing center, but it was a rare night when she didn't bring work home.

With a certain resignation she slogged into the cluttered room. This Christmas marketing plan for their new line of Pioneer Dolls was vital; seasonal sales contributed the largest portion of a doll company's profit. This year, for the new line, she'd thought up an advertising campaign based on nonprofessional models, children of company employees. Briskly she picked up the briefcase.

She dropped into the swivel chair, her minuscule burst of energy withering like that drooping vine. Enthusiasm for Christmas was difficult to sustain during the heat of August.

Sometimes, she thought guiltily, enthusiasm for the entire doll business was difficult to sustain. Not that she wasn't happy with the success of Andkit, Inc., of course. The financial rewards astonished her, and the money had enabled her to fulfill that pledge to herself to someday refuse Ben's tainted money. She also had to admit that seeing herself referred to as the "financial brains" behind the company was a terrific boost to the ego.

She was even more pleased with what the business had done for her mother. Andrea loved the creative work; she'd blossomed into a new woman, outgoing and confident. Kit still couldn't quite think of her mother as *Andy*, the name she'd affectionately acquired from the daughter of one of their employees, but Andrea often used it herself now. She bubbled with new ideas for future projects, reproductions of antique dolls, a Brides of the World series, some sturdy, old-fashioned baby dolls. She even had an idea for a series of books built around the doll characters.

Kit often wished, sometimes almost desperately, that she could "bubble." She knew that any number of classmates from her college days would kill to be in her successful entrepreneurial position. Yet sometimes she felt not so much successful as trapped. Trapped by responsibility, trapped by circumstances, even trapped by success.

Because leaving the high-flying future they were building here would make no sense. And abandoning Andkit would also undercut and betray her mother's hopes and dreams, which was totally unacceptable, of course. Andrea had made wonderful strides, but she knew little about the financial workings and strategies of the company. They were still in debt for the Small Business Administration loan for which Kit had fought fiercely to get the company going.

But if, by some miracle, Andrea *could* take over...

Kit stared at her shadowy reflection in the dark computer screen. If she didn't have to devote her future to Andkit, what would she do?

With a jolt of guilt, she felt a rush of envy for Tyler and his *World of White Water*. The thrill of unknown rapids, the excitement of new sights around each river bend, perhaps finding, somewhere on the wild edges of the world, a river that had never been run! Yet beyond those adventures, she knew there was something even more important she wanted.

Marriage, family, home...

She smiled softly, seeing in the dark screen a crowded vision of children, dogs, cats, backyard barbecues, love and laughter and family worship. And, in hazy shadows of far-off future, grandchildren and growing old together...

The vision deteriorated abruptly. Growing old with whom?

There was no man in her life to be the loving husband in that cozy vision, the devoted father, the leader of family worship. She'd dated; she'd gone through an almost frantic spell of it after learning Tyler was engaged. But no guy ever seemed to measure up to what she wanted in a man, and she'd quickly dump one and rush on to another. Then she'd angrily chastise herself, knowing she was subconsciously comparing every guy to Tyler, and that was both foolish and unfair. Tyler was no perfect role model; he was no more trustworthy than her father had been!

Eventually, however, the whole process had worn itself out, and she hadn't dated since sometime last fall. Not that she had much time for dating or a relationship anyway. She often put in ten- or twelve-hour days at Andkit.

Resolutely she turned on the computer. The gray-white screen efficiently blotted visions and reflections, and she dug into the marketing plan. Three hours later it was roughed into shape, and she felt a satisfying weariness of accomplishment. She was trying to stretch the kinks out of her back, wondering where her mother was at this late hour, when the phone rang. She picked it up thinking that it must be Andrea calling to say she'd gotten into a deeper individual discussion of a divorce problem with someone from the group and had lost track of time.

"Hello." Kit stifled a yawn.

"Kit?"

She recognized the voice instantly. She just as instantly denied recognition. How many times had she thought she'd caught a glimpse of him only to realize it was someone who only marginally resembled him? Now she was doing the same thing with voices.

Briskly she said, "Yes, this is Kit Holloway."

"This is Tyler." Then, deliberately mocking the formality of her use of her own full name, he added, "McCord. Tyler McCord."

ELEVEN

How many times had she thought of this moment? Tried out dialogue ranging from distant and angry to witty and sophisticated. But now that the moment was here all she could do was whisper an inane repetition of his name. "Tyler."

Was he married? She felt a sudden feverish burn to know the answer. Surely he wouldn't call if he *were* married!

Or perhaps he would. After three years, how well did she know Tyler? Sometimes, after the canyon split between them, she wondered if she'd ever really known him, if she'd been in love with an illusion.

Then she was angry with herself for even a pinpoint of interest in his marital status. She'd long ago put her feelings for Tyler into the same naïve-mistakes-of-my-adolescence category where she'd dumped her idealized view of her father. Blurting out such a question would also horrify any expert in etiquette. Yet it was pride more than good manners or lack of interest that finally stopped her from asking the question. She would *never* let him suspect how devastated she'd been when she heard about his engagement!

With his next words, she realized marital status was utterly irrelevant to this phone call.

"I'm sorry to interrupt you at this hour, but something has happened." The tinge of mockery in his voice was gone now, the brief sword-crossing replaced by worry and concern. "Ben and Rella left day before yesterday in the Cessna on a flight down to Mexico. They were taking a Mexican businessman and his son who had been on a river trip with them to a ranch somewhere in the Sierra Madre mountains. They should have been back in Page yesterday, but they've never shown up." He paused abruptly before adding, with a hint of defensiveness, as if he suspected she might simply snarl at him for bothering her with this information, "I thought you might want to know."

"Yes, of course I want to know! You're saying the plane is missing? That it could have gone down somewhere?" She felt strangely weak as she stood there clutching the phone. Something such as this had never entered into her wildest imaginings about a call from Tyler.

"It's a strong possibility. I haven't been able to talk to the businessman personally, but the authorities down there say the plane did arrive at the ranch day before yesterday. Ben and Rella spent the night at the ranch—apparently it's quite an elaborate estate—then took off again the following day. It's possible they stopped somewhere along the way, of course, rather than heading directly home."

"Surely there are all sorts of regulations about flying across the border! Clearances or something they'd have to get. Didn't they file a flight plan?"

"They did for the trip down. But the ranch has just a small, private airstrip, and no one seems to know anything about a flight plan for the return trip. Maybe they just waved and took off. You know Ben. He doesn't always think rules and regulations apply…"

Tyler broke off, as if realizing that statement could be applied to more than Ben's attitude toward flying regulations. Kit didn't jump in with condemning comparisons about how her father had also broken the moral rules of marriage. She just searched wildly for some explanation rather than the one that filled her with terror, not stopping to examine why it filled her with terror after she had so long denied any feelings for Ben and Rella.

"But there are explanations other than a crash," she insisted frantically. "Dad might have seen something that interested him and just decided to drop down and take a look. And stayed a while. Or maybe they had some minor engine problem, or needed fuel, and detoured to some small Mexican airport, and the authorities just don't know that. There are any number of reasons why they might not have returned to Page yet!"

"Yes, that's certainly true. That's why Mrs. Altman in the Canyon Cowboys office wasn't overly concerned when they didn't show up yesterday. So it wasn't until today, when she really did become worried, that she contacted local authorities to find out if they knew anything about the plane." Tyler paused and then added reluctantly, as if he hated to squelch one of Kit's hopeful possibilities, "The ranch owner told authorities that Ben filled the fuel tanks on the Cessna there at the airstrip. He keeps a supply on hand for his own plane."

Kit tried to look on the up side. "At least that means they didn't crash because they ran out of fuel over some isolated area."

"Kit, I'm hoping for the best. Ben is a good pilot. But I know he had some engine problems with the plane last winter. It's also rough, mountainous country down there, lots of canyons and cliffs, which could mean dangerous down and updrafts. And there were thunderstorms scattered all over the area that afternoon."

A terrifying vision swept through Kit—the vulnerable little Cessna storm-tossed and helpless, electricity crackling in evil witch-fingers of lightning around it, the fragile wings spiraling downward, slamming into a ragged mountainside like a discarded toy, pieces scattered like bits of shrapnel. Ben and Rella injured and helpless—

"They're looking for the plane, aren't they? Surely someone is out searching for them!"

"I think so, but things down there don't operate exactly the way they do here, so I'm not certain how much of a search it is. It's also possible, if the plane did go down, that it could have happened on this side of the border, which puts it out of Mexican territory. But the authorities on this side are convinced that they'd have known if the plane did cross the border, so it's all kind of muddled."

"We've got to do something!" She shifted the phone to her other ear. Her hands shook with the frantic helplessness of their situation. "We can't just sit around and wait!"

"My thoughts exactly. I've hired a private plane to fly me down there. We'll leave at daybreak and go directly to the ranch. I want to talk to Ben's passenger personally. Maybe Ben mentioned something to him about plans or a route for the return trip, which will give us a better idea where to search. Then, if there isn't already an official search under way, I'll get one going. And take part in it."

The threat and determination in Tyler's voice promised bad

news for anyone who balked or stood in the way of that search, and Kit felt a quick wash of relief. Tyler wasn't helpless; Tyler knew what to do.

"I'll come along and help...."

A small silence, although Kit was uncertain whether that indicated surprise at her offer or that he was taking time to consider accepting.

"There's something else you could do that would be of more value at the moment."

"Yes, of course, anything."

"Basically, with both Ben and Rella gone, no one is running the show back in Page."

"Aren't you there?"

"No." He didn't elaborate. "They apparently didn't plan to be gone more than overnight and didn't leave specific instructions about anything. Mrs. Altman is more or less running things at the moment, and everyone knows their duties for routine matters, but you know how things start to come apart when no one's in charge."

Something sank inside her. "You sound as if you don't expect them back anytime soon."

"I'm just saying someone needs to be in charge there. Ben and Rella also have a launch scheduled for Friday. I'd go up and take care of everything there, but I think it's more important that I get down to Mexico and find out what's going on."

"Where are you now?"

"At my apartment in Oceanside."

Kit was taken aback by this information that he lived in southern California, that he apparently wasn't, as she'd assumed, now a partner in Canyon Cowboys. She had a dozen curious questions, but this was no time to ask them.

"So what you're asking is for me to go up to Page and run Canyon Cowboys temporarily."

"Yes. And pilot one of the rafts on this upcoming trip." Then, as if the thought had just occurred to him, he asked sharply, "Do you still have your commercial operating certificate?"

"Yes." There had been no real reason to renew when the certificate was about to expire, but she'd done it. Maybe for the same not-quite-explainable reason Ben had kept up his membership in the Professional Cowboys Rodeo Association long after he knew he'd never rodeo again.

Tyler didn't ask for explanation. "Good," he simply said briskly. "There's an experienced pilot who occasionally fills in when they need someone extra, Kyle Anderson, older guy, maybe you know him?"

"Yes, I remember him. He taught at the grade school during the winters and piloted for Canyon Cowboys in the summer."

"Right. So the two of you can take over Ben and Rella's places on this coming river trip."

"Tyler, I haven't been on the river since…well, you know the last time I was on the river! I also don't know all that much about running the company."

There was more. She hadn't really been thinking about details when she impulsively offered to assist with the search; the frantic need to *do* something had simply burst out of her. But what Tyler was asking was a commitment of at least ten days, because once she started down the river, even if Ben and Rella returned home, she'd have to finish the trip. She couldn't be away from Andkit for that long! Someone needed to be in charge *here*.

"I'm not worried about your competence. But, if you prefer, Kyle can officially be lead pilot, and you'll be second. As for managing the company, just put the management skills you've used to make a big success out of Andkit to use in running Canyon Cowboys. You can do it."

Surprised, she realized he knew about their company and its sudden rise to success. "I'm not sure Dad and Rella would want me involving myself in their business even in an emergency."

"I think they'd appreciate it." He hesitated. "They've always hoped for a reconciliation with you."

"I've never seen any evidence of that!"

"Look, this isn't the time to get involved in old arguments and accusations and bitterness. Do you want to do this or not?"

Kit hesitated, thoughts and emotions and fears tangling like tornado-twisted strands of barbed wire. Even if she could somehow figure a way to leave Andkit temporarily, did she want to do something for these people she had cut out of her life? And there was so much to be done at Andkit! New additions to the Teddi-Cat family. The new line of Pioneer Dolls. A meeting in New York next week with the head of a national chain of stores. Conferences about advertising and marketing, meetings with suppliers. Why should she take any risks with Andkit in order to preserve Ben and Rella's business? They'd never shown any concern for her! Maybe they'd just made an impulsive stopover at some romantic hideaway and would come in holding hands and laughing.

But they could be stranded in a desert wasteland, injured and hungry and thirsty. She refused to think they were dead. She simply would not think it. Whatever her differences with Ben and Rella, she didn't want them dead.

Okay, she *could* get away for a few days, she decided slowly. Not easy, definitely not convenient, but possible. Rearrange schedules, delegate responsibilities, postpone the trip to New York, tell Andrea she'd have to handle the meetings with suppliers. Kelli could be a big help. Her former roommate was working for Andkit as Kit's assistant now, and she'd proven to be a marvel of efficiency and bright ideas.

Tyler apparently interpreted her silence as foot-dragging rather than a whirlwind of planning going on in her mind. "If you don't want to do it for them, you might consider doing it from the standpoint of protecting your own interests."

Both his words and the scornful cynicism in his voice confused her. "My own interests?"

"If the plane has crashed and neither of them survive, you're in line to inherit Ben's half of Canyon Cowboys. You wouldn't want the company falling apart just when you might own half of it, would you?"

Outrage that appealing to her own self-interest might be more effective than merely suggesting Ben and Rella needed her help almost made her slam the phone down. Angry retorts and insults and accusations of her own blazed like headlines across her mind, but in the end all she did was say tightly, "I'll arrange to fly to Page late tomorrow afternoon. You'll keep me informed of what's going on?"

"Yes. As much as I can. I don't know what conditions I'll encounter down there or what contact will be possible if I'm on a search."

She ended the conversation with remote politeness. "Thank you."

She thought she heard him say something else, maybe her name, but the phone was already too far away from her ear to catch the word, and she didn't snatch it back to ask for a repeat.

TWELVE

K it arrived in Page just before dark on Wednesday evening. The Canyon Cowboys office was closed, but she immediately called Mrs. Altman at home to let her know she'd arrived to help out until Ben and Rella returned. She didn't know whether or not Tyler had informed Mrs. Altman that Kit was coming, and she wondered if the long-time, competent, but occasionally grumpy office manager might simply tell her she had no business butting into Canyon Cowboys' affairs now and refuse to cooperate with her. The woman surprised her by being both friendly and conscience-stricken.

"I'm so sorry I didn't report Ben and Rella missing that very first day," she fretted. "I keep thinking that if I had, maybe a search would have been started sooner and they'd be found before—before it's too late."

"We don't know that it is too late," Kit soothed. She felt a stomach-plunge of apprehension. "Unless you've heard from Tyler?"

"No. Not a word."

"Then there's still the possibility the plane didn't crash. Or, if it is down, that Dad and Rella are fine and just waiting to be rescued. And I'm sure if anyone can find them, Tyler can. I'm just grateful that you reported them missing when you did."

By now, however, in spite of her assurances to Mrs. Altman, Kit was reluctantly convinced the plane had crashed somewhere, that Ben and Rella hadn't impulsively made a casual stopover or side jaunt. But she clung to a reassuring mental picture of her father, big and muscular and invincible, hiking to safety, more annoyed at being dumped on a Mexican desert than frightened or injured. And lean, tough Rella striding along right beside him.

"I've been wondering about your mother." As if afraid that sounded like snooping, Mrs. Altman hastily added, "I read a nice piece in the paper some time back about both of you."

"Mom's doing fine. We're both concerned about Dad, of course."

Actually, Andrea hadn't seemed to know quite what to do with her emotions when Kit gave her the news. She'd worked so hard at ending her feelings for Ben, of letting go of her relationship with him. For a moment she'd looked almost blank, as if she had to search behind closed doors in her mind to remember who these people were. Then empathy for Kit's worries about her father took over, and she wrapped her arms around her daughter and murmured words of support and comfort. "Can we *do* anything?" she'd asked finally, and then Kit said she'd told Tyler that she'd go to Page and help out with Canyon Cowboys for a few days.

Andrea hadn't protested or complained about the inconvenience or problems this would pose for Andkit; she simply threw her wholehearted support into making it possible. They put in a frenzied day of rearranging plans and schedules, making hurried decisions, and briefing Kelli on her new responsibilities before Andrea drove Kit to the airport that evening.

Just before they reached the parting point at the terminal, Kit asked impulsively, "Mom, how do you really feel about all this?"

"About your going to help out? Or the possibility that something may have happened to your father and Rella?"

"Both."

"Still nervous that some big problem will come up, and you won't be here to solve it," Andrea admitted. She smiled with a hint of tears glistening in her blue eyes. "But so very proud of you for putting your hurt and bitterness aside and jumping in to help when they need it."

"I don't deserve your being proud of me," Kit said unhappily. "The only reason I agreed to do it was because Tyler said something that made me angry. Now..."

"Now you're having second thoughts?" Andrea asked with a mother's intuition. "Don't. You're doing the right thing. Kit, we've never talked about this, but if you haven't already forgiven them, do it. It's like letting go of an enormous burden when you do."

"You've forgiven them?"

Andrea nodded. "Although now that this has happened..." She sighed and shook her head. "I still feel guilty."

"Guilty?"

"Guilty because for a while I *wanted* something terrible to happen to them, and now perhaps it has. Rationally, I know my past wish for avenging thunderbolts has nothing to do with what's actually happened now, but I feel so guilty for ever having had such terrible thoughts."

"Mom, we spent a long time last night praying for Dad and Rella, remember?" She gave her mother's shoulders a little chastising shake. "Don't feel guilty. Just keep praying, okay?"

And right there in the Phoenix airport, with people swirling around them, they had joined hands and bowed their heads and prayed once more.

Now, here in the Page airport, Kit briefly leaned her forehead against the phone. Ben and Rella couldn't be dead. No matter how angry she'd been with them, she thought as she had so many times since Tyler's phone call, she didn't want them dead! *Please, Lord, guide Tyler to them!* She swallowed and changed the phone to her other ear so she could dry her damp palm on her pants leg.

Aware that two people were standing behind her impatiently waiting to use the phone, Kit hurriedly jumped into the next problem of the moment. "I understand there's a river trip leaving Friday. Is everything set up and ready?" she asked Mrs. Altman.

"There are a few problems. There always are, as I'm sure you remember. Kyle, the substitute pilot, will be here, but he had to go out of town and won't be home until late Thursday night. The truck barely made it back from Pierce Ferry with the rafts on the last trip. It's in the shop, but is supposed to be out tomorrow in plenty of time for the launch Friday. The market that supplies our meat called and said they can't get the steaks Rella ordered for the trip. I don't usually handle these matters," Mrs. Altman added, sounding both apologetic and flustered. "Ben and Rella always do these things themselves, you know. My job here in the office is mostly with reservations and payments and payroll and such."

Yes, Kit knew. Canyon Cowboys was still one of the smallest commercial outfits on the river. Most of the others were big companies, often running trips on multiple western rivers, their offices staffed with several people, a local manager running the show and owners from outside the area not personally involved. Not like Canyon Cowboys, which was very much a hands-on business with Ben and Rella involved in every aspect of it.

"We'll manage. I'll be in the office first thing in the morning."

"Are you staying at the house?"

Kit stopped herself from gasping an appalled *No!* In years gone by, she'd spent many nights at the ranch house, but staying there now that it was Ben and Rella's home had never occurred to her. She was willing to help out in this crisis; she desperately wanted Ben and Rella to be alive and safe. But this was definitely not a welcome-home week. "I'll get a motel room."

A little awkwardly, as if hearing in Kit's voice the aversion to going anywhere near the house, Mrs. Altman said, "The Canyon Cowboys office is at the ranch now. They built onto the front end of the warehouse."

So she couldn't avoid the ranch, then. She found herself wondering if that antique carriage Rella had restored for the wedding was still in the barn. Even more, she wondered what had become of the ring that had once symbolized the love and promise between herself and Tyler.

But all she said was a brisk repetition of her earlier words. "I'll see you there in the morning, then."

She took a taxi to the motel near the edge of town in the direction of the ranch. Along the way, she saw sights both familiar and new. The hamburger stand where everyone had hung out in her high-school days was gone; in its place a mini mall of gift shops, video rentals, an espresso shop, and an outdoor-clothing store. The old movie theater gave her an unwanted twinge of nostalgia, and a parking lot where something had been, but she couldn't remember what, made her feel oddly like some old-timer returning after an absence of many years.

Their route didn't go past her old church or the house. At the motel, she thought about people she knew whom she might call, but she'd deliberately cut ties here, and reviving them now seemed pointless. Yet, as she crossed the street to a restaurant later, she was aware of just how much she'd missed this little town in which she'd grown up.

She breathed deeply of evening air with no blight of urban pollution, an untarnished scent with sweet undercurrents of sagebrush and river and open space. It made her remember solitary cross-country rides when her wonderful horse Sandy was young and strong and sometimes bucked a little for the sheer joy of life. Winter nights on an old-fashioned hay ride with the church youth group, clip-clopping down the road trailing the scent of alfalfa hay and the sound of choruses of praise. She gazed upward at emerging stars, undimmed by city lights and haze, and thought of crisp fall nights, football games, magical night boat rides on the lake.

And then she abruptly cut off all such reminiscences, because memories of Tyler wound through them like a scarlet ribbon, brilliant and inescapable. And painful. Briskly she ate a grilled chicken sandwich and salad. She called her mother when she got back to the motel room, and they went over details of a purchase agreement on some fabrics that they'd missed discussing earlier that day. Afterward she spent a strengthening hour with her Bible and prayer before finally feeling ready for sleep.

In the morning she took a taxi out to the ranch. The day promised heat, but it wouldn't be the relentless furnace blast of summer in Phoenix. She purposely gave the white two-story ranch house no more than a fleeting glance. It held too many memories of the closeness between the McCord and Holloway families, shared holidays and barbecues and family celebrations, a closeness now twisted by change and betrayal into an ugly caricature of what it had once been. Yet she couldn't help noticing that the house was still more old-shoe comfortable than stylish, the yard fence of old wagon wheels still tilting a little to one side, the big cottonwood trees shading the house unchanged. But the hand-carved McCord sign that had hung over the arched gate was gone, the short chains once holding it now dangling empty.

The warehouse doors were open, two young guys in shorts busy loading supplies into the neoprene rubber rafts for tomorrow's launch. The big pontoons on either side of the thirty-seven-foot rafts weren't inflated yet, which Kit always thought made the rafts look a little forlorn, like big, ungainly birds stripped of their wings. She went directly to the office, where Mrs. Altman put a hand over the phone and asked whether she should take more reservations for the oar trips in the fall. Kit, after a small hesitation, told her yes.

The busy day kept Kit from wallowing in worry, though worry lingered in the back of her mind like a festering sliver. She took over Rella's desk in the office, finding everything reasonably well organized. By phone she located another supplier who promised to get steaks to them that afternoon. The price was higher than Rella usually paid, according to the records, but Kit didn't quibble. She dealt pleasantly but firmly with a woman on the phone who was canceling for tomorrow's trip and wanted her money back, even though the signed agreements specified no refunds at this late date. Mrs. Altman didn't volunteer any personal information about Tyler, and Kit didn't ask.

About eleven o'clock, the big truck, something like a double-decker car hauler, pulled into the yard, relieving Kit of one worry. She and Mrs. Altman both went out to take a look, and Mrs. Altman made introductions to the crew, whom Kit suspected gathered around more out of curiosity about her than interest in the truck.

The wiry little truck driver, Red Sizemore, cheerfully assured her that this rig could now run to New York and back, if need be, purring all the way. Old Mike, who supervised repair and maintenance on rafts, motors, and other equipment, and had been with Canyon Cowboys for years, greeted her warmly.

The two pilot-trainees, known as swampers, who'd been loading the rafts eyed her with keen interest, not necessarily professional, she suspected. In preparation for more than office work, she'd dressed in cuffed shorts and a cotton tee, and Brian, the boyishly cute, dark-haired one, gave her bare legs an unabashedly thorough inspection. With a flirty, engaging grin, he said, "Call me JoJo." Both he and the other swamper, tall, slim Ryan, were probably not much younger than Kit, but she had a peculiar feeling of seeing them from the viewpoint of some much older generation.

At noon she went to the kitchen at the rear of the warehouse.

It had been remodeled since she'd last seen it, with a huge new freezer and a walk-in, refrigerated room to hold supplies for the river trips. JoJo was making sandwiches from some leftover supplies and offered her one.

"See?" He flashed that grin, which she assumed he knew was quite devastating. With a cheerful lack of modesty he said, "I'm not only gorgeous, I can cook, too."

"Good. I'll expect to eat a lot of your cooking on the river, then." She sat at the wooden picnic table and chomped down on the inch-thick ham sandwich.

"I'm also very good at tossing pliers."

Kit laughed. "They still do that?" Tossing pliers at a bucket set about twenty-five feet away had always been the system for settling who had to get up first and get the coffee going for breakfast, while the other guides slept a few minutes longer. She'd finally become quite expert at the toss.

JoJo swung a muscular leg over the bench and sat down opposite her. "I don't mean to be disrespectful to Ben and Rella, joking around while they're missing," he said apologetically. "We're all pretty shook up about it. They're great people, the best."

Kit made some noncommittal murmur.

He gave her a sideways glance, openly curious. "I never knew they had a daughter. I've met Rella's son, Tyler, but nobody's ever mentioned you." He was obviously fishing for information. When she didn't oblige, he opted for a more direct question. "He's what, your half brother?"

Tyler had been her best friend, her fiancé, and her ex-fiancé. Technically, after Ben and Rella's marriage, he might even be something like her stepbrother. She felt a certain relief knowing that she and Tyler, and the triangle between her parents and Rella, were not subjects of current gossip. Yet she was surprised also to feel a small twinge of something—pain, resentment—that Ben and Rella had apparently relegated her to some skeleton-in-the-closet status where her name was never mentioned. In any case, she had no intention of explaining to JoJo all the messy details of her finished relationship with Tyler. She detoured to a different subject. "This is your first season with Canyon Cowboys?"

"Yeah. I'll be in my junior year at the University of Washington this fall. History major. You in college?"

"No." Before he could ask more nosy questions, she jumped in with another question of her own. "How'd you happen to get the name JoJo?"

Sooner or later, almost everyone here acquired a nickname, usually an inside joke from some personality trait or incident on the river. Sometimes the nicknames also changed according to new events. Everyone had laughingly called Tyler BB&H for a while after a flirty passenger had addressed him as, "Hey, Big, Blond, and Handsome."

JoJo grinned again. "I guess I'm kind of a clown, and somebody said the name for a clown was JoJo. It kind of puts a dent in my macho hero image, but I guess I can live with it."

"JoJo, the lady-killer clown," Kit mused teasingly.

"I do my best," he agreed cheerfully. "Did you have a nickname when you were on the river?"

"Shorty." She hadn't been fond of that reference to her petite size, but it was better than the other embarrassing nickname she'd acquired later on, which she hoped no one now remembered.

Kit spent the afternoon working in the warehouse, getting the remainder of the supplies packed into the ice compartments of the rafts, and checking that all the necessary items such as fire extinguishers, first-aid kits, water filtration equipment, tool kit, and fuel were on board. She also did a job that had been her assigned task from as far back as she could remember. Eggs in cartons didn't survive long on a rough river trip and were also a waste of space, so all the eggs were cracked and slipped whole into gallon plastic containers, yolks floating in a sea of whites. The result looked a little like some bodyless but many-eyed alien creature trapped inside the jar, curious yellow eyes peering out from all sides. She'd always secretly enjoyed this little task, although she remembered once, long ago, when she and Tyler had wound up in big trouble for getting in a wild egg-throwing battle.

Once she turned and saw a tall figure silhouetted against the open doors of the warehouse, and her heart whipped into a strange frenzy. Tyler! Tyler was here!

Then the figure turned, and she realized it was much heavier around the middle than Tyler. It was in fact a deliveryman bringing the promised steaks. She let Ryan go to meet him. She turned back to the eggs, blinking rapidly—a speck in her eye, she assured herself, nothing more—but unaccountably crushing and ruining the next egg.

With Ben and Rella missing, everyone's manner was more restrained and subdued than Kit remembered from previous years. JoJo occasionally livened things up. He juggled spoons once, ending with a comical pratfall that brought spoons raining down on his head. But there was little of the good-natured teasing and kidding around that had always enlivened these hard-work days in the past.

At the end of the day, Red backed the big truck up to the warehouse and, using the electric winch, they loaded the rafts, the one that went on the top layer of the double-decker going on first. She left the warehouse a little after five o'clock, appropriating a company pickup for her personal use. The day was not yet ended, of course.

She arrived at the lodge on the edge of Lake Powell fifteen minutes before the scheduled seven o'clock time for the get-together orientation meeting with tomorrow's passengers. She knew from the very first moment JoJo's appraising glance touched her that he'd talked to someone, probably Mike, and acquired a rundown on past history of the Holloways and McCords. She had also done a little background investigation of her own about the swampers. Mrs. Altman had characterized Ryan as quiet, shy, and dependable, JoJo a little show-offey but good-natured and rock-solid in an emergency. He also, she'd added, had a self-confident belief that it was his duty to supply any unattached female on a river trip with a little taste of canyon romance.

The lead pilot usually ran these meetings, but Kyle Anderson wasn't there and this wasn't something swampers usually did. Kit felt a little awkward taking charge and debated with herself how much to tell the group about Ben and Rella. Their disappearance hadn't made a big splash in the news, except locally, but some might have heard of the situation. She finally made only brief mention of it, then briskly went into demonstrating to the rafters how to pack their sleeping bags and other gear in the wetbags to keep everything waterproof. She explained about the ammo cans in which small items needed during the day could be stored, when the wetbags were unavailable, and JoJo and Ryan distributed the cans. They also handed out guidebooks that gave detailed, mile-by-mile information about the river and the rapids.

She explained safety procedures, what to do if you unexpectedly found yourself dumped in the water, and the government rules and complexities about garbage and human-waste disposal while on the river. She answered questions on various subjects, from danger of snakes to the likelihood of flash floods and contact with the outside world.

"If there's an emergency, we can radio out for help," Kit answered in response to that last question. "If you just want to keep in touch with your stockbroker, forget it. Cell phones are useless in the canyon."

The guy who'd asked that question took some ribbing from his buddies about Kit "having his number," and his thirteen-year-old son whistled screechy approval of her answer. Apparently he was hoping for some exclusive Dad-time on the river.

Afterward, she circulated among the twenty-eight guests as they nibbled on fruit, cheese, and crackers. Among a few of the passengers she detected doubt as well as curiosity about her; a woman pilot was not what they had expected.

One older man came right up and felt her arm muscles. "You sure you can do this, little lady?" he asked doubtfully. "From what I hear, this is a pretty rugged trip."

Little lady, indeed! Kit momentarily felt like flipping him with one of the karate moves she'd learned in a class at the health club, but instead she gave him her most disarming smile. "Brains and experience count for more than brawn going through the rapids with a motorized raft, and I've been running the river with my dad since I was about six years old. So I think you'll be safe with me."

A moment later JoJo confirmed her suspicion that he'd checked up on her history. "A bold and confident speech," he whispered, "for someone with the nickname of Wrong-Way Holloway."

Kit groaned. There it was. That long-ago error had happened not long after she'd received her certification as a full-fledged river pilot. She'd been feeling proud and confident with her new status, but in leaving a camping site in a calm area of water she'd somehow blithely headed her raft loaded with passengers upriver instead of down. And after that embarrassing error, "Wrong-Way" had replaced "Shorty" as her river name. She glanced at the man who had already expressed doubts about her competence, then back at JoJo. She gave him her most threatening glare. "You wouldn't!"

"It'll be our little secret," he assured her with a wink and another of his flirty, boyish grins. "Although a small bribe in the form of missing the bucket with the pliers wouldn't hurt. I need my beauty sleep, you know."

"You look plenty beautiful to me," Kit assured him.

He wiggled his eyebrows and pretended a leer. "Likewise."

Kit left the orientation meeting feeling confident about tomorrow's launch. The passengers looked like a good-natured, congenial group, swampers JoJo and Ryan competent and fun. She could even think optimistically that by the time she was back in Page again, Ben and Rella would be home safe and sound. She went back to the motel room, showered, and washed her hair, the last real shower she'd have for a week. She was settling down with her Bible when the phone rang.

It was Mrs. Altman saying she'd just gotten off the phone with Tyler. No real news, just a call to tell them that he'd been on a search flight all day, without results, and would be going out again tomorrow. For a moment Kit felt a twinge of disappointment that Tyler had called Mrs. Altman, not her. But there was no need for him to give the information directly to her, of course.

"So I suppose no news is good news," Mrs. Altman concluded hopefully.

Kit dutifully agreed, but inside, her upbeat feelings spiraled like a falling plane. At some point that old adage fell apart, and no news was *not* good news.

She spent much time in prayer for Ben and Rella, and also Tyler, as well as for her mother back in Phoenix. And, as she had always done in the past on the night before a river trip, she prayed for the safety of all the passengers and for wisdom and good judgment for herself as pilot. Because in spite of the fact that thousands of people safely enjoyed the river every year, this was no amusement park ride that could be turned off with the flick of a switch. The Colorado River was different than it had been before man-made dams changed its flow, but it was no less powerful and dangerous, no less savagely beautiful and wild.

Which was perhaps why she loved it more than any other spot the Lord had created on this earth.

Then, in spite of worry and apprehension and fear about Ben and Rella, she couldn't help a guilty surge of exhilaration and anticipation. She'd never have chosen these circumstances under which to return to the river. She desperately regretted—along with other less clearly defined regrets of the heart—this reason for being here. If there was any possible way she could change the situation, she would.

Yet the tingle of excitement remained: tomorrow, the river!

THIRTEEN

K yle Anderson was already at the warehouse when Kit arrived shortly after daybreak, climbing on the truck to give the rafts a last-minute check of his own. He was a plain-looking man of sixty, retired from teaching now, his neat khaki shorts and shirt offset by a disreputably battered, wildly multicolored hat. He shook Kit's hand, said, "Good to see you again," and offered quiet sympathy about Ben and Rella.

"No word about them yet, I take it?" he asked.

"No, but Tyler is down there helping with the search."

"It's in good hands then."

Kit believed that. But she now couldn't help a gut-wrenching worry about Tyler as well as Ben and Rella. He'd said the area in which they were missing was rough and dangerous. What if, in the search for them, his plane went down too? *Keep him safe, Lord,* she again begged silently.

Kyle returned to his inspection, and Kit tried to take her mind off her dark visions by busying herself with some last-minute paperwork in the office. She was grateful for Kyle's maturity and quiet air of competence. She'd floated the river many times, but every year there were changes, beaches forming or eroding, flash floods in side canyons sending new boulders crashing into the main river and altering the rapids. She also hadn't piloted a raft since the summer before her breakup with Tyler, and the river wasn't shy about testing courage and skill. She was glad she had Kyle to rely on for this first trip.

They had the rafts off the truck and in the water at Lee's Ferry an hour before the passengers arrived from Page. When the leased bus pulled into the parking area, Kit was just attaching the nylon drag bags filled with soft drinks to the rear of the pontoons; the drinks would stay cold in the river's bone-chilling forty-five degree temperature.

The group exited the bus with whoops and hollers, cameras in hand or dangling from straps draped around necks, dressed in everything from jeans to Hawaiian-print shorts to a skin-baring, fringed bathing suit on one young woman—an outfit that jerked JoJo to immediate attention. Children as young as nine were allowed on these motorized trips, but on this trip the youngest were a couple of thirteen-year-olds. They hit the sandy beach like twin whirlwinds.

Life jackets were fitted and assigned, wetbags securely fastened in the rafts with netting, ammo cans secured with a cord run through the handles. Kyle went through some of the basic instructions with the group again: lifejackets were to be worn at all times on the raft. Swimming allowed only in areas the pilot designated as safe. All trash, including cigarette butts, was to be bagged and hauled out. If you went overboard, keep calm and float with your legs and feet headed downriver in front of you, knees bent so if you bumped into something you could push yourself away from it.

And then they were off on their 175-mile journey, Kyle and Ryan in the lead raft, Kit and JoJo following. JoJo launched the trip with a flourish by christening the raft with a can of Pepsi before jumping in. Kit stood in the horseshoe-shaped area at the rear of the raft with her hand on the long handle attached to the motor. The outboard-style motor was small, more for guiding purposes than power. She wore a heavy slathering of sunscreen lotion, T-shirt and lightweight khaki shorts that would dry quickly, plus rubber-soled Teva sandals and fast-dry socks. River adventures were not fashion shows.

The water at Lee's Ferry flowed gently, the first dance of sun-silvered ripples a mile downstream at Paria Riffle. On the one-to-ten scale of rating river rapids, Paria was barely a one, and the big raft bounced through the ripples with haughty grace. The motor purred comfortably, and the passengers were barely water spattered, even those riding three abreast in the center area up front appropriately known as the "bathtub." Kit, wanting everyone to first become acquainted with both the river and the raft, wasn't yet letting anyone straddle the pontoons or grab the thrill rides on the horn.

They passed under the Navajo Bridge, Kit thinking back on

that time she had said good-bye to the river from there. Now her feelings were so mixed: joy at being on the river again, sorrow that it was under these ominous circumstances. A few miles downriver they came to the first real challenge, Badger Creek Rapid. It wasn't a heart stopper, but it had a dangerous hole known as a "keeper," a place that could trap and spin a raft in a dizzying whirl of white water. She and Tyler once rescued three rafters here whose oar-powered, noncommercial raft had flipped.

Kit followed Kyle's lead and maneuvered into the slick, V-shaped tongue of the *safe* route—safe being a relative term, she thought as she braced herself against the onslaught. White-toothed waves loomed over the raft, like an open mouth waiting to eat the unwary alive, and then avalanched into it. The raft plunged down, bucked up, the handle lunging against her hand. Squeals of the passengers mingled with the roar of the rapids and the shrill whine of the motor as it momentarily lifted out of the water.

Then they were shooting out the bottom side of the rapid, everyone drenched, talking, shaking off water, JoJo saying approvingly, "Hey, Shorty, you've done this before!"

Kit wiped a shaky hand across her wet face. It had been a long time! But she also felt more confident now that she'd conquered the river's first challenge. "You had doubts about my abilities?" she asked with pretended indignation.

He grinned. "I was ready to take over if you couldn't handle it."

"Sonny, I was runnin' this river when you were still in diapers," Kit proclaimed grandly. She wasn't sure of that, but she liked the sound of it.

JoJo grinned again and said, "I like older women."

The morning went smoothly, with just enough rough water to keep Kit too busy to worry about Ben and Rella, almost too busy to recall adventures she and Tyler had shared here. They stopped for lunch on a narrow stretch of sand with a few frothy tamarisk trees for shade. Kit and the men put up a table and set out coleslaw and the makings for sandwiches: ham, turkey, two kinds of cheese, lettuce, pickles, onions, tomatoes, mayonnaise, and various other dressings and mustards, plus several kinds of bread. Kit, with a roaring appetite after a skimpy breakfast and the adrenaline flow of the rapids, piled her rye bread high with ham, Swiss cheese, and tomato, adding several hefty slices of onion. She carried her sandwich and soft drink to a nearby rock. JoJo followed and plopped down cross-legged in the sand beside her.

"Well, I believe I'll think twice before kissing you," he stated as he eyed her generous stack of onion slices.

"You'd better think more than twice about it," Kit retorted.

"Hey, how come?" JoJo sounded indignant. "You and Tyler McCord split up a long time ago. I thought the field was clear."

"The gossip mill still spins, I see."

"I had to give it a little push to get any information," JoJo admitted. "But it definitely said you and Tyler were a thing of the past."

"Maybe I'm involved with someone else now."

"Are you?" he asked bluntly.

"For a clown, you're awfully nosy," Kit grumbled. "And shouldn't you be busy romancing the passengers or something?"

JoJo glanced across the sand at the attractive girl in the fringed swim suit. She was shivering under a towel now, apparently having learned from cold experience that the clear, green river water was not a comfortable arena for exposing curves.

He stood up. "Ah yes." He sighed as if this were some heavy responsibility. "Duty calls."

Afternoon brought Soap Creek and Sheer Wall and House Rock Rapids, plus Boulder Narrows, where the river current separated and slid around a huge rock in the center of the river. They camped near the mouth of a side canyon. As usual on landing, willing passengers were recruited to form a line to help with the unloading. Everything from wetbags to food and kitchen equipment was passed from hand to hand to a safe spot well above the waterline. The water level of the river fluctuated considerably, depending on releases from Glen Canyon Dam, and unprepared campers had been known to have supplies and equipment, even rafts, drift away in the night.

JoJo and Ryan, shirtless in the heat of late afternoon, set up the portable toilet equipment. Kit started the water filtration system.

Kyle helped inexperienced campers get their gear ready for the night, including small tents for a few people who wanted them. All four guides chipped in on the dinner preparations for broiled salmon, broccoli in cheese sauce, rice, and salad. Kit was already starving again, but guides ate last, of course. And as everyone lined up to fill their plates, she made an unhappy discovery.

"Where's the silverware?"

Kyle glanced around their semiorganized stack of equipment and supplies. "Should be in a plastic box around here somewhere..."

No plastic box. No silverware. Twenty-eight hungry passengers lined up to eat, presumably not expecting to do it with their fingers.

"Who was supposed to see that it was on board?" Kit demanded. "Isn't there a checklist?"

"Figure out who to blame later," JoJo muttered. "Right now, look for silverware. *Make* silverware."

Ryan finally found a box of kitchen utensils with some old bent and discarded silverware in the bottom. The first people in line grabbed the few bent-tined forks, others got a single knife or spoon, until, at the end of the line, people just took whatever was left. Kit expected unhappy grumblings, especially from those who wound up with a pancake turner, paring knife, or wickedly long barbecuing fork as their sole eating utensil. But JoJo saved the day and had everyone laughing as he stood and gave an elaborate lesson in the proper etiquette of eating with a potato peeler.

"Pieces of meat, fish, or plain vegetables are delicately speared with the tip of the utensil. One at a time, of course. One does *not* stack them up as if one were stabbing fish in a pond. And scooping is *most* boorish and will not be tolerated," he warned severely. He demonstrated proper technique with outstretched little finger and the haughty dignity of one teaching the uncouth how to handle some imposing array of silverware at a fancy dinner.

"The proper form for eating vegetables *en sauce*, however, is dramatically reversed. In that situation one uses the utensil to slide and twirl the vegetable gracefully so that a small amount of sauce may be scooped up with it. Not an excessive amount of sauce, however," he warned with a shake of forefinger, "or one may find oneself in the gauche position of dribbling on one's bare belly button."

By this time that lean-muscled area of JoJo's belly was spotted with cheese-sauce dribbles from his leaking potato peeler. "Although in such unfortunate instances one may discreetly ask the waiter for an extra napkin, of course."

He looked off into space, hand extended in the negligent manner of one accustomed to having servants scurry to supply whatever he wanted. Kit, bowing obsequiously, supplied him with a paper towel with which he daintily swabbed his tanned belly.

"And at the end of the meal," he added, still demonstrating, "one lays the utensil with the point exactly in the center of the plate, cutting edges downward please."

"Thank goodness for clowns," Kit said with honest appreciation after he bowed to the applause and dropped to the sand beside Kit to finish his meal. She ate her own meal with fingers and the awkward assistance of a large wooden spoon.

After dishes were cleaned up and pliers tossed—a competition in which Kit, long out of practice, was the definite loser—most of the group lingered to watch the stars come out and hear Kyle talk about the human history of the canyon. Kit wrapped her arms around her knees and listened with rapt attention. She had heard all this many times before, told it herself occasionally, about the Indian cultures that had come and gone in the canyon and the artifacts that had been found. It never failed to capture her imagination.

There was also the adventure story of John Wesley Powell's first dangerous exploration of the river in 1869. But the tales Kit especially loved were about the legendary Georgie Clark. Georgie, whom Kit had actually met a few times, was a fabulous woman who, before Glen Canyon Dam changed the flow and temperature of the water, had actually floated the river in a life jacket all the way to Lake Mead. She had also pioneered commercial use of the big rafts, lashing three together, to take larger-scale groups on adventurous trips through the Canyon. Kit sometimes thought dreamily that when she was an elderly lady she'd like people to remember and tell tales about her exploits on the river as they did about Georgie Clark.

JoJo then offered a different form of entertainment, the dramatic reading of a narrative poem about a woman in love with a faithless rogue of a river guide. He was surprisingly good, voice inflections and timing dramatizing both the love story and the danger. He stopped at a Perils-of-Pauline high point, story to be continued the following evening.

Kit felt good as she helped close their "kitchen" for the night to keep out small marauders, then washed her face in the river with biodegradable soap. She sagged with weariness by the time she stretched out on top her sleeping bag, because the night was too warm to crawl inside it.

Yet, even tired as she was, she didn't instantly fall asleep. She cushioned her head on her hands and gazed up at the stars soaring above the dark walls of the canyon, the worry she'd avoided all day now settling around her.

Where were Ben and Rella tonight? Safely on their way home? Or looking up at these same stars, trapped and injured in some isolated Mexican canyon? Or dead? She shivered in spite of the hot night, arms prickling with fear.

No, not dead, she once more vowed in fierce rejection. Tyler would find and save them and bring them home.

Then a thought she hadn't considered before hit her. Ben and Rella would return home to cheers and congratulations and rejoicing. But after that, what?

She still couldn't embrace Ben and Rella's lifestyle and the choices they had made. That hadn't changed. She still couldn't ignore what they'd done. Time didn't alter the wrongness of betrayal and adultery and the ruthless selfishness of what they had done to Andrea.

But she could tell them she still loved them, she decided with a sudden rush of joy, let them know that she was glad they were safe and alive! Because that was true.

A sound jerked her to a sitting position, a rustle, a thump. It seemed to be coming from her ammo can. Cautiously she unfastened the lid and jumped when two tiny mice leaped out and skittered into the brush. She laughed delightedly. The mice must have gotten inside when she left the can open while she went to wash in the river.

Okay, then, it was decided, she thought as she relaxed and settled back on the sleeping bag, squirming a little hollow in the sand for her hips. When Ben and Rella got home, she would tell them she loved them. No condoning of what they'd done, but forgiveness and an acknowledgment that love still existed. She felt an unexpected sense of peace settle around her, as if a weight she hadn't realized was there had been lifted.

But in spite of peace with the decision, sleep didn't come.

Because the little incident with the mice reminded her of a much more formidable encounter, the time she and Tyler had come face-to-face with a rare mountain lion on a canyon trail. And the way Tyler had instantly pushed her behind him to protect her, shielding her with his body until the animal turned and ran. Then memories of adventures they'd shared on the river rushed down on her like some flash flood roaring out of a cleft in the canyon wall.

Mishaps: a raft flipping at Bedrock; getting a raft hung up on a rock at Hance; running out of propane for the stove and having to eat cold food for the last two days of a trip; making a batch of biscuits so hard the passengers wound up tossing them around like balls instead of eating them.

Accomplishments: rescuing a woman who slipped on a rock and tumbled into the river; going through Lava Falls for the first time alone, without aid of an older pilot; giving a paraplegic a safe and memorable trip.

Fun: swimming in the turquoise pools of Havasu Creek; floating in life jackets down the Little Colorado; learning to jitterbug in the sand from a spry old couple who supplied '40s music on a little cassette player. Playing tricks on each other, such as the time Tyler, for several days running, by sleight of hand slipped her a much heavier pair of pliers than the other guides were tossing, bewildering her about why she could no longer hit the bucket.

And always, always, that first kiss at Elves Chasm.

Seven days, she suddenly thought bleakly. Back in Phoenix,

busy at Andkit, she sometimes managed several days without even thinking about Tyler. But here, the memories were everywhere. Could she take seven days of being reminded of Tyler at every rapids, every campsite, every sunset, every sunrise?

In the morning she wakened to the muffled rumble of the alarm clock stuffed under her sleeping bag so the sound wouldn't disturb anyone else. Overhead the sky had paled to a powder-puff blue, stars withdrawing for the day, canyon walls still caught in shadows of the night, river flowing dark and mysterious. Even in this serene stretch, the river was never silent; always it whispered and gurgled, dull growl of rapids never far in the distance. She'd heard a passenger complain about the sounds the previous evening, but she loved this ever present song of the river. A canyon wren rustled in a nearby thicket of willows, going about its important bird business without regard for human invaders. Kit breathed deeply of the morning air that was just a little fresher, a little sweeter here than anywhere else on earth. Scents of river and willows and...*coffee?*

Yes, definitely coffee. She hastily dressed in the shelter of the sleeping bag and found JoJo already at the propane stove mixing batter for hotcakes, the scent of coffee filling the air with heady fragrance.

"What's this?" she demanded. "I lost the pliers toss."

"The results aren't written in stone. I figured you deserved some special treatment your first morning on the river." He handed her a steaming cup.

Kit thought about protesting; she was no fragile flower who needed special treatment. Instead, feeling the sore muscles in her shoulders protest when she lifted her hand to accept the coffee, she just smiled appreciatively. "If you're trying to make points with the temporary boss lady, it's working."

She made the comment teasingly, but for a moment their eyes met, and they were both aware of the reason she was "temporary boss lady," and the tragic possibilities lurking outside this canyon.

"Sleep okay?" he asked quickly.

"Yes. Slept great." The realization came as something of a surprise. In spite of those bleak moments when she'd felt grim about the prospect of seven days of being constantly reminded of Tyler, she had slept soundly. And she was again starving even as she remembered mornings like this when she and Tyler had shared these breakfast duties, sneaking kisses as they cut cantaloupe and oranges into wedges and set out syrups and jams.

Within minutes some early-bird passengers were up and about, most of them making good-humored comments about wanting to get in line early so they could grab one of the few real forks in the box. Kit got the bacon sizzling and started cooking eggs to order to accompany the hotcakes JoJo flipped with reckless flourish.

They were on the water long before sunshine reached the river, the line of golden warmth moving slowly down the canyon wall. Most of the passengers, on advice of the guides, wore rain gear this morning. Not because of rain, but because the combination of cool morning air, deep shade, and regular drenching with cold water as they crashed through the rapids could be almost bone chilling.

The rain gear came off as the day warmed, and then people were eagerly vying for positions on the horn. They floated past Vasey's Paradise, where water poured right out of the canyon wall to create a lush garden of green below. Kit remembered exploring there with Tyler one time, and how indignant he was when he came down with a horrendous case of poison oak, and she hadn't so much as a single itchy blotch. They stopped at Redwall Cavern to play volleyball; how many times had she and Tyler done that? Farther on Kit pointed out, in the area known as Marble Canyon, the site where some people had wanted to build another dam, and only fierce protests had kept it from being constructed and inundating much of this majestic hallway of stone. Tyler had done a paper at college on that subject.

At camp that night Kyle made a great discovery as he dug out tools to make a minor adjustment on a motor: the box of silverware, neatly tucked in where it had no place being, behind the tool kit! Everyone happily returned to eating the conventional way, all except the thirteen-year-olds who preferred potato peelers and had a great time showing off their messy technique. Kit didn't try to establish blame for the error of the misplaced box; actually the shared inconvenience had worked to bring the group together as a kind of big, sharing family.

A radio communication that evening surprised Kit. The radio system was not such that they could keep in touch with Mrs. Altman in Page or any other fixed station outside the canyon. It was basically an emergency, ground-to-air system that required communication through a plane or helicopter overhead. But this pilot knew Ben and Rella and just wanted to let Kit know that there hadn't yet been any more news from Tyler. Kit appreciated his concern and thanked him. Yet she also thought if she heard that helpful no-news-is-good-news phrase one more time that she might just cover her ears with her hands and scream.

"I've heard stories about some of Ben's exploits," JoJo said as Kit tucked the radio back in its space on the raft. Most of the passengers were gathered around Kyle, who was tonight telling them about the geology of the canyon. "If anyone can survive a crash I'm sure it's Ben and Rella. I wish I could do something to help."

Kit managed a smile. "You are helping. You cheer me up and keep my mind away from worrying." She'd laughed and clapped along with everyone else when he'd earlier done an impromptu Elvis imitation, the Styrofoam lid of an ice chest as his pretend guitar. "C'mon. I want to hear some more of that poem about Belle and the villain she's in love with. I'm hoping she comes to her senses and wallops him with a frying pan."

Which reminded her of a time on a chilly, first-of-the-season trip when she and Tyler tried to soften their hard Snickers candy bars in a frying pan and wound up with a mess that Rella grumbled was "sticky enough to trap a dinosaur."

Oddly enough, however, the memory held more laughter than pain. They'd put water in the pan to try to dissolve the sticky mess, then gleefully named it Snicker-soup and slurped it up.

Next morning they reached one of Kit's favorite places on the river, the point where the milky turquoise waters of the Little Colorado joined the river. Kyle and Ryan stayed near the mouth while Kit and JoJo led the rafters upstream. There they showed them how to fasten their life jackets on upside down to keep from getting bottoms scraped on the rough rocks and sent them off on a wild water-coaster ride through the shallow rapids. Kit and JoJo careened after them, and as Kit bounced along, hot sun and clear blue sky overhead, tumble of turquoise water swirling around her, toes scooting ahead, an unexpected thought flashed through her mind.

Home. This is where I want to be. This is where I belong. Home.

The thought was still with her as she lay on the sleeping bag that night, the moon, not yet risen, making a glow like some great silver fire just beyond the canyon rim.

I wish I could stay here. I wish I didn't have to go back to Phoenix and Andkit and spend day after day trapped in an office. I don't want to go back!

Phoenix and Andkit were the right place for her mother, so very right. Andrea was blooming there, happy not only with their successful business but growing in her faith, eagerly sharing it. But Kit, in spite of the painful memories that assaulted her here —memories not only of Tyler but of Ben and Rella, too—would so much rather be on the river, in the canyon she loved. Hearing the song of the river, not the hum of computers or clatter of sewing machines; seeing moonlight and blue-shadowed canyon, not cost and sales estimates; feeling the heat of the canyon night, not manufactured coolness of some unseen air conditioner.

She suddenly remembered what Tyler had said, that she was in line to inherit her father's half of the company if he and Rella didn't come back. She was instantly appalled that the thought had so much as entered her head. If it could bring Ben and Rella back, she'd eagerly promise to spend twenty-four hours a day for the rest of her life in a Phoenix office! And once more she turned to prayer for them.

The trip continued on as if following the script of some idyllic sales brochure. Even though August was the "swampy" season for thunderstorms and occasional downpours, the weather remained picnic perfect. They saw deer and a herd of bighorn sheep, and the two boys happily caught and released several fish. Time after time she was awed anew with the grandeur of the Lord's work here: towering red walls with only a ribbon of blue sky between them, then opening to a grand vista of layered, multicolored cliffs stretching to a rim miles in the distance. Here an amphitheater in stone, there a narrow side canyon sculpted into a work of art, everywhere fantastic arrangements of rocks and sand and cliffs.

The rapids were satisfyingly scary, avalanche after avalanche of white water crashing down on the rafts. Crystal Rapid, which they scouted from shore before taking the rafts through it, loomed every bit as big and dangerous as Kit remembered. Its treacherous holes and boulders and standing waves tested her capabilities to keep the raft headed downriver and not turn sideways, because meeting those waves sideways was a pathway to disaster. They hiked to Elves Chasm, and Kit waded the pool and climbed behind the tinkling waterfall, letting herself appreciate the elfin charm of the spot and not even trying to avoid the memory of that first magical kiss. Because some memories, she thought almost fiercely, were worth cherishing no matter what the outcome.

Kit was nervous about Lava Falls, the Colorado's most notorious challenge, where the river dropped some thirty-seven feet within a hundred yards. Lava was always a ten on that one-to-ten scale of rating river rapids. Even a mile upstream at Vulcan's Anvil, which was the dark core of an old volcano blown into the river at some time in eons past, the roar was audible. Not loud but menacing, like the ominous growl of a waiting predator. It was the custom for each rafter to try to place a penny on one of the narrow, rough ledges of the Anvil; if your penny stayed on the ledge you were assured safe passage through the rapids below. If it fell off, look out! Kit had always preferred a strong prayer to superstition, and she offered one now.

They headed downriver from the Anvil, the water deceptively slick and calm before it turned into a writhing, roaring monster of treacherous holes and lurking rocks and white-toothed waves, the unyielding wall of stone on the right waiting to punish errors of judgment.

Yet on this day Lava treated them almost like honored guests, giving them a wild ride and briefly burying them under a breath-smashing thunder of water, but spitting them out at the bottom drenched and triumphant. Prayer answered again, Kit thought thankfully. She always looked forward to Lava and was always relieved to be through it.

On the last night JoJo finished his reading of the long poem, everyone satisfied when the heroine found true love with the good man who rescued her from the watery grip of the river, and the unfaithful villain vanished downstream. They also had a little ceremony to award certificates that proclaimed each person now an official "river rat" for successfully completing this adventure.

Next morning they had only a short float to the helicopter pad at Whitmore Wash. The helicopter appeared minutes after they arrived, stirring brush and sand as it settled to the pad in a shimmer of whirling blades. It carried five people at a time out to a nearby ranch, from where they would be flown by plane out to Las Vegas, the South Rim, or back to Page. The crew would deflate the pontoons, lash the rafts together, and continue on to Pierce Ferry, almost a hundred miles downriver, where the truck would meet them to transport the rafts back to Page.

Right after the first group lifted off in the helicopter, Kit saw Kyle, Ryan, and JoJo with heads together in conference. Then they approached her as a unit.

"We think it would be a good idea if you flew out with the passengers," Kyle said.

Kit started to protest. Going all the way to Pierce Ferry was part of the pilot's job. She even rather liked that peaceful time without passengers, floating through the night without stopping, the water mostly calm. But she was also, with still no news from Tyler, anxious to get back to Page.

After only a momentary hesitation, she nodded. "Okay, guys. I'll do it. And thanks."

She went out with the last load of passengers. JoJo squeezed his arm around her shoulders just before she automatically ducked to go under the whirling blades to the door the pilot held open. "Hang in there, Shorty. I hope there's good news when you get back to Page."

Impulsively Kit kissed him on the cheek. "Thanks, JoJo."

She intended to shower and wash her hair in the ranch's modern facilities, but there was an empty seat on a six-passenger plane taking off for Page in five minutes, so she grabbed the chance to be on it. An hour and a half later she was in a cab on her way to the Canyon Cowboys office where she had left her suitcase and the pickup.

A figure stood in the shadowy doorway of the warehouse, his back to the broad opening. Over the clatter of some power tool in the rear of the warehouse, he was unaware of her arrival. How, she wondered, could she ever have mistaken someone else for him? Because, even with his back to her, this was so unmistakably him. Tall, lean, shoulders filling a shirt with ripped-out sleeves, hair still that thick, unruly blond.

She got out of the cab, shut the door, and paid the driver. When she looked up as the cab pulled away, he was facing her. They stared at each other across the graveled yard, across the intervening years.

FOURTEEN

S he looked less like the polished young executive in the newspaper photo and more like the sweet, fresh-scrubbed river-girl he remembered from years gone by. She must have flown out on the helicopter at Whitmore Wash, then come directly here from the airport after the plane flight back to Page.

She could still be sixteen, Tyler thought with a peculiar pang. She wore no makeup, her skin as naturally fresh and sun kissed as the first time he kissed her, her dark hair wind blown and tangled. She lifted a hand to brush a strand of it away from the corner of her mouth. Her shorts and T-shirt were rumpled, a faint shimmer of sunburn-pink on her legs. She looked tired, worried, blue eyes desperately haunted, but never more beautiful.

She stood motionless as he finally walked toward her. He suspected she knew what he had to tell her, yet some frantic hope made her ask, "Are they here? Are they all right?"

He put his hands on her shoulders. There was no way to alter the harsh facts or break the news gently. "They're dead, Kit."

"You know this for certain?" she demanded wildly, her unwillingness to believe flashing blue sparks in her eyes. "You found them? You saw them?" she challenged.

"Another plane spotted the wreckage. It was almost hidden in a brushy canyon, miles away from the main area where we were searching. The pilot didn't see any sign of life, but we got a helicopter with a medical team there within a few hours."

"And?"

"They weren't there."

"Not there!"

"I didn't see how they could have survived the crash, the way the plane was smashed up and scattered. But they did survive. There was some blood, but not a lot of it, and we could see where they'd eaten the few supplies they had with them. They had also built a fire, either to stay warm, because it's chilly there in the mountains at night, or to try to signal for help." For a brief time he'd blazed with hope. *It wasn't too late! They were alive!*

"And then they tried to walk somewhere? But they should have stayed with the plane! Shouldn't they have stayed with the plane?" she added with less certainty.

"It looked as if they did stay with the plane for a couple of days, but there was no water in the canyon, and they had very little with them. When they ran out they must have decided their only chance was to get to higher ground where they might be spotted. Or maybe they even hoped to find a ranch or village."

Kit didn't speak, just shook her head helplessly, too stunned even to cry.

"They made it only about a dozen miles from the crash site, but the terrain was so rough, so rocky and brushy, it took us three more days to find them. The bodies were almost a mile apart. I don't know what that meant. Or which of them died first." He swallowed convulsively. "They weren't badly injured, and if they'd had water they might have survived. But…"

He felt her shudder as she contemplated death from thirst. He would not tell her more. It had been a devastating sight.

"Where are the…the bodies?"

"The authorities have all been very helpful and cooperative, and I've arranged to have the bodies flown here. They should arrive tomorrow. The funeral home will pick them up at the air-port. We'll have to discuss the funeral and cemetery arrange-ments."

She didn't respond to that. Instead she said, "I guess I should call Mom," but she just stared into space, and her slim body didn't move.

Tyler realized his hands were still on her shoulders. He let them drop, again overcome with the guilt that had haunted him ever since the bodies had been found, the desperate feeling that he had failed Ben and Rella. And Kit, too.

"Kit, I'm so sorry. I keep thinking if we'd found the crash site just a little sooner, if we hadn't been looking in the wrong area, if I'd demanded that the search keep going at night so we could have spotted their fire, if it hadn't taken so long to find them after we located the plane…" His voice broke with the desolate regret of hindsight and failure.

Her gaze suddenly targeted him. "Tyler, if you're blaming yourself, don't! You did everything you possibly could. Don't feel guilty."

She threw her arms around him, and they clung together there in the dusty yard. Tyler was aware of her as a woman, the warmth and softness of her, the feel of her silky hair against his cheek, but he was more aware of her simply as someone who shared his agonizing sense of loss. At this moment their differences didn't matter; they were united in suffering and grief.

"I just can't believe it," Kit whispered. He felt the trickle of her tears dampening his shoulder now. "I always thought Dad was invincible. I had this mental picture of them, hiking out to safety, Dad fuming because someone wasn't there to rescue them in fifteen minutes."

"I can't believe it, either," Tyler agreed. And, again, the guilt. The awful guilt. "I should have done more.…"

Kit leaned back in his arms. "More? Tyler look at you! You must have lost ten pounds. Your hand is bandaged, and your face and arms are all scratched!"

He hadn't eaten regularly in the past week, although he hadn't thought about that until now. Food just hadn't mattered. And he'd spent nights in prayer and studying maps rather than sleeping. He wiggled his stiff fingers within the bandage. "The hand injury isn't anything serious. I just slipped on a rock and cut it. I got the scratches when we were searching in the brush around the crash site."

With a tenderness he hadn't expected, she lifted his injured hand and kissed the exposed tip of a finger. Strangely, that more than anything else made him blink to hold back the tears. All along he'd kept telling himself that he couldn't break down, that he owed it to Ben and Rella to be strong, to see this through for them. But this almost did him in.

"I prayed for them, Tyler," Kit suddenly said brokenly. "Over and over I've prayed for them. And so has Mom. I didn't want them to die! I never wanted them to die."

He pulled her back into his arms and smoothed her tangled hair with the oar-callused palm of his good hand. "I know."

"At a time like this, I can understand how faith can falter and fail! You pray and pray, and still the unthinkable happens."

"Don't lose your faith, Kit. In the end, it's all we have."

"But Dad and Rella didn't have it."

So painfully true. Rella and Ben had died without turning to Jesus, without ever knowing him as Savior. Tyler felt he had failed there, too, and that was perhaps the most painful and heaviest burden of all.

Kit pulled back. Tyler hesitated a moment, not wanting to let her go, then took a step backward himself, opening space between them. Tears streaked her face now. She fumbled in the pocket of her shorts for a tissue but couldn't find one. He had nothing to offer her, and finally, like a bewildered child, she stretched the short sleeve of her T-shirt and awkwardly wiped her eyes with it.

"What now?" she asked bleakly.

"Did Ben have relatives we should notify?"

"Maybe some aunts and cousins. I'll have to ask Mom. Dad wasn't much on keeping up family connections."

Not even with his wife and daughter, Tyler thought briefly, but from Kit's dazed expression he doubted that bitter connection had even occurred to her. Rella had a half brother he probably should notify, although she, too, hadn't been much on keeping up distant family connections. In happier times, the Holloways and McCords had always been family for each other.

He touched her shoulder lightly. "Why don't you go call Andrea? Then we'll figure out what to do next."

Kit, after accepting an emotional murmur of sympathy from Mrs. Altman, called her mother from the office. The receptionist at Andkit put Kit on hold while they located Andrea, whose overseeing of the doll construction was very much a hands-on supervision. She stared out the office window as she waited. Nothing had changed about the old ranch house lazing in the shade of the big cottonwoods, but somehow it already seemed to have taken on an aura of lonely desolation and abandonment.

"Kit?" Her mother's voice, hopeful, yet with an undercurrent of dread.

"The plane crashed." Briefly, Kit told Andrea what she knew about the accident and return of the bodies.

"Kit, sweetie, I'm just so terribly sorry." Andrea's voice broke, and Kit knew she was feeling something deep and personal that went beyond sorrow for Kit's loss. For several long moments neither of them spoke. Finally, taking two tries at getting her voice to work, Andrea asked huskily, "Is there anything I can do?"

Kit thought of her naïve decision to tell Ben and Rella, when they returned, that she loved them. She could never do that now, and the guilt born of stubbornness and postponement swirled like some tornado of the mind and heart. "It's too late to do anything."

With instant remorse Kit realized her mother might misinterpret the words as accusation for something she had left undone. "I didn't mean you, Mom! I meant..."

"I know what you mean, hon," Andrea said gently. "Sometimes we all regret things...undone. What about the funeral?"

"I don't know yet. I'll have to call you. Do you want to come?"

Kit could feel some internal conflict waging within her mother in the brief silence that followed, before Andrea finally said, "Under the circumstances, I don't think it would be appropriate. This should be a time for people to show their respect and grief, not a time to arouse old scandal and gossip."

A lesson in how to behave with class, Kit thought with renewed respect as she realized her mother was putting consideration for Ben and Rella's memory ahead of herself. "Are there people we should notify?"

Her grandparents on both sides had been dead for a long time, but there were the aunts and cousins she'd mentioned to Tyler. Christmas-card relatives, she'd always thought of them, because that was the only time they seemed to exist.

Andrea, now more-or-less thinking out loud, dredged up a few names. "Ben's Aunt Cora lived in Indianapolis, and there was an Uncle Henry somewhere, plus some cousins in Texas. But I didn't keep any addresses when we left Page," she added with apologetic guilt. "You might find something if you look through your father's things."

Kit doubted that and suspected her mother did also. Most of what Ben thought worth remembering he kept in his head. "I'll tell Tyler. Is everything going okay at Andkit?"

Again Andrea hesitated, but finally she simply said lightly, "There have been a few minor bad hair days, but we're managing."

An early crisis at Andkit had happened when doll hair tangled in one of the machines, and before they got everything under control, doll hair had spewed like some gigantic blond spiderweb over everything. After that, their way of referring to any new crisis had been to call it another bad hair day.

Kit suspected these "bad hair days" since she'd been gone may not have been so minor, but at the moment, if the company wasn't in complete collapse, she just wasn't up to digging into details. "I'm not sure when I'll be home."

"That's fine. Don't worry about things here. We've postponed a few decisions until you get back, but Kelli's doing great holding things together."

She went back out to the warehouse where Tyler was helping Mike straighten the aluminum framework of a raft bent in collision with a rock on a recent river trip. She reported what her mother had said about Ben's relatives. Tyler said he'd see if he could locate anything.

"I suppose the first thing, then, is to make the arrangements about the funeral." Kit was surprised that her voice sounded controlled and professional even though inside she felt wobbly and lost. "I don't suppose Dad and Rella left directions about what they wanted?"

"No."

They both knew Ben and Rella were people who made plans for living, not dying.

Kit picked up the suitcase she had left in the office, and they drove to the funeral home in separate vehicles. As soon as they arrived Kit wished she had gone to a motel and showered and changed clothes first. Her clothes and river sandals felt too rumpled and sandy, her hair too straggly and unwashed in the silent, serious dignity of this place. It had no specific scent or sound or sight of death, yet an aura of death lingered everywhere. In the heavily padded carpet, which absorbed their footsteps soundlessly, in the subdued lighting, in a faint scent of unseen flowers. She fought a terrible urge simply to turn and run. The only other time she'd ever been here was when Tyler's father died.

Was Tyler thinking about that now? Thinking how different things had been then? She glanced sideways at him, but behind the grim compression of his lips, she couldn't tell what he was thinking. She'd once romantically believed they thought as one on everything important, but three years ago she'd learned that that wasn't true.

The discreet, deferential manager led them to the office, where he said that Tuesday afternoon was the earliest time the service could be scheduled.

Tyler looked questioningly at Kit. "That okay with you? I know it's been difficult for you being away from your work for so long, but you'll be able to fly back to Phoenix that same day. I'll try to arrange a preliminary discussion with the lawyer about the wills on Monday."

"There's a river trip scheduled to launch on Wednesday."

"Right. Kyle and I can handle it, so there won't have to be any cancellations for Canyon Cowboys."

Very smooth, very efficient. Yet Kit also felt a faint twinge of resentment that Tyler assumed she'd instantly be rushing back to Phoenix. Maybe she planned to stay on. She didn't like thinking about Ben's will, but it was something she had to face. If what Tyler had said earlier was true, a share in Canyon Cowboys would now be hers.

But he was right, of course, she acknowledged with an inward sigh; she did have to get back to Phoenix as soon as possible. Whatever decisions her mother and Kelli had postponed demanded her attention.

"Yes, Tuesday will be fine," she murmured.

Without argument they also agreed on the caskets, music, flowers, obituary, the programs for the service, pallbearers, burial, and who to officiate at the service.

Finally they were outside again. The final arrangements had all gone smoothly, yet at the same time everything felt so unfinished. Kit blinked unsteadily in the blazing sun. The asphalt parking lot wavered like a black sea. Tyler steadied her with a hand on her elbow.

"You okay?"

She automatically nodded. She clutched a railing beside the steps for support and took a steadying breath of the fresh air.

"Kit, I want to apologize," he said, suddenly sounding hurried, as if he thought she might get away before he could say this. "That night I called to tell you that Ben and Mom were missing, I made some totally uncalled for comments about reasons for you to come here to run Canyon Cowboys for a few days. I was upset, but that's no excuse, and I am sorry. I tried to apologize on the phone, but I was too late, and you were already hanging up."

"Thank you." She hesitated and then, feeling she should apologize for cutting him off that same night, added, "I'm sorry if I hung up too soon." The pickup looked like a distant metal island shimmering in the sea of asphalt.

"There are still arrangements to make at the cemetery, but I can take care of them, if you prefer."

"Yes, I'd appreciate that."

"Where are you staying?"

She named the motel where she'd rented a room before the river trip. "I didn't keep the room while I was on the river, and I neglected to make a reservation for when I'd be back. But I can probably get a room there anyway."

He glanced at the watch on his tanned wrist. "Would you like to go somewhere for lunch first?"

After the funeral home, food was the last thing she wanted. Just thinking about it made her feel queasy. She tightened her grip on the railing. "No, thank you."

He eyed her less than steady stance on the steps. "Perhaps I should follow you to the motel?"

She straightened her slumping shoulders, suddenly defensive. Did he think she was coyly trying to play helpless female and work some sympathy angle to snag his attention?

"I'll be fine. I can manage on my own." The words came out in a more hostile tone than she intended, but those brief moments of closeness, of shared grief, in the parking lot at the warehouse seemed long ago and distant now.

"I'm sure you can. I just thought...Kit, I'm not trying to resurrect our old relationship or make some embarrassing pass at you, if you're concerned about that." Now he sounded impatient, half angry.

"I didn't think that!" she gasped. Which was certainly true. Nothing even close to that thought had occurred to her.

"Sorry," he muttered. "Look, we're both tired and tense and probably not thinking too clearly. At least I know that's how I am. Let's just call a truce for the next few days so we can get through this, okay?"

"What happens at the end of the 'next few days'?"

He hesitated, as if there were some subject of possible conflict between them, but all he said was, "Just a figure of speech."

She nodded and began the seemingly endless trek across the asphalt to the pickup. She could feel his gaze following her, but his own pickup roared out of the parking lot before she reached her vehicle. They had not, she realized, made any arrangements for further communication between them.

FIFTEEN

A s it turned out, the motel where she'd stayed before was full and she had to find another place. Once finally settled in a room, she showered and washed her hair, then simply collapsed on the bed. She was always pleasantly tired after an intensive river trip, but this time weariness of the mind and soul was added to physical tiredness.

She didn't feel angry with the Lord for what had happened to her father and Rella; she wasn't angry that all the prayers both she and others had offered for their safety and their lives had not been favorably answered. Her faith was not destroyed. In the sonorous words of Ecclesiastes, there was a time to be born and a time to die, and Ben and Rella's time had come. Yet the guilt that she'd never told them that she still loved them settled around her like some inescapable fog. Even worse was the desolation of knowing that their lives had ended with their hearts still rejecting the salvation Jesus offered.

Unless...

She sat up as an arrow of hope stabbed through the fog. Had Tyler thought about this? She could call him at the ranch. Just as quickly the quick hope disappeared, and she slumped back to the bed. It was possible, but, more likely, just wishful thinking on her part.

She forced herself to go out for a sandwich and a walk in the pleasant, small-town dusk, but not to dwell on nostalgic memories or sad, regretful thoughts about Ben and Rella. Instead she determinedly thought about the postponed sales trip to New York, how to cut costs on the packaging for the new line of pioneer dolls, if they should pay off the Small Business Administration loan early or put the money into expansion of the company.

The following morning, although the Canyon Cowboys office was usually closed on weekends, she drove out to the warehouse.

She did it partly because she needed to keep busy, more because she didn't want to give Tyler any chance to think she was avoiding him. Because if he thought she was avoiding him, he might also think she awarded some inflated importance to their meeting again. It was, she recognized wryly, a convoluted train of thought. It was also wasted mental energy because, except for handyman Mike, she was alone at the warehouse.

Working from the list of reservations for the next river trip, which included a request for a special diet from a man with numerous food allergies, she busied herself ordering supplies. She fielded phone calls from people seeking general information and others who already had reservations. She also accidentally found Rella's address book in the desk, which, not to her surprise, did not include names of any of Ben's Christmas-card relatives.

She made a sandwich in the kitchen for lunch and afterward spent several hours looking into records about the financial status of the company over the past couple of years. Later, after locking the office for the day, she took an impulsive detour to the old barn.

She unfastened the latch and pushed the big sliding door open just enough so she could slip inside, taking a moment to let her eyes adjust to the dimness. The old barn was silent now, apparently unused. No welcoming nicker of horses or stamp of hooves, no Rella lustily singing some old cowboy song as she cleaned stalls, no scent of fresh saddle soap from the tack room.

Yet a faint scent of hay still lingered, old but sweet, and she heard a familiar scurry of tiny mice feet in the loft. Dust motes danced in the sunlight shafting through the open door, and the hard-packed dirt floor beneath her feet still held the faint, curved impressions of old hoofprints. But the storage area near the front of the barn was empty now, no antique carriage stood there in restored glory.

She felt a sudden heart pang for everything that was gone along with the carriage. The marriage that never was, her father, Rella, the old close family friendships. The tears trickled down her cheeks, silent leakage from a well that she sometimes thought would never completely run dry.

A shadow suddenly blocked the shaft of sunlight and she whirled, not so much frightened as embarrassed at being caught here, caught crying.

Caught by Tyler, of course, the last person she wanted to see in this incriminating situation. She recognized him even though he was only a faceless silhouette against the bright light. She swiped her fingers across her eyes, surreptitiously dried them on her shorts.

He shoved the sliding door open wider, instantly spotting her in the empty space where the antique carriage had once awaited their marriage. "I'm sorry. I didn't mean to startle you. I saw the door open and thought someone was trespassing."

He said the last word awkwardly, because it was so obvious that what she was doing wasn't just trespassing; she was snooping. Okay, why hide it? she asked herself defiantly.

"I was just wondering if the antique carriage Rella restored was still here."

"She finally sold it last spring." He shrugged lightly. "It was never used. There didn't seem much point in keeping it."

"Oh? From what I heard, you certainly didn't waste any time getting engaged again after we split up!" She mentally kicked herself as soon as the words tumbled out. They sounded spiteful, petulant, and childish. And also as if she'd kept a magnifying glass on his activities, as if she *cared*.

"If you didn't also hear that it was a short-lived relationship, I can assure you it was. I'd be happy…" He broke off, his wry smile humorless. "Well, not *happy* to tell you about it, but willing, if you're interested."

She was uncomfortably poised between curiosity and a determination to remain aloof from even a minimal display of interest when a sound outside made them both peer out the sliding door. It was the double-decker truck carrying the rafts just pulling into the yard.

JoJo waved after instantly spotting her standing in the barn doorway. "Heard anything about Ben and Rella?" he called.

If Kit had wanted to hear the story of Tyler's romantic relationship, and she was not certain she did, it was too late now. Not only JoJo but also Ryan and Red, the truck driver, were striding across the yard toward them.

She let Tyler report the tragic news, and the shock registered on their faces. Tyler also asked JoJo and Ryan to be pallbearers, to which they somberly agreed. The two pilots and two swampers on the rafts that were on the river now, a trip that had launched a few days after Kit's trip, would not be back in time for the funeral. Tyler himself would be a pallbearer, and Kit impulsively asked if she could also be one.

The men all looked at her in surprise, and even Kit didn't know if this was appropriate, if women were ever pallbearers. But she simply looked at them defiantly; she was strong enough to do it! Finally Tyler half smiled and nodded.

"I think that would please Ben very much."

That evening she called her mother to tell her the funeral was scheduled for Tuesday and that she'd be home later that same evening. Near the end of the conversation Andrea apologetically brought up a problem about accident insurance payments for a worker who had been injured on the job. Kit told her whom to have Kelli contact and what to do to be sure the worker was properly taken care of, and they also went over a problem with the bank statement.

She went to her old church on Sunday morning. The pastor was new, Pastor Ron and his wife having left to go into missionary service. She didn't really want to see people or have to deal with their sympathy and curiosity, but she needed this time in the house of the Lord. She spotted Tyler in a pew on the far side, but she didn't know if he saw her. Afterward, she fielded handshakes and sympathetic murmurs and hugs from old acquaintances but escaped as soon as she politely could. That afternoon she drove out to a favorite place along the shore of Lake Powell, where she simply lay back on a blanket and let herself drift with the slow drift of clouds across the sky.

JoJo called that evening, saying he'd called every motel in town before he found her. He asked if she'd like to go out for a hamburger. When she demurred he told her she *should* go out for a hamburger, that he was going to nag her until she did, and finally she gave in. Afterward, she appreciated his persistence. He wasn't clownish this evening, just sweet and concerned and comfortingly companionable.

She went to the Canyon Cowboys office again early on Monday, but left about midmorning because she had to buy something to wear to the funeral. She hadn't brought along anything remotely suitable. Operating in unfamiliar territory, where she had no idea what a woman pallbearer should wear, she finally chose a simple navy blue linen dress with matching jacket and dark shoes with low heels. When she returned to the office, Mrs. Altman said Tyler had called. He had an appointment for them with Ben's lawyer that afternoon.

He was waiting when she got out of the pickup at the lawyer's tile-roofed office at two o'clock. She'd changed from her usual shorts to tan pants, but Tyler was still in khaki shorts. Ben would have approved, she thought. He always said he'd put on a suit for weddings, funerals, and presidential visits, but other than that, he wasn't getting out of his Levi's or river shorts for anyone.

Lawyer Jim Blake was friendly, unhurried, and sympathetic. He took time to reminisce about a river trip he'd taken with Ben and Tyler's father years ago, laughing when he recalled that on it Kit and Tyler had gotten in trouble for accidentally drenching a passenger in an after-dark water fight. He glanced back and forth between them, as if also recalling there had once been more than childish play to their relationship. He discreetly did not ask questions, however, and briskly launched into an explanation of the provisions of the wills, which he had written.

Ben and Rella had the company under a type of joint ownership that enabled each to name a separate heir to their share. Ben's will specified that, if Rella did not survive him by thirty days, Kit inherited his half of the company; Rella's will said Tyler got her half if Ben didn't survive her by thirty days. This, the lawyer pointed out, eliminated any problem determining which of them had died first. The ranch and warehouse, as part of the company assets, were included in this division. On both wills, anything else they owned jointly or individually went to Tyler. Jim Blake called the situation generally "straightforward and uncomplicated," but warned that, even so, the probate process could move with frustrating slowness.

"I think the plane was insured, but if there's any life insurance, I'm unaware of it," Jim Blake added.

Tyler nodded, and again they were all aware that Ben and Rella concentrated on living, not dying.

"What about operation of the company until probate is settled?" Kit asked.

"That's something the two of you will have to work out between you. If you plan to sell Canyon Cowboys, it can't be done until probate is complete. However, it should be possible to enter into a binding agreement with a buyer so that the actual transfer of ownership would be more or less a formality when probate is settled."

He gave Tyler a sheet detailing information he needed about Ben and Rella's assets and asked for addresses and phone numbers where both Tyler and Kit could be reached. Kit gave her home and Andkit phone numbers. Tyler, after a brief hesitation, said his permanent address was Oceanside, but that the best place to contact him for the next few weeks would be through the Canyon Cowboy offices. There were a few papers to sign. Handshakes. More sympathy. Another blinding blaze of sunlight hit them when they stepped outside, but this time Kit had a firmer grip on herself.

Their pickups were parked side by side in the small parking lot, and Tyler paused between them. "I know the wills left everything but Canyon Cowboys to me, but if there are any personal belongings of Ben's that you'd like to have…?"

"I don't think so, but thank you. If I do happen to think of something I'll let you know."

"You looked a little shocked when Jim mentioned selling Canyon Cowboys."

"Yes, I suppose it did shock me for a moment. I just hadn't thought about it. But selling is the logical course of action. I have Andkit. You have *The World of White Water.*" Which, she now knew, was a year-round commitment, that he'd never actually joined Ben and Rella in the company.

"I suppose that's true. Although it would be possible to keep the company in joint ownership and hire a manager." He hesitated. "Somehow it seems almost a betrayal to sell what our families worked so hard for so many years to build up."

"*Betrayal?*" Kit repeated in an angry gasp. He dared talk about betrayal after what Ben and Rella had done to Andrea?

He scowled, twin furrows cutting between his thick blond eyebrows. "Maybe betrayal wasn't the right word."

"I don't feel I'm under any obligation to preserve anything for Ben and Rella. And I don't owe them anything!"

"You still don't forgive them, do you, Kit, not even after they're dead," he said, an angry statement, not a question.

"This has nothing to do with forgiveness! Mom says she's forgiven them, and so have I." She swallowed the hard knot in her throat. That hadn't come out sounding very forgiving, but it was true. There on the river she'd finally done it. "I even intended to tell them when they got home that I still love them. Because I do. But that still doesn't mean I want to erect a memorial to their marriage!"

"So you do want to sell the company?"

Kit hesitated, feeling caught in an unexpected trap. She didn't feel any obligation to hold on to the company just because Ben and Rella had worked hard to build it. Yet, sell it? That brought an equally unexpected spike of dismay. A bit stiffly she detoured a flat yes or no answer. "I don't see buyers lining up, so that isn't a problem that must be decided at this moment."

He didn't argue, simply nodded, got in the pickup, and drove away.

Kit went back to the motel, angry and upset, uncertain exactly what she did want. However, as she'd said to Tyler, a decision about Canyon Cowboys was not the problem of the moment.

Getting through the funeral tomorrow was.

SIXTEEN

Heavy scent of flowers. Perspiration welding her dress to her back in spite of the artificially cooled air. An astonishing number of people crowding the chapel at the funeral home, many spilling into the hallway. The new pastor at the church officiating at the service, Tyler offering the brief eulogy, Kit seeing him only as a dark-suited blur through a veil of tears. The closed caskets gleaming softly in the subdued light, matching blankets of roses spilling across them. The music...

Kit felt as if she were choking, as if she couldn't grab a breath, as the organ played the majestic strains of "The Old Rugged Cross." She'd chosen it because she remembered Ben's big voice booming it out on the Easter occasions when he usually went to church with them. Now she wished she'd chosen something that didn't feel as if it were slicing her heart to ribbons.

Tyler had chosen for Rella a poem called "The Cowboy's Prayer," recited by JoJo with an accompaniment of soft background music. Kit couldn't see JoJo clearly, either, but she had a blurred impression of dignity and maturity, no trace of the boyish clown now.

Tyler came back to sit beside her after the eulogy. They were the only family members present. They rose together when the time came to transport the coffins to the two waiting hearses. This she wasn't sorry about, she thought fiercely as she felt the heavy weight of the coffin drag against her arm. No matter what people thought, she was glad she had chosen to make this final last trip with Ben. *I love you, Dad,* she whispered inwardly. *You and Rella, too. I still love both of you. I'm sorry I never told you.*

Another brief service at the open grave sites, words she couldn't hear because of the roaring in her ears, the final ritual of tossing a few chunks of earth on the lowered coffins, the soft, lonely thunk as they hit. Tyler's strong arm around her shoulders, his voice murmuring something wordless but comforting. More people coming by to offer sympathy, grieving pats, hugs.

Finally Tyler walked with her back to the dark car in which they had come, which the funeral home had provided, his arm still around her. Thunderclouds were building off to the west, a faint scent of summer storm in the air. A sudden puff of wind stirred her hair.

"I need to talk to you," he said after he opened the door and helped her inside. "When are you planning to leave?"

"My flight is at six o'clock. I've been thinking, if you wouldn't mind, I think I'd like to have my father's old rodeo trophies and buckles after all."

"Of course you can have them! Look, a few people are coming to the house now. People have been bringing food ever since they heard, and the house is overflowing with casseroles. Would you like to come out to the house, too? You could pick up the trophies and buckles."

Kit hesitated, halfway drawn to the old house and people who had cared about Ben and Rella, halfway repulsed by both. "No, I don't think so," she said finally. "Thanks anyway. Perhaps you could have Mrs. Altman box up the trophies and buckles and ship them to me."

"Kit, I know this is a difficult time, but I do wish you'd come. And I must talk to you. It's important." His tone was suddenly urgent.

"Perhaps you could come by the motel later?"

"Okay, I'll do that, just as soon as I can get away."

In the motel room, Kit changed to her tan pants for the flight and packed her suitcase. That took fifteen minutes, and she still had three hours until her flight. She felt shaken by the funeral, guilty for avoiding the good-hearted people gathering at the ranch house, depressed at the prospect of going back to Phoenix and her office at Andkit. Maybe, after the Christmas frenzy, she could get away for a long vacation.

She paced restlessly around the bed, uneasily wondering why Tyler wanted to see her. From her perusal of the records, finances at Canyon Cowboys did not appear to her to be particularly robust. Business was good; the files contained numerous letters with glowing praise from happy customers, many of whom had made repeat trips with Canyon Cowboys. But, as she already knew, both Ben and Rella cared more about good times on the river than details about money. Or perhaps it was something more personal Tyler wanted to discuss with her, something about their relationship. Was she ready for that?

A knock at the door surprised her. Tyler already? She composed her face into a neutral mask and opened the door. The mask broke in surprise. "JoJo!"

He was in his familiar shorts and T-shirt again, and he grinned with a boyish embarrassment that instantly lifted her spirits. "I know it's terrible manners to show up unannounced like this, but I wanted to tell you good-bye in person before you left."

"I'm glad you came. Because I want to thank you for the beautiful reading you gave today."

"I was glad Tyler asked me to do it. I thought a lot of Rella." His gaze skipped sideways as if he realized this perhaps wasn't an appropriate thing to say to her, and Kit realized that he now knew all the messy details of the past.

She impulsively squeezed his arm. "That's okay. I thought a lot of Rella, too."

"I also figured you probably hadn't eaten anything all day." He brought out a sack he'd been hiding behind his back.

He was right, of course. All she'd been able to manage at breakfast was coffee, and she'd skipped lunch entirely. But now, in spite of everything, the tantalizing scents coming from the sack told her she was definitely hungry. The thunderclouds had passed over with only a few warning rumbles, and sunshine had already dried the spattering of raindrops.

"Let's eat out by the pool," she said.

She tacked a note to the door to tell Tyler where she was, and they found lounge chairs under an umbrella beside the blue-bottomed pool. JoJo spread the lunch on the metal table between them. Fried chicken, french fries, coleslaw, soft drinks.

"The best junk food in town," he proclaimed proudly.

Conversation came easily with JoJo, devoid of the undercurrent of emotional tension that seemed to accompany any dialogue with Tyler. She was laughing over his story about his first cooking-for-himself experiences in an apartment at college when a shadow fell across them.

"Am I interrupting something?" Tyler asked.

Kit hastily set her drumstick on a paper napkin and wiped her greasy fingers. "No, of course not." She felt suddenly guilty for laughing on this sad day and wondered if it was that inappropriate laughter that had brought the scowl to Tyler's face.

Tyler's pointed glance at JoJo suggested JoJo perhaps had important business elsewhere, but JoJo didn't take the hint. He just dragged up another chair with his toe. "Chicken?" he offered, pointing to the box.

"No, thank you." When JoJo still made no move to leave, Tyler said even more pointedly, "I have some private business to discuss with Kit."

JoJo looked to Kit for confirmation that this was okay before leisurely crumpling his napkin and soft-drink carton. "Maybe I could call you in Phoenix sometime?" he suggested.

Kit smiled. "That would be nice." She and Tyler both watched JoJo saunter to the door in the block wall surrounding the pool.

"Nice kid," Tyler muttered after the stocky figure disappeared. "I didn't realize you'd become quite so friendly already."

Kit almost laughed at the somewhat sarcastic emphasis he put on "friendly," and the caustic tone in which he said "nice kid," as if to emphasize the few years of difference between their ages and JoJo's. In former times she'd have jumped on this and gleefully teased him about being jealous, but at the moment that thought was so incongruous, so unlikely, that she simply said, "What was it you wanted to talk to me about?"

"Two things. First, Kyle was really apologetic about dumping this on us at the last minute, but he can't make tomorrow's river trip after all. His son was mowing the lawn this morning, and somehow the mower kicked up a rock and hit Kyle in the eye."

"Oh, no! How bad is it?"

"Bad enough that the doctor says he has to stay flat on his

back to let the eye heal for the next few days. You probably noticed he wasn't at the funeral."

Kit hadn't noticed, but then there were undoubtedly many things she hadn't noticed beyond her blur of tears.

"Which leaves us short one pilot for the trip. Can you stay over for another week, Kit? I know it's a lot to ask," he added, even as she was already shaking her head negatively.

"JoJo is dependable and responsible. I let him take the raft through Nankoweap and the jewel rapids…"

"JoJo is doing great. And so is Ryan. But Nankoweap and Sapphire and Turquoise aren't Crystal and Lava, and neither JoJo nor Ryan is experienced enough to be second pilot."

Kit shook her head, feeling a little helpless. Her mother and Kelli were counting on her to be back tonight. "What's the other thing?"

"I've had an inquiry about selling Canyon Cowboys. They apologized for bringing this up so soon but said they did want to make us aware of their interest if we're considering selling."

"They do know you're not the sole owner and can't make the decision alone?"

"I told them."

Thinking back to their earlier hostile discussion outside the lawyer's office about selling the company, she asked warily, "What if this is something we can't agree on?"

"Then we may have a problem."

Kit didn't pursue that line of thought. "Who are they?"

"It's a company that has been doing tour excursions and houseboat rentals on Lake Powell for a couple of years. They want to expand into raft trips through the Canyon, but, as you know, that's practically impossible unless you buy out someone who is already on the river and has the necessary commercial permits. Which Canyon Cowboys does, of course. I suppose it would be foolish to turn down a good offer."

"Yes, that's true."

"They also said that even though the deal couldn't actually be finalized until after probate, they'd be willing to take over operation of the company immediately."

"Immediately!"

"By immediately I don't mean tomorrow," he amended. "We still have thirty passengers to start down the river tomorrow, most of whom are already in town."

"I think Canyon Cowboys needs some better backup system for substitute pilots in case of emergencies. It always seems to be just one man—or woman—away from disaster and having to cancel trips."

"Agreed. We might make that suggestion to the potential buyers. But that doesn't do anything to solve the problem *today.*"

"I suppose I could call Mom and see if there's any possibility they could get along without me for another week," Kit finally said doubtfully.

Tyler watched as Kit slipped through the same door by which JoJo had left. So slim, even fragile looking, but so strong in a crisis. He had heard some surprised whispers about her being a pallbearer, but he felt as proud of her as he knew Ben and Rella would have been. And so unproud of himself for that ridiculous crack about JoJo a few minutes ago. What had brought that on? JoJo *was* a good kid, talented, hard-working, dependable. So why had he made the comment sound more snidely derogatory than complimentary?

Maybe because JoJo and Kit's easy laughter had reminded him of how he and Kit used to laugh—and didn't anymore? Now their conversations revolved only around grim and serious matters. Death. Business. And, except for those brief moments in the yard at the warehouse when they'd clung together, always with the canyon of the past between them.

Kit returned a few minutes later. She reached for her soft drink, found it empty, but didn't remark on the fact that he'd obviously finished it. Instead, sounding a little surprised herself, she said, "I'm staying."

"You are? Hey, that's great!" Great because Canyon Cowboys needed her as a pilot. Great because…well, just great.

"Mom wanted to know about returning some unsatisfactory

fabric, and Kelli had some questions about a contract with another of our suppliers. And a few other things are piling up for me to take care of when I get back, but basically they're getting along okay without me."

I'm not.

The thought hit him like a sneak blow from behind. He instantly rejected it and didn't even waste time mentally listing all the reasons it wasn't true. He simply stood up briskly. "There's the orientation meeting tonight, but if you'd rather skip it…"

"Oh, no. I'll be there."

She arrived at the lodge at five minutes to seven, emotions under control and feeling upbeat, like a kid unexpectedly let out of school. Seven more days on the river!

But within five minutes she had her first warnings that this river trip was not going to be as brochure-perfect as the last one had been.

SEVENTEEN

T he first problem was that for the first time in Kit's memory, there was a mix-up with reservations at the lodge, and the room they always used for orientation meetings had been assigned to a convention of vacuum-cleaner salesmen. Sorting out Canyon Cowboys' passengers and shuffling them to a new room took a good fifteen minutes, and then, of course, the usual snacks and coffee and juice weren't ready for them.

Tyler looked harried, and Kit guiltily suspected all this confusion about the meeting room was somehow her fault for not double-checking with the lodge. Only JoJo retained his cool, and, after giving Kit a surprised but enthusiastic hug when he heard she was staying, he joked and teased some disgruntled members of their group into a better humor.

Kit, who was standing with Ryan at the rear of the room, counted heads while Tyler started the meeting with the usual greetings and information. Three short. She was just about to slip out to see if the three missing people were still wandering around lost because of the room change, when the door opened and three men swaggered in.

Kit tried not to typecast people on first impressions, but these three, a little too loud, a little too arrogantly macho, almost blared *ex-jocks and proud of it*. All three had obviously been muscular and athletic at one time, but now the hairlines were receding and the muscle dissipating into fat. Everyone turned to look at the small commotion they created. Her first thought was that she hoped the crude slogans plastered across their sweatshirts were not their philosophies of life.

Within a few minutes she unhappily decided they probably were.

The three slouched into seats in the back row of metal folding chairs. They didn't say anything, but there was something disruptive about the very way they sat there with arms folded, chairs noisily tilted back, expressions bored while Tyler explained about the wetbags.

After less than five minutes the short, stocky one muttered, "C'mon let's get outta here. We're wasting our time. Who's so dumb they can't figure out how to stick their stuff in a waterproof bag so it won't get wet?"

"Hey, wait a minute. Aren't we supposed to get some eats and drinks? First we get the runaround on where the meeting is, then this."

"Yeah, what kind of cheapskate outfit is this, anyway?" This guy had curly blond hair that looked a lot like Tyler's, although his body was far from Tyler's lean fitness. "Considering what this is costing, we ought to be getting a prime-rib dinner and champagne."

Kit, who was only a few feet away, quietly approached the men and whispered that there had been a delay with the food, but it would be available a little later. A mistake, she realized instantly. She had to bend forward to speak to them, putting her T-shirt at their eye level, and all three instantly leered at her as if she were the snack.

Cracking their crude-thinking heads together was what Kit wanted to do, but she forced herself to be more diplomatic and add politely, "Please be patient. We're taking care of everything as quickly as possible."

"Okay, sweet thing, whatever you say," the blond guy said in a sweetly patronizing tone. "You gonna be our cook and waitress on this little raft party?"

At the same time she distinctly felt a hand on the back of her leg.

"I am not your 'sweet thing' or your cook and waitress," Kit stated in a whisper fierce enough to singe their ears. "I'm one of your river guides, and I can and will, if necessary, remove you from the passenger list for objectionable behavior."

The businesslike threat made an impression. The hand left her leg. The three men exchanged glances, until finally one of them snorted and said, "Feminist," in a disgusted tone, which apparently was the ultimate put-down among this trio.

She glanced up at Tyler as she retreated to the back wall and was relieved that apparently neither he nor JoJo, busy with the equipment demonstrations, had noticed this small disruption.

The three men pointedly ignored Kit after that. They whispered and snickered crudely during Tyler's instructions about human waste disposal on the river, acting far more childish than the four preteens sitting quietly up front. They grumbled when they found the drinks were nonalcoholic. Kit suspected they'd already spent a little too much time bellying up to the bar before reaching the orientation meeting.

By the next morning, however, when the three guys climbed off the bus at Lee's Ferry, she concluded they were obnoxious jerks with or without alcohol. Passengers were often enthusiastically noisy, but these three were offensively loud and rude. One of them, while they were playing Frisbee before the rafts launched, almost ran over the oldest woman in the group. They pointedly excluded the friendly, enthusiastic kids from their game. Usually the pilots left it up to the passengers to decide which raft they wanted to ride on, but this day Tyler snapped out orders that sent the three guys to his raft.

Kit was grateful. With the Three Toads, as Kit had privately named them, several hundred yards away from her on the river, she enjoyed the day. Because of a change in the water level, the hungry waves at Badger Creek Rapid were larger and more treacherous—and more fun. People in the "bathtub" up front got an especially rough dunking. JoJo took the raft through Soap Creek Rapid and did an admirable job of it. And by midafternoon, they had more important matters than the Three Toads to worry about. Tyler pulled his raft in at a narrow beach and waved Kit in for a consultation.

"What do you think?" he asked, head tilted upward. "Storm going to hit us?"

At river level it was often difficult to tell what was going on beyond the canyon rims, and a distant storm could send a flash flood roaring down a narrow side canyon without warning. But now menacing mounds of summer thunderclouds already peered over the towering walls, and a sultry breeze ruffled the leaves of a sprawling Arizona Grape clinging to the sand. The feeling in the air was ominously electric.

"Good chance of it, I'd say." A deep rumble of thunder emphasized Kit's words. They'd earlier decided that on this first night they'd camp at one of the larger camping areas several miles beyond Boulder Narrows, but now Kit asked, "Are you thinking we should make camp early?"

"How about that area just beyond the Narrows? We'll have to make sure people don't sleep right in front of the side canyon in case it flash floods, but an earlier stop will give everyone time to set up tents and get out of the rain when it hits."

"Sounds like a good idea to me. How are you and our three, ummm, personality-challenged passengers getting along?"

Tyler grinned at her phrasing. "In all these years I've never tossed anyone overboard, but there may be a first time. They're smart-aleck know-it-alls, the kind of guys about whom Ben used to grumble, 'You can tell 'em, but you can't tell 'em much.'" He rolled his eyes. "And if any of them calls me 'Cowboy' one more time…"

Thankfully, such passengers were extremely infrequent. Almost everyone who took a raft trip was there to have a fun, safe float down the river. Kit had memories of many wonderful people, good-humored even under sometimes adverse conditions. But on rare occasions there was an unpleasant or troublesome passenger, and this trip looked like trouble times three.

Dark clouds covered all the visible sky above the canyon by the time they headed onto a boulder-strewn shore and planted stakes well above the water line to secure the rafts. Everyone helped with the unloading, and then Kit and JoJo worked at top speed setting up the kitchen and toilet facilities. Tyler and Ryan handed out tents and helped those who had problems getting them set up.

The small, dome-shaped tents weren't complicated, but trying to set one up in a hurry, with thunder rumbling ominously and the dark clouds threatening a deluge at any moment, could be frustrating for someone who had never done it before. Erratic spurts of wind billowed the filmy nylon and sent a couple of unanchored tents flying, and, inevitably, there was the occasional missing metal rod or stake. Everyone was cooperative and uncomplaining, however, most people even joking and laughing as the round-topped tents sprouted like red mushrooms among the boulders.

The four kids, three boys and a lively tomboy of a girl, seemed energized by the prospect of a storm. They dashed around playing king of the mountain on the boulders, chasing lizards, pretending to "morph" into powerhouse crime fighters. Kit laughed at their antics, glad they were along. Kids always made river trips extra fun.

She would gladly have traded the Three Toads for three more kids. They grumbled and complained that when they went on safari in Africa, guests were expected to take it easy and have a drink while the guides did all this grunt work.

It took the efforts of all four guides to drape a wildly-flapping tarp over the kitchen area in hopes that when it started to rain they could keep the food more or less dry. They anchored the tarp with ropes and stakes, but it still skittered like an oversized kite trying to take flight.

"Everything going okay?" Kit asked as Tyler knelt in the sand beside her to rummage in the tool kit for something. She had to raise her voice to be heard over the snapping and flapping of the tarp.

"Guess who put their tents right where I told people not to, right in the path of the water if a flash flood comes roaring out of that side canyon," he muttered. "Then ripped a hole in one of the tents when they were moving it. And then complained about our 'cheap equipment.'"

A flash of lightning somewhere beyond the canyon rim illuminated the camp in an eerie, blue-silver glow. A few moments later a sharp *crack* split the air, the sound rattling from wall to wall in the canyon.

Tyler raced off with the wrench to do something, and Kit dug out the steaks for the meal. Les, the blond guy Kit was reasonably certain had put his hand on her leg at the orientation meeting, came up and dug around in the cans of soft drinks she had placed in a bucket at the end of the serving table.

"Where's the beer?"

"We don't supply anything alcoholic. Passengers who want alcoholic beverages must bring their own."

"You mean we're stuck out here for a week with no beer?" He sounded as outraged as if this were the equivalent of surgery without anesthetic. "How come nobody told us that until now?"

"It's in the instructions supplied to all our passengers, and you also were told at orientation. It's the general policy of all the commercial river-running outfits, as far as I know."

Still grumbling as if this were some regulation she'd invented specifically to ruin his trip, he grabbed three soft-drink cans and headed back to give his buddies the bad news. "Don't overcook our steaks," he tossed over his shoulder. "We'll send 'em back if they're overcooked."

JoJo had just come up beside her with a jug of fresh water from the filtration system and heard the grouchy warning. "Your steaks will be so rare you may need a lasso to catch them," he muttered.

The rain held off during dinner, although the sand whipped by gusts of wind made eating a gritty experience. No complaints from the Three Toads that the under-doneness of their steaks had been carried a bit too far, although that may have been because they had now decided to play macho survivalists and were busy scoffing at any hardships here compared to some trip they'd taken in Canada. Tyler decided to skip the storytelling and program this evening as a few warning spatters of rain sent most of the passengers scurrying for their tents.

Kit hadn't yet put up her own tent, and she now had to find a place for it in the dark with the threat of rain even closer. There was very little space between the jumbled boulders, but with a flashlight she finally found a tiny island of sand just large enough for the tent. JoJo showed up to help, whistling cheerfully as he helped thread the flexible metal rods through the narrow tubes of nylon to form the supporting framework for the tent. The gusting wind had died down now, leaving the air oppressively thick and heavy.

"I was sorry to hear about Kyle's accident, but glad it meant you were making another river trip," JoJo offered.

"Me, too."

"What's going to happen with Canyon Cowboys now?"

"I don't know. Tyler says he's had an inquiry from someone who's interested in buying it. But he seems reluctant to sell." Kit put her weight against a metal stake to push it into the sand. She straightened suddenly, thinking she heard a rustle on the other side of the largest boulder beside her tent, but when she peered around she didn't see anyone. "In case you didn't know, Tyler and I are each inheriting half of the business."

"No, I didn't know that. Interesting." He gave her a speculative, sideways glance. "What do you want to do with the company?"

"I'm not sure. It's all a rather awkward situation. Tyler and I don't exactly see eye to eye on various things. If it weren't that I have to go back to Phoenix…" She let the thought drift off unfinished, not certain even in her own mind where it was headed.

"Who says you have to go back to Phoenix?"

"My conscience, I suppose. My mother and I started our business together, and she can't handle it alone."

"But there's still something going on between you and Tyler even if you don't always see eye to eye."

She squatted back on her heels and pushed a lock of hair, gritty with windblown sand, out of her eyes. "No, there isn't. Why would you think that?"

"Maybe because of the little glances you give him when you think no one's looking. Maybe because of the way Tyler looked at me as if he hoped I'd choke on a chicken bone when I asked if I could call you in Phoenix."

"If anyone chokes on a chicken bone, I hope it's one of my three least-favorite passengers," Kit declared. If JoJo noted that was a diversionary tactic to get away from the high-voltage subject of Tyler and their relationship, he didn't let on.

Kit thanked JoJo for his help, then went down to the river to wash up. The song of the river was sluggish tonight, sullenly gurgling around rocks at water's edge. The water level had risen several inches in the last hour, letting the rafts sway lightly in the current.

172

They were pale, shapeless blobs in the darkness, the cliffs on the opposite side of the river featureless walls. The muggy air hung motionless, an odd, breath-held quality to it, as if everything was suspended waiting for the circling storm to attack. More warning drops of rain spattered Kit's face as she walked back to her tent.

She crawled through the small opening and zipped it shut behind her. She changed to her shorty pajamas, found a brush in her duffel bag, and bent over from her knees to brush the sandy grit out of her hair. And instantly found herself sweating from the minor exertion.

Outside, the motionless air had been uncomfortably muggy; inside, the nylon tent felt airless, smothering, unbearably oppressive. The perspiration clung to her skin rather than evaporating. Okay, she'd sleep outside, she decided.

She had no more than wrestled her sleeping bag halfway out the small opening when another handful of warning raindrops spattered her. Thunder rumbled again, as if the canyon had trapped the thunderheads and wouldn't release them. Kit suddenly wished it *would* rain, pour down, drench everything, get rid of this unfinished, something-is-going-to-happen feeling. Tyler had made certain everyone, even the Three Toads, was safely out of the way if a flash flood roared down the side canyon, so there was no danger, and she loved that wonderful, fresh-washed scent and clean feeling after a storm.

Maybe it was coming now, she decided as a few more sprinkles pattered the tent. She dragged the sleeping bag inside again, now feeling as if she were wallowing in a bath of her own perspiration. After a few sweltering minutes stretched out on top the sleeping bag she decided to give up on sleep for a while. She dressed again, stopped in the kitchen for a quick drink of water, and made her way quietly to the river's edge. She could hear voices here and there and saw a few shadowy figures, as if others were as restless and sleepless as she was. Clouds blotted the moon, but an occasional shift in the roiling mounds let an uneasy flicker of light skitter through.

She sat down and leaned against a boulder, letting her bare feet extend into the water. The cold tug of the current cooled her skin, but the oppressive heaviness of the air, the feeling of something waiting, something unfinished, remained. A storm unfinished. Which was sometimes how she felt about Tyler and herself.

Footsteps whispered in the sand somewhere beyond the boulder. She peered around it, thinking that if it was the kids out adventuring in the dark—something she'd done many a time!—she'd warn them to stay back from the water. But what she saw, a glimmer of pale blond hair moving toward her, made her draw back against the boulder. Les? She wasn't *afraid* of him. The Three Toads had apparently decided to scorn her as a female, but that didn't make her any less reluctant to encounter one of them out here in the dark.

She pressed her body against the head-high boulder, palms clutching its dark surface, ears straining to hear more. Nothing except for the muted whisper of the river and the faint trill of some night bird. Okay, she'd just quietly take a roundabout route back to her tent so she wouldn't accidentally run into him at the kitchen.

She slipped around the far side of the boulder, pushed her way through a rough thicket of willows, and tumbled straight into his arms.

EIGHTEEN

K it!"

"Oh, Tyler, it's you! I thought…" She didn't relax in his arms, but she stopped fighting like a terrified wildcat.

"What are you doing out here?" he asked.

"I'd forgotten how airless a tent can be on a hot night. What are you doing wandering around?"

"Just wandering around." Thinking about her, although he didn't intend to admit that. Neither did he want to dwell on how good she felt in his arms now that she'd stopped struggling. "Making sure everything's okay."

He wondered if she remembered how Ben always did this, often getting up in the night to make sure the rafts were secure and nothing unusual going on. Now she lightly pulled back and, after a small hesitation, he reluctantly let her go.

"You seem a little jumpy," he suggested.

"Just the storm, I suppose. I wish it would rain and get it over with." She backed off another step. "Well, I guess I'll head back to the tent. I left the flaps up, and maybe it's cooled off in there now. We forgot to toss the pliers, but I'll start coffee in the morning."

"Looks as if the water has risen. I think I'll tighten the tie lines."

"I should have thought of that. I'll help."

They circled the boulder, and he tugged one of the rafts up solid against the sand while she shortened and tightened the rope holding it.

"Need a flashlight?" he called as she bent over the stake.

"No, I can manage."

Her agile fingers always were better than his at tying knots. As she'd once proved when she sneaked up to his sleeping bag and expertly tied his shoelaces together in the dark when they were kids.

They repeated the process with the other raft, and once more she said, "Well, I'm going back to the tent and try to get some sleep."

"We could…just sit here for a few minutes," he suggested tentatively. He tried to think of some persuasive reason, but the only one that came to mind was, "I have a Snickers in my pocket." He instantly felt foolish. She no doubt dated suave, cosmopolitan guys now, ones with something much more sophisticated than a candy bar to offer.

He expected she'd smoothly turn him down, but after a moment's hesitation she laughed lightly. "I guess I've always been a sucker for a guy with a Snickers. There's a nice place over there by the boulder. I sat there for a while before you came over."

The space where she'd been sitting turned out to be almost covered with water now, so they had to move around to the back side of the boulder. The clouds shifted to reveal a curve of silver-white moon for a moment, then hid it again. Kit squirmed a place in the sand to sit, and he did the same beside her.

"I came over earlier to see if you needed help with your tent, but you already had some eager help." He inwardly groaned as soon as the petulant-sounding comment was out. *Great going, Tyler, the perfect way* not *to start a conciliatory conversation.*

She did not leap on it, however. Instead she simply countered lightly, "Since when have I needed help putting up a tent?"

"True," he agreed. Kit was a very self-sufficient woman. So what did *that* thought mean? he challenged himself wryly. That he wished she weren't so self-sufficient so she'd perhaps feel some need to lean on him? As if to emphasize that self-sufficiency, as he was patting his pockets looking for a pocketknife, she immediately produced one from the pocket of her shorts and handed it to him.

"I always watch for the *World of White Water* on TV," she said, surprising him, as he cut the Snickers in half. This time she didn't demand that he measure it down to the fraction of an inch, as both of them had always done when they were kids. "It's a wonderful program. How did you get into doing it?"

He handed her half of the candy bar. "The producer is a guy named Royce Morrison. I met him during my senior year at college, through that professor I worked for. He had a full crew lined up to start production on this series, but I told him if he ever had a place for me, I'd be interested. A couple months later he contacted me. My job with him right after graduation was definitely low man on the totem pole, much like our swampers, but that fall his number-two video cameraman decided to quit. So I took a crash course at UCLA, and Royce let me take a stab at the photography." He laughed. "I made some big, dumb mistakes at first. Stuff like getting more of my foot than the rapids in one sequence. Accidentally wiping out about ten minutes of important film on another. But I've improved, and I'm head cameraman now."

"The few times you're actually shown, you always look as if you're having such a wonderful time." Her head was leaned back against the boulder as she ate the candy bar, the shifting moonlight flirting with the sculpted lines of her face, emphasizing the curve of her cheek and dark sweep of her eyelashes. Did she sound a little wistful? No, of course not. She had city life and the big-business excitement of Andkit now. After a moment's hesitation she added, "I guess I've wondered why you didn't go into partnership with Ben and Rella in Canyon Cowboys."

He'd wondered about that himself. Would he have gone into business with them if Royce hadn't come along and offered him this job exploring the wild rivers of the world? He'd never wanted to cut Ben and Rella out of his life as Kit had done; he'd always felt he owed Rella too much to do that. Prayer and digging into the Lord's Word had also convinced him it wasn't what the Lord wanted him to do. But neither had he ever felt quite comfortable with Ben and Rella together. Now he just shrugged lightly and said, "Maybe I would have, if this other chance hadn't come along."

A faint scent of rain drifted up the canyon now, but the threat of a drenching on the campground was receding. The clouds were breaking up, the silver-white half-moon peeking through more often. The air had cooled, and the boulder, still retaining some of the heat of the day, now felt pleasantly warm against his back.

"I remember your dad used to like to camp at this place," Kit said, surprising him with the change of subject. He had braced himself for another argument about Ben and Rella. She laughed softly. "He had some wild tale about UFOs he liked to tell here."

"And another one about Indian ghosts that was better than any scary movie."

"Do you still miss him?" she asked.

"I'll always miss him."

"I missed Dad and Rella even when I was so angry with them. It seems unreal to think that they'll never be here on the river again." He heard the soft rustle of her hair against the boulder as she shook her head. "Even after the funeral, even after helping carry the coffin and knowing he was in there, I still keep expecting them to just...be here."

He didn't feel that way. He missed Ben and Rella, was reminded of them at every rapids, every twist of the river, but he'd seen their bodies, and the fact that they were only memories now was all too real to him.

"Tyler, did either of them ever make any move toward acceptance of the faith you and I have? Did they ever show any interest at all?"

"Last Christmas Rella came to church with me on Christmas Eve. I didn't get back to the ranch often, and she was careful to say that she was going only because she wanted to spend more time with me. But afterward we talked about the service, and I thought she possibly had a little different perspective on Christmas. We talked lots of times, actually. She'd always listen, sometimes appear interested, but she'd also always just seem to shrug it off."

"And Dad?"

"One time a couple years ago when he was laid up with a pulled muscle I caught him reading the Bible I'd left on the coffee table in the living room. He said something about there being some 'real red-blooded guys' in it. I agreed there were, including the most 'red-blooded' of them all, Jesus. I left the Bible there, but I don't know that he ever picked it up again. Maybe the only reason he picked it up that time was because he had to move it to get to his *Rodeo Sports News*." Tyler tilted his head reflectively. "But he liked to listen to gospel music, if it was country-and-western style."

"Sometimes I prayed for them, even when I was so angry with them." She made an odd little sound, as if a sob had caught in her throat. "But not as often as I should have."

"Yeah. Me, too."

She dug her heel in the soft sand, making a little furrow. The moon was fully exposed now. It shone on her bare leg, and under its glow the skin gleamed as if silvered.

"I sometimes had the impression they weren't totally closed against the Lord. I certainly never gave up hope that they would accept salvation," he added. He shook his head. "But..."

She sat up straighter, crossing her legs. "But you don't always know what's going on inside people. I always thought Mom was such a devoted Christian. You know how she was always so faithful about going to church, always busy with church activities. But after Dad left her for Rella, she confessed to me that her faith was all a fraud, just empty busywork. She said she'd wanted terrible things to happen to them. That if there was a God and he cared anything about good and bad, that he'd have punished them. He wouldn't have let them be so happy and her so miserable."

"I'd certainly never have guessed that was what was going on inside Andrea," Tyler agreed, honestly astonished. "And now?"

"And now, as she once put it, she isn't a fraud anymore. She truly gave her heart to the Lord. We prayed together for Dad and Rella."

"I'm glad. And I'm glad things have worked out so well for her. But I'm not sure Mom and Ben were as deliriously happy as Andrea probably thought they were."

"They were unhappy, sorry they'd done it?"

"No, I don't think so. But one time I asked Mom squarely if they were happy. She said..." He paused, trying to remember Rella's exact words. "'Mostly' was the word I think she used. Mostly happy. But that guilt was not a strong foundation for top-of-the-line happiness, that it was not easy to be happy when you knew your happiness came at the expense of others' unhappiness."

Kit picked up a handful of sand and let it drizzle over her foot. "I suppose at one time I'd have been glad to hear that. Now it just seems so very sad. Such a waste of lives."

"I'm also fairly certain that, much as I'd like to think it, neither of them was concealing some secret relationship with the Lord from me. Unlike Andrea, their lack of a spiritual life was right up front. What you saw was what was there. That's what hurts the most about their deaths, of course. Knowing that they died without ever making the commitment that would save them for eternity. Every day I think about how I failed them. How, if I'd been better at getting across what I believe, I could have opened their eyes. That if I'd somehow done something differently, I could have shown them the way. But I didn't. I failed them."

Kit didn't jump to offer easy condolences for his feelings of disappointment and failure. Instead she turned her head to give him an odd, speculative look. "Maybe not."

"What do you mean?"

"Tyler, how long a time was there between when the plane crashed and when they died?"

"I'm not sure. We figured they'd stayed with the plane for at least two days. It may have been another two or three days after that before they actually died."

"What happened in those days? How does anyone know what happens when it comes down to the bottom line, when there's nothing left except you and the Lord?" He heard a note of excitement in her voice.

"You're suggesting they may have turned to the Lord in a last-minute plea to help them out of a desperate situation?" He also heard a twinge of disparagement in his own voice. "How many people make promises and then forget them when the crisis is over? How real is that kind of conversion?"

"It could have been that way," Kit admitted. "Or maybe they knew the situation was beyond desperate, that it was hopeless, and they came to a last-minute recognition that in the end everything you'd been trying for so long to get through to them was all that really mattered! There was time, Tyler. Time! And maybe that time was a special gift from God, not something he grants to everyone. Maybe this tragedy was what it was all about, what it took to get through to them. The *only* way to get through to them.

Maybe everything either one of us ever said to them about our faith was all stored in reserve for those last hours when its meaning would become real to them. Maybe all of it, my rejection of them, your not rejecting them, the plane crash, maybe it was all part of God's plan. A harsh plan, perhaps, by some standards, but his plan. The Lord doesn't hold it against people who come to him late. Remember Jesus' parable about the men who came late to working in a vineyard earning the same as those who came early."

Tyler considered the passionate words tumbling out of her. Ever since Ben's and Rella's deaths he had dwelt solely on the unhappy truth that he had never heard or seen the spiritual change in them that he had long hoped and prayed for. But that didn't mean it hadn't happened in those last hours!

Kit leaned back and sighed. "I thought about this earlier, at the motel. I even thought about calling you at the ranch and talking to you about it."

"I wish you had."

"But then I also thought, maybe it was all just wishful thinking."

"That's possible," he agreed, nodding soberly. "But it's also a wonderful possibility that had totally escaped me before."

She stood up, dusted sand off the seat of her shorts, conscientiously crunched the Snicker's wrapper, and put it in her pocket. "I guess it really is time for bed now."

He turned her to face him, hands lightly holding her waist. "Thanks, Kit. Thanks for talking to me like this."

She smiled lightly. "Maybe we don't have to argue or get into some big conflict every time we have a conversation. Maybe sometimes we can just talk."

"I hope so."

Although, to tell the truth, he hoped for much more.

NINETEEN

K it crawled out of the tent before dawn. The morning smelled fresh washed even though the rain had detoured the campground, the day full of joyful promise. Cloudless blue ribbon of sky overhead, fluffy white trail of a jet plane like a fairy-tale bridge across the canyon, cheerful, wake-up warble of a canyon wren.

She felt fresh washed, too, as if the long talk with Tyler last night had cleansed something between them. She started the burner on the propane stove and was humming a cheerful praise chorus when Tyler, yawning, running his hands through his still sleep-rumpled hair, joined her in the kitchen.

For a moment Kit thought he was going to kiss her, which was how he'd always greeted her in the past when they met first thing in the morning to start breakfast on the river. She was reasonably certain he thought about it, the way he looked at her. She was less certain how she felt about his actually doing it, although, with a skitter of a heartbeat, she doubted she'd turn and run.

Whatever his original intentions, after their eyes caught and held for a breathless moment, he simply grumbled cheerfully, "Hey, where's that coffee you promised to have ready this morning?"

She flicked a forefinger of water at him from the blue-enamel pot she was filling. "Whatever happened to, 'Good morning. Isn't this a lovely day?'" she chided.

"Actually, it is a lovely day," he said. His meaningful glance, targeted on her rather than the canyon awakening around them, told her that their talk last night played a large part in making the day lovely.

They worked companionably together to start breakfast. Their talk was of everyday matters: the rapids they'd encounter today, the possibility of another summer thunderstorm, the fact that the water level had dropped considerably in the night, far lower than it had been earlier. He cut oranges and grapefruit into wedges; she set out jam and plates and silverware. She baked biscuits in the Dutch oven while he made the sausage gravy to ladle over them. Most of the passengers were cheerful and upbeat at breakfast, although the Three Toads grumbled that all the fuss putting up tents was a big waste of time since it hadn't rained after all.

They stopped at Redwall Cavern again that day and also at Vasey's Paradise because a botanist on board was especially interested in the lush plant life there. They saw a golden eagle drifting gracefully on lazy air currents overhead, a rare sight in the canyon in these days when the number of the magnificent birds was sadly dwindling. She pointed out to the passengers the place high on a cliff where bits of an old Anasazi footbridge remained. JoJo took over in the motorwell for a couple of long stretches, leaving Kit free to laze in the sun and even nap a little between rough rides through rapids.

After lunch, one of the men who was especially enthusiastic about photography wanted a photo of all four guides together. He lined them up beside the rafts, Kit and Tyler in the center, JoJo and Ryan on either side, arms linked around each others waists. At the last moment, just as the man snapped the photo, Tyler and JoJo lifted Kit off her feet and swung her high in the air. It was a warm, companionable moment, full of shrieks and laughter, yet an unexpected last-times feeling shivered through Kit.

Because it was last-times, of course. She'd be going back to Phoenix at the end of these seven days. Back to the hum of machines, sales conferences, advertising strategies, the rough competition to get ahead and stay ahead in the toy world. But her thoughts kept returning to the question JoJo had asked: Who says you have to go back to Phoenix?

That afternoon, as they drifted through the timeless red walls, she took the thought further. So far she'd handled several problems at Andkit from a distance. Would it be possible, if she spent winters working with the company in Phoenix and kept in touch through the summer to assist with larger problems, that she could run Andkit without being there full-time? And gradually hand more and more of the management over to her mother and Kelli until the responsibility was all in their hands?

She felt a sudden burgeoning of hope—of potential freedom! Yes, maybe it could work!

Or would following her own dream be troubling for her mother? Kit thought again about her father's betrayal of her mother. Would Andrea be all right if Kit left for long periods of time? Could Andrea take such a change just as she was getting back on her feet? Or would she see it as another betrayal?

Perhaps the whole idea was utterly foolish. Andkit had the potential to be a "money-making machine," as one enthusiastic magazine writer had called it; most people would never comprehend her dissatisfaction there. But no matter how many "doll dollars," as Kit and her mother sometimes laughingly called them, Andkit produced, it didn't have the canyon or the alternating raw excitement and serene peace of the river. Andkit wasn't what she *loved*.

When it was time to set up camp, Kit brought her thoughts back to matters at hand. They camped in an area where the canyon widened to reveal a magnificent vista of layered, multicolored cliffs soaring to the distant rim, a view that always made Kit feel physically insignificant against the grandeur of this backdrop of the Lord's creation. And, at the same time, marvel that he knew and cared about each individual in the midst of all this, that she wasn't insignificant to him.

This was Mexican night, and JoJo livened the preparations for a taco and rice and chili dinner by producing an enormous if battered black sombrero with dangling silver bells and pulling Kit into an improvised Mexican Hat Dance. The kids enthusiastically joined in, the little tomboy, Lisa, leading the way as usual. And then…disaster.

The food was all set out and ready: a big pot of chili on the stove, Spanish rice, tortilla chips and fiery salsa, warm tortillas and all the makings for tacos, a big bowl of mixed fruit, and an icy jug of fruit punch.

JoJo hit the triangular gong that announced dinner. "And now, señors and señoras, señoritas and niños," he called, bowing grandly, "if you will just step this way…"

He transferred the enormous black sombrero to Kit's head, where it promptly fell over her eyes. So she never was quite certain what happened next.

Running footsteps. Squeal. Swish of sand. A yell, "Hey, kids, be careful!"

A crunch, shrieks, thuds. "Grab the stove, it's tilting!" And then Kit was flung flat on her back on the sand, weight squashed on top of her.

She struggled out from under the sombrero, shook her head, and blinked in appalled disbelief. The fallen table had her pinned against the sand, food everywhere. A bowl of salsa overturned on her chest, splashes of salsa on her arms. Something sticky in her hair, tumbled mounds of Spanish rice all around her. Tortilla chips scattered like fallen leaves, the pot of chili upside down on the stove, chunks of fruit salad sparkling in the sand like fallen jewels, fruit punch dribbling from the ice jug, shredded cheese, lettuce, and tomato draped in a tangled web over everything. Four kids in a frozen tableau of horror, everyone staring, not making a sound.

The tableau exploded to life. Shocked parents grabbing kids and scolding, JoJo lifting the table off Kit, Tyler helping her to her feet, Ryan handing her a paper towel to daub at her shirt and arms. She'd been the only one in the main flyway path of the food, although they all bore various splotches. Shredded cheese dangled from Tyler's left ear, shredded lettuce from Ryan's glasses.

The food mess was so incredible that for a minute all they could do was simply stare at it, hardly knowing where to begin. With just a little rearrangement, what had been appetizing food only a few moments earlier was now garbage. Spying an ant already busily making off with a shred of cheese, JoJo said, "We'd better hurry up and do something before the ants take over. I think they're already sending smoke signals to notify their friends."

The little girl, Lisa, tearfully apologized first, then the boys, and the parents were also apologetic for not watching and controlling the kids better. The explanation for the disaster was that the kids had been romping and playing after the Hat Dance, exuberantly skidding and falling in the sand, though neither they nor anyone else seemed sure exactly how the en masse crash into the table had occurred.

They should have been more careful, of course, but Kit couldn't be too angry with any of them. She and Tyler had caused their share of youthful disasters, too.

Tyler handed out garbage bags and both crew and passengers tackled the cleanup. Tyler and Ryan scooped up the larger messes with a shovel; little Lisa helped with a spoon. Nothing edible was salvageable, and every scrap had to be picked up for hauling out of the canyon with the usual trash. After the worst of the mess was packed away, Kit went off to wash sticky stuff and sand out of her hair and change clothes. The children, who were very quiet now, were still working, carefully picking the last small shreds of cheese and lettuce out of the sand.

Afterward, all they could do for a substitute evening meal was set out the makings for sandwiches, the same as they usually had for lunch. No one seemed too upset by the change in the dinner menu, and Kit heard laughter and scraps of various tales of disasters and escapades from people's own childhoods.

Just as Kit was setting out more Swiss cheese for sandwiches, the little girl, Lisa, came up. She looked a little scared but determined as she said, "I'm sorry your blouse got ruined. I'll give you two dollars now and send you fifty cents out of my allowance every week until it's paid for." Her tomboy knees were skinned, her snub nose bore the scab of some encounter, and the shoelace on one red tennis shoe dangled untied.

Kit hugged her, especially impressed because she knew this was something the girl was doing on her own, not something her parents had pressured her to do. For a moment she didn't know what to say. She didn't want to minimize the children's carelessness and the inconvenience it had caused so many people, but neither did she want the money. "Do you go to Sunday school?" she asked impulsively.

"Sometimes."

"How about if you promise to go every Sunday for at least the rest of the summer, and the first time you go you give the Lord your two dollars? Then each week you give him fifty cents until you think the T-shirt has been paid for. And talk to the Lord about being more careful about doing something that might hurt others after this."

Lisa considered the proposal solemnly. "You mean pray?" she asked finally.

"Yes. That's what talking to the Lord is."

"I think I kinda prayed the first time the big waves crashed down on us. But I don't pray much," the girl said doubtfully.

"Then this would be a good time to start."

The girl considered the entire proposition again as Kit tied her shoelace for her, obviously not one to make careless promises. Finally she nodded. "Okay, I promise. Fifty cents every week and praying."

Kit smiled as she watched the little girl run off. Then she realized that Tyler, who had been off doing something with the balky water-filtration equipment, had returned and seen the small exchange.

He smiled. "You know who she reminds me of?"

"No."

"Yes, you do. *You*. Right down to the skinned knees."

He was right, of course. Lisa did remind her of herself at that age, shins or knees or some other vulnerable portion of her anatomy usually skinned up, often in trouble, always repentant. But all too often blithely rushing on to get in some new tomboy trouble. They looked at each other, and Kit wondered if he was thinking the same thing she was. About the family they'd once planned to start together, a little girl of their own who might have been like her, a boy like him.

Then someone interrupted to ask for more rye bread, and by the time Kit got it she saw that Tyler was absorbed in cleaning up the stove. Perhaps she'd been mistaken in her speculations about what he was thinking.

A mother of one of the guilty boys reached the table almost at the end of the dinner line, and she, too, apologized again. "I'm just so very sorry. It's been such a wonderful trip. We live in an apartment back in Detroit, and the kids don't often get a chance to play so exuberantly. They really overdid it." She smiled ruefully, and Kit could see she was trying hard not to cry. "Is there anything I can do to help make up for…"

"You could keep your brats under control," Les, the blond Toad, growled as he slapped mayonnaise on a slice of bread. His wraparound, reflector-type sunglasses perched on top his head gleamed with an iridescent shine in his blond hair. "Or better yet, you could have left them at home so you wouldn't ruin everyone else's trip."

Kit gasped at the blunt, viciously spoken words. "Accidents happen," she said as diplomatically as she could. "Having sandwiches isn't as much fun as the Mexican meal, but I doubt anyone's trip is *ruined.*"

Les was hardly suffering from ruined appetite or lack of food; this was his second time through the line, and he piled enough ham and cheese on his sandwiches to start his own deli. Kit also suspected this minor disaster would become a high-point memory of the trip for many people, a story to be told and retold with laughter.

"I think we're all going to survive," she added, straining her vocal cords to sound cheerful and her face to smile.

"People who don't know how to make their kids behave shouldn't even have kids," Les muttered as he piled pickles on his already oversized sandwich.

The woman made a strangled sound, dropped her half-made sandwich in the trash, and fled. Les didn't even glance her way, apparently unperturbed at how he'd upset the woman. "Isn't there any Dijon mustard?" he grumbled.

"Didn't you ever do something a little careless and boisterous when you were a boy?" Kit challenged.

"If I'd done anything like what these kids did, my father would have blistered my fanny until I couldn't sit down for a week. All these brats got was a little, 'Now you should have been more careful, children.'" His voice went high pitched as he mocked the scolding the children had received, which had actually been more severe than that. "Mustn't damage their delicate little self-esteems, of course," he added disdainfully.

"Accidents happen," Kit repeated.

"Of course, who's really to blame is you people."

"Us?"

"You shouldn't even allow kids on these trips. They just get in the way and cause trouble and ruin everyone else's fun. If I were running this outfit, there'd be a rule: no one under sixteen allowed. Maybe even eighteen."

"Well, you aren't running it, and I like children," Kit retorted flatly. "And as long as I have anything to do with Canyon Cowboys, children will always be welcome." She was tempted to add, *Who we ought to disallow is loud-mouthed, ill-tempered ex-jocks,* but she managed to shove a bite of cheese into her mouth to shut herself up.

"This isn't the kind of meal we paid for," Les added as he yanked his reflective sunglasses down over his eyes and stalked off.

"If you care to apply at our office for a meal refund, I'll make certain that you get it," Kit snapped after him.

They spent much of the next morning swimming and playing in the Little Colorado, even the Three Toads apparently enjoying bouncing through the shallow rapids, although they disdained doing it in the usual manner with life jackets fastened on upside down. Kit suspected their superior attitude cost them some scratched or bruised bottoms, but they didn't acknowledge that, of course. Kit went down twice, both times floating side-by-side with Lisa, whose mother didn't care for any closer contact with the water than what she got on the raft.

Would she ever have a child of her own? Kit wondered a little wistfully as she and Lisa held hands to whoosh down a swoop of milky turquoise water and crash with whoops of laughter into a froth of white water.

The fluctuation in water level of the main river, caused by variations in the amount of water released through Glen Canyon Dam, had roiled the river, turning the usual clear green water a murky brownish green today. It emphasized the gorgeous turquoise of the Little Colorado where the two joined, until the larger volume of murky green-brown swallowed the turquoise.

Because the water level was now much lower, Tyler suggested they scout Hance Rapid, which could be extremely treacherous at low water because so many more rocks were exposed. Leaving Ryan and all but the most energetic passengers with the rafts just above the rapids, Tyler, Kit, and JoJo hiked down to the best vantage point from which to check out the situation. A side canyon joined the river here, with a wide space between the cliffs and the water, but the sand was covered with jumbled rocks and low but rough shrubs, making walking difficult.

Many more rocks were definitely exposed in the rapids than the last time Kit and JoJo had gone through Hance, white water leaping around the dark rocks in a menacing dance of danger. Kit mentally picked a route through the river-wide gauntlet of rocks, a deceptive jumble that could sometimes be more dangerous than rapids with larger waves and holes but a clean route with plenty of space between boulders for a raft. The sight of all those treacherous rocks waiting to ambush them didn't make Kit nervous, but it did make her cautious.

"Looks like a herd of alligators out there waiting to gulp us down," JoJo observed.

Tyler nodded. "Very hungry alligators. With big, dangerous teeth."

Together they chose what looked like the safest route through the jumbled barricade of boulders, Tyler standing behind Kit once so she could sight down his arm and pinpoint a particularly vicious rock where the best route was to the right. Even with her mind on the rapids and the treacherous route through the boulders, she was very conscious of him, his nearness, his left hand lightly holding her shoulder, his right arm brushing her hair as he pointed.

"Just as a precaution, how about having the passengers walk around?" Kit suggested. She remembered a time when a raft, fortunately not one belonging to Canyon Cowboys, got so disastrously hung up on a rock at Hance in low water that a helicopter had to be brought in and passengers lifted off one by one. Getting hung up could happen to the best of guides, as they all knew.

"That's a good idea," Tyler agreed. Wryly he added, "Guess who's going to object?"

He was right.

As soon as Tyler announced that the passengers would walk around the rapids while the guides took the rafts through, Les, apparently the leader and head griper of the trio, objected strenuously.

"We're on this trip for the thrills and excitement. We *paid* for thrills and excitement, not to be treated like a bunch of little old ladies. We have a right to be in the raft."

"Sorry," Tyler said. "We want to make every trip as exciting and fun as possible, but it is also our responsibility to consider the safety of the passengers first. With the water this low on this particular rapids, there's just too much chance of a raft getting hung up or flipping. Taking such a chance would show a careless disregard for our passengers' safety. And lives."

"If you ask me, what it shows is a lack of guts," Les sneered.

Tyler's mouth compressed with anger, but he held back a harsh response and simply said stiffly, "I'm sorry you feel that way."

Then Les turned to look at Kit, and now it was her turn to come under his fire. "Or maybe you're afraid your girl guide here just isn't competent enough to handle the rough stuff," he added scornfully.

Tyler's fists clenched, and Kit could see that his usual even temper was near the exploding point. So far the Three Toads had ridden only where Tyler had assigned them, in his raft, but given the current tension Kit decided she'd better shoulder her share of their unpleasant company.

Drawing on a charm she didn't feel, she smiled and said lightly, "After we get past Hance, perhaps Les and his friends would like to ride in my raft. If I'm so incompetent, they're sure to get plenty of thrills and excitement riding with me."

"You *are* walking around Hance," Tyler added with grim certainty.

Les looked as if he were tempted to challenge Tyler's authority, but finally he shrugged, muttered something unrepeatable, and backed down. In all her years on the river, Kit could never remember encountering anyone even half as obnoxious.

The passengers, no one else complaining, started walking toward the far end of the rapids where the rafts would pick them up.

"Hey, Girl Guide, you want to go first?" Tyler called after both sets of pilots were in their rafts, motors running.

He grinned, and Kit grinned back, appreciating the teasing vote of confidence. "Sure, I'll go first. Easy as floating an inner tube across a swimming pool," she called back.

Although, a few moments later, as she faced the next several hundred feet of river with the maze of boulders lurking like dark booby traps, she didn't feel nearly so confident.

TWENTY

A quick glance at shore showed Kit that most of the passengers were lined up to watch. From here, with the raft already in the grip of the current, the view was even more ominous than it had looked from shore. From water level, she also couldn't see the complete route they'd chosen. She had to remember where the spaces between rocks were wide enough to slip a raft through, where to duck right or left. And there was no turning back now.

She gripped the long handle extension on the motor and braced herself, easing the raft into the rapids at the point they'd chosen. Then she whipped sideways to slide around a boulder straight ahead, slithered between two sharp rocks with barely a finger width to spare.

"Doing great!" JoJo yelled from his position near the front of the raft.

"Then why are you holding on like a scared kid on a roller coaster?" Kit yelled back, just before white water crashed over the horns.

White water surrounded them now, a roaring maelstrom of it, like some angry creature trying to leap into the raft with them. The bathtub and horns disappeared in another wild explosion of white water, then instantly bucked upward, momentarily blocking her view. Exposed rocks surrounded them like a hostile army, and she could feel submerged rocks beneath her feet, the raft bumping over them until an unseen vortex whirled them sideways. She called on the little motor for more power, and it responded, shooting them across the whirling water. Into a slippery hole, past a rock with a treacherous ledge concealed beneath the surface, through another drench of white water.

"We made it! Good job, Girl Guide."

Beyond the white water, Kit guided the raft into shore, happy with the triumph that successfully conquering a challenging rapids always gave her. And also a little weak with relief.

Then she turned to JoJo suspiciously. "What's with this 'Girl Guide' stuff?"

"Doesn't it fit?" JoJo asked innocently.

Kit groaned. "No! It's awful. And sexist."

JoJo just grinned, and Kit knew she was stuck with it. Well, she thought philosophically, it was better than Wrong-Way Holloway. Then they both turned to watch Tyler and Ryan make the same run they'd just finished. There was one tense moment when the raft momentarily hung up on a rock caught between the left horn and the bathtub, but Tyler expertly maneuvered away before the treacherous flow of water locked the raft immovably against the rock.

The passengers climbed on, Les and his co-Toads taking Kit up on her offer to ride on her raft. Les had a comment to make, of course.

"Didn't look to me as if it was all that big a deal," he scoffed. "I'll bet I could have piloted a raft through there myself."

Yeah, right, Kit responded silently, *and I could race a car in the Indy 500*. But she didn't argue with him. The trio hogged the horns in the rapids but otherwise didn't give her any problems. Thunderclouds massed off in the distance again, but they were so far away that no sound of thunder followed the webbed lightning occasionally flashing out of the dark mounds.

They made camp just above Grapevine Rapid, where a rough, red wall rose straight from a sloping sandy beach. Launches were regulated so that, even though at any given time a number of people were floating the river, there was usually no feeling of being on a white-water freeway. Sometimes a planned camping site would already be in use, but often they seemed to have the river to themselves. This day, however, two smaller, oar-powered rafts drifted by, carrying supplies for a dozen or so people in individual kayaks. Kit, cooking pork chops for dinner, watched with interest as the kayakers rhythmically dipped their paddles from one side of the kayak to the other. Kayaking was something she'd never done.

"Looks like fun," Tyler commented. He was baking biscuits in the Dutch oven, JoJo and Ryan rearranging some supplies on the rafts.

"How come we never tried kayaking?" Kit asked.

"We still could." Tyler grinned and bent his arm to flex an impressive bulge of muscle. "We aren't exactly over the hill yet. In fact, Royce is thinking about filming an ocean kayaking trip along the British Columbia coast for *The World of White Water.*"

Kit rejected a momentary flash of disappointment that Tyler's "we" was merely a figure of speech, not a real *we* with the suggestion of a possibility of the two of them doing something new together. Which was entirely accurate, of course; they wouldn't be kayaking or doing anything else together. They had reached a cautious level of cooperation and friendliness on this trip, and sadness at the loss of Ben and Rella had created a tentative bond between them. But any deeper relationship was a thing of the past, which was exactly how she wanted it.

Lisa and the boys fished after dinner, under the watchful eye of one of the fathers. Lisa yelled for Kit to come when she caught something. "Look, it has funny whiskers!"

Kit identified Lisa's catch as a small catfish. Regulations required that several protected species must be returned to the river, but catfish could be kept. "Want me to cook it for you?"

Lisa, after stroking the unlovely creature with a forefinger, said, "No, I want to let him go."

Kit ruffled the girl's hair approvingly. That's what she'd have done, too.

With the potential storm the first night, and the dinner disaster the second night, JoJo hadn't started one of his continuing suspense stories for this trip. But this night quiet Ryan produced a harmonica, and JoJo led everyone in exuberantly singing "Row Your Boat" and several other songs suitable for round singing. The Three Toads chose not to participate, of course, and went off somewhere by themselves, but everyone else had a rollicking good time.

Tyler was correcting a small problem with his raft's motor when the singing started, but a few minutes later he slid into an empty spot on the sand beside Kit. They sang on different rounds of the songs, the groups of male and female voices cheerfully competing to drown each other out rather than cooperating musically. Then JoJo got them all into a cooperative effort on an old Beatles' song, where everyone swayed back and forth in rhythm with the music.

Tyler's shoulder brushed Kit's frequently as they sang and swayed, and once he draped his arm around her shoulders when he whispered, "Reminds me of our old youth group choir practice."

"Rather different songs," Kit pointed out.

"I guess it's just the singing together that reminded me, then. All the fun we used to have."

Kit smiled. "I'm having fun now."

He gave her a long, thoughtful look. "So am I."

After the singing, everyone gathered around the kitchen for snacks before heading off to their sleeping bags. A sluggish breath of hot breeze sighed up the canyon, and no tents had sprouted tonight. A bat hunting for night-flying insects swooped low over Kit's head as she went down to give the rafts a final check. She didn't want any unpleasant surprises if the water level rose or fell in the night.

She was climbing out of the raft when Tyler's lanky silhouette approached through the darkness. The moon wasn't visible yet, but the light it shed from beyond the canyon rim gave a soft radiance to the night. "Oh, there you are. I was wondering where you'd gone," he said.

"Everything's secure for the night. But I'll have to gas up in the morning. I didn't get around to it tonight."

"I've already taken care of it."

"Hey, thanks!"

"Glad to do it, Girl Guide."

Kit groaned. Several people had quickly picked up on the name and called her that at dinner. She'd wondered if it would make Les angry because the name actually made fun of his condescending attitude toward her, but apparently he was too dense to notice.

"You did a good job at Hance today," Tyler added approvingly.

Kit had the odd feeling that he was searching for some way to keep the conversation going. She was undecided if she wanted to help. "You, too."

He tried again. "You seem to have found a real buddy in little Lisa."

"She's a great kid. She tried to pay me for the T-shirt that was ruined with salsa stains."

"I saw that she released her little catfish. That's what you always used to do, too." He laughed lightly. The Holloway and McCord males had always teased Kit about her untomboyish squeamishness in this area. She liked the thrill of catching a fish, but she also preferred to see the fish swimming free rather than sizzling in a frying pan.

"Good thing my living comes from making dolls, not fishing," Kit agreed.

"I suppose you're anxious to get back to work. I understand your company has made quite an impressive showing in the doll world."

Kit circumvented his comment about her being anxious to get back to work. "Mom is very creative." Somehow it seemed disloyal to Andrea to admit how *un*anxious she was to return to Phoenix and Andkit.

"But you like being back on the river again," he suggested shrewdly. "This hasn't been the greatest trip so far, but you've still seemed happy. At least as happy as possible under the circumstances."

"I never wanted to leave the river." She didn't mean that as an accusation, but she suspected it sounded that way. Tyler didn't leap to a defense, however.

"Neither did I," he said slowly.

"But things changed."

"Maybe they could change back again."

Kit's head jerked in surprise as she wondered what that meant. Was he suggesting renewing their relationship? He instantly stepped forward and placed a finger across her lips.

"Don't ask what that means. Because I'm not sure myself."

She took a step backward, away from the strange feeling that arced through her when he touched her. "Okay, I won't ask. Now if you'll excuse me…"

He leaned against the horn, feet crossed at the ankles. "Are you in a big hurry to hit the sleeping bag?"

She hesitated. The silvery curve of moon was now peeking over the canyon wall. And moonlight and the river and Tyler were a powerful combination. What was she afraid of? she scoffed at herself.

"Not necessarily," she said, a little coolly.

"I just thought maybe we could sit and talk awhile. As you pointed out the other night, we don't have to argue. We could just talk. We used to talk about everything."

He patted the taut skin of the inflated pontoon, but Kit didn't instantly respond to the invitation to sit beside him.

Instead, leaning against the pontoon of the other raft a few feet away, she said, "You could tell me more about working on *The World of White Water.*" But unexpectedly she remembered something that made her laugh. She picked up a slender scrap of driftwood and reached over to tuck it between his nose and upper lip. She considered the results critically.

"What's this?" he asked, moving his lips carefully to keep the stick from slipping.

"You had a mustache on one of the programs in the series. Very dashing."

He grimaced and laughed, displacing the bit of driftwood. "Also very itchy, as I recall. But if you want me in a mustache, I'll sure grow one." He twirled an imaginary mustache with a villain-foreclosing-on-the-mortgage swirl. "You just say the word."

Kit laughed, a little surprised at his obvious eagerness to please. "I'll think about it."

He went on to tell her about his disastrous first trip with *The World of White Water*, which was on a river in Russia. It had never been shown on TV because most of the film had been lost when one of their rafts was literally torn apart in a rapids. "We were lucky to get out with our lives, let alone any film or equipment."

He went on to tell about their most recent experiences on the

Yangtze River in China, which would be shown on PBS sometime in the fall.

"I'll be sure to watch for it," Kit said. At some point during the conversation he had moved across the gap between the two rafts, and now they were sitting side by side on the fat pontoon, not quite touching, but almost.

"You might especially watch for a Chinese guy who always had a big grin," Tyler said. "Unless Royce edits it out, there's a good scene of him pulling me out of the water after my raft flipped. We hired several helpers there, but he was the only one who spoke good English. He was extremely interested in the little New Testament I always carried, and we had some interesting discussions. He was of the belief that there are many paths to God, that Jesus is just one of many ways. And the best way to get to heaven was just to be good and do good."

"Did you change his mind?"

"I showed him the Bible verses, but he scoffed and said there were other books that told of other pathways, and why should he believe this book over the others? I had to admit I was not overly knowledgeable about other religions, but I asked him if he thought he was really good enough to get to heaven on his own. And for once he lost that big grin and admitted he probably wasn't that good, and then I told him about how God, through Jesus, offers salvation as a free gift, not something you have to earn."

"Wasn't it C. S. Lewis who pointed out, in some discussion about the world's religions, that one thing that differentiates Christianity from all other religions is grace?" Kit said. She went on to tell about a young woman who worked at Andkit for a while and was involved with a New Age group that believed in reincarnation. "I was undecided whether I should try to learn more about her beliefs in order to refute her misguided ideas or if I should stay totally away from it."

They discussed both sides of that issue for a while, then drifted on to talking about Kit's experiences searching for a church in Phoenix and Tyler's similar experiences in Oceanside. And eventually that led to laughter about Tyler's first attempts at surfing on the California coast and then to the strange doll-hair disaster and other "bad hair days" at Andkit.

Finally Kit reluctantly said, "I guess it must be bedtime. I think we're the only ones still up."

She slid off the pontoon—and into Tyler's arms. For a moment she thought it was simply an accidental movement on his part, a swift reflex action to catch and keep her from stumbling when her feet touched the sand. And then, as his arms tightened around her, she knew it was no accident.

"It's been wonderful talking to you, Kit," he said huskily. "I've missed you. We always could talk about everything. And laugh."

She swallowed and then admitted honestly, "I've missed you, too."

His fingers rubbed the spot between her shoulder blades. Vaguely she remembered reading once that this was the most insensitive part of the human body. Her shaky thought at the moment was, *Couldn't prove that by me!*

"I'm sorry about Kyle's accident, but I'm so very glad you're here," he whispered.

She lifted her head to look into his eyes. Moonlight glinted on his blond hair and eyebrows, but it darkened the blue of his eyes to almost black. She didn't remember putting her arms around him, but they were there, clasped across his strong back. "Maybe I was looking for an excuse to stay anyway."

He lifted his right hand and brushed the hair away from her temple, then cupped her jaw in the curve of his fingers.

"I should go…" she whispered. Yet her legs made no move to put the thought into action, and her arms made no effort to release him.

He dipped his head, pausing a moment with his mouth hovered a fraction of an inch from hers, as if he were momentarily having second thoughts. Then he closed the space and kissed her.

Kit didn't instantly respond. She simply accepted the kiss, reveling in its tender passion and gentle urgency, floating with the sweet arousal of old memories and breathtaking new possibilities.

He lifted his mouth, his lips still brushing hers as he tentatively whispered, "Kit?"

And this time, when he closed that heartbeat of space between them, she kissed him back.

TWENTY-ONE

Kit had won the pliers toss, so she didn't have to get up first the next morning. She simply lay there in the sleeping bag when she woke, breathing deeply of the canyon air, listening to the faint sounds of the camp awakening, smelling the first tantalizing scent of coffee brewing, watching the glimmer of a last star overhead fade into the pale blue of the morning sky. The river's song was softly musical this morning. Or was it some special music humming in her heart?

She wanted to extract each magical moment from the night before, hold it up and examine it from all sides, relive and glory in it. The companionable conversation, Tyler balancing her silly stick-mustache on his upper lip, the muscular warmth of his arm brushing hers as they sat on the pontoon, the laughter. The kiss.

The sweet-shivery memory of the kiss was what did it. Instantly she grabbed her clothes from under her pillow and started dressing. The kiss, although she couldn't bear to think of it as a *mistake*, was like a few words taken out of the context of a paragraph. It had nothing to do with their real lives. And she definitely must not enter the danger area of reliving it.

A position unexpectedly emphasized by the view of an outsider.

Kit and JoJo were cleaning up the breakfast dishes. Tyler and Ryan had taken about half the passengers on a short hike, Lisa and the boys among them. Hands in soapy dishwater, JoJo gave her a speculative glance.

"You and Tyler were getting rather friendly last night."

An uncomfortable heat warmed Kit's cheeks, but she chose to assume JoJo meant the fact that Tyler and she sat together during the singing. "We used to sing in our church's youth-group choir together."

Her hopeful assumption was wrong, of course.

"I'm talking about much later in the evening. The *very* friendly scene when you were down by the raft."

"What were you doing? Peering around with your top-secret, spy-in-the-night kit?" she grumbled.

"It hardly took a spy-in-the-night kit to see the two of you in the moonlight." He put his hands on his hips and stared at her. "And the sudden blaze of color in your cheeks just now, Girl Guide! Is there such a thing as moonburn?"

"So I blush easily," Kit muttered. "This is a crime?"

JoJo ignored the rhetorical question. "Does what I saw mean you and Tyler are getting back together?"

"No! It was just…" She couldn't think of a logical or appropriate ending for that statement and instead chose to scrub a frying pan with furious energy.

JoJo tactfully didn't embarrass her further. All he said was, "He hurt you once, Kit. Don't forget that."

"It wasn't one-sided. We hurt each other."

"Just be careful, Kit."

In spite of that warning and her own rather apprehensive feelings, the day turned out to be fantastic. Perfect weather, the blazing heat punctuated by cold white water avalanching into the rafts at Horn Creek and Granite and Crystal Rapids. They stopped to explore the Anasazi ruins, spotted a herd of bighorn sheep grazing on a slope so steep that Lisa said their legs must be longer on one side than the other, watched hikers cross overhead on the Bright Angel Bridge to Phantom Ranch. Even the Three Toads seemed relatively mellow, although Les slid so far to the side of the horn going through Crystal Rapid that only a quick grab by one of his buddies kept him from plunging into the torrent.

Tyler was friendly, but nothing about his manner suggested that he thought the kiss meant anything was changed between them. She was careful to act the same way, friendly but distant. She didn't want him to read more into the kiss than was there or give him the mistaken idea that it had some special meaning or importance to her. Although it would help, she thought wryly, if she could erase the way she felt, as if she'd been sprinkled with stardust.

By the second to the last night on the river, when the four guides were in a huddle discussing plans for the following day, she'd come to the conclusion, with a certain internal embarrassment, that she was the one who'd mistakenly read more into the kiss than was there. Stardust? No. Just a minor incident, a combination of moonlight and hormones and nostalgia; certainly no big deal to Tyler.

That conclusion, however, unexpectedly made her feel less reluctant to approach him about something that was on her mind. She decided she'd do it as soon as this meeting was over. They were gathered around the motor well of Tyler's raft, where he had been replacing the rough-running motor with one of the spares they always carried. Tomorrow they'd hit Lava Falls, and that was the last place any of them wanted a motor to conk out.

"What about riders on the horns through Lava?" JoJo asked.

Occasionally, when passengers were particularly competent and conditions of raft and river just right, they did allow riders on the horns through Lava. Kit had ridden there herself several times, of course, although each time she'd concurred with Frank McCord's assessment that riding the horn through Lava was a little like "riding a bronc through a tidal wave." But this time Kit quickly shook her head negatively.

"Some of our passengers aren't quite the hotshot horn riders they think they are."

The others didn't need names to know who she meant, and Tyler nodded agreement.

The short meeting broke up, but Kit didn't accompany JoJo and Ryan when they jumped out of the raft. "Could I talk to you for a minute? About a business matter," she added hastily in case Tyler mistakenly thought she was looking for a repeat of that other night.

He glanced up but went back to tinkering with the motor. "Sure. What's up?"

"I don't have this all worked out yet, and there are a lot of details concerning my responsibilities at Andkit to consider, but when everything is settled with the probate, I'd like to buy your half of Canyon Cowboys."

He straightened and looked at her so strangely that she fumbled for further explanation.

"I know you expressed a reluctance to sell to the outside company, but this would be more or less keeping it in the family."

"With full ownership in your hands, you'd also be free to sell out completely whenever you wanted." The statement fell short of an accusation that her motive in this was to dismantle the company to keep it from becoming a monument to Ben and Rella, but the hint of such a suspicion was there.

"No. That isn't what I have in mind. I want the company because of this." Kit's arm swept the scene around them, the strangely carved layers of rock where they were camped, the river flowing deep and green, the walls of multicolored rock climbing to the distant rim. "This is where I want to be."

"And just how would you manage this?"

"I don't know what your half of the company is worth, of course, but Andkit made a good profit last year and I have funds available…"

"I'm not talking about money." He sounded almost impatient. "I mean *how*. I can't see you simply abandoning Andrea and your responsibilities at Andkit."

"No! Of course not." She explained how she thought she could manage by spending winters with Andkit in Phoenix and handling problems long-distance during the summer until she could gradually turn management over to her mother and Kelli. "Mom much prefers the creative end of Andkit, but I think she can handle management, too. She's a different person than she used to be."

Unspoken were the condemning words, *before Dad abandoned her*, but Tyler undoubtedly knew she was thinking them. She was desperately sorry Ben was dead, that he'd died before she could tell him she still loved him, but that didn't change her feelings about the wrongness of what he'd done.

"Very interesting, your wanting to buy my half of Canyon Cowboys," Tyler mused. "Perhaps it's proof that great minds do think alike. Although it does present a certain complication."

Great minds think alike? What was that about? But his statement about a "certain complication" concerned her more. "What do you mean?"

"I mean that I was planning to ask you to sell your half of the company to me."

"But you can't run it," Kit objected instantly. "You're in Russia and China and Alaska and Chile and…"

"Yes, and I love exploring the wild rivers of the world. But the Colorado River and the Grand Canyon are *home*. I always figured on coming back here eventually. I think I could also split my time: work with Royce and *The World of White Water* in the winter, run Canyon Cowboys during the summer. Although, as you and I used to discuss, I'd like to expand Canyon Cowboys into other rivers, which would make it a year-round job."

A definite complication. In dismay she asked, "What if we can't agree on who sells out to whom?"

"I don't know. Toss a coin? Hire lawyers and sue each other? Of course the problem also comes with an obvious solution." He smiled lightly.

"Which is?"

"Keep Canyon Cowboys in joint ownership and run it together."

She'd been leaning against the inflated tube of the raft. She surged to her feet. "You can't be serious!"

He straightened, screwdriver still in hand. "I couldn't be more serious."

"I couldn't work with you!"

"It seems to me we're working together just fine."

"Only because it's just temporary!"

"It doesn't have to be temporary." He dropped the screwdriver and grabbed her by the shoulders. "And it doesn't have to be just a business partnership between us."

Kit just stared at him, feeling strangely light-headed. Had she hoped for this moment? Wanted it so she could icily say, "Never!" and remind him that time hadn't closed the canyon of differences between them? Or wanted it so she could recklessly ignore the past and fall into his arms?

"Kit, I didn't intend to say anything about this, about *us* yet." He rubbed his palms up and down her arms. "I didn't want to scare you off by coming on too strong too soon. But we can't let our relationship deteriorate into some squabble over ownership of Canyon Cowboys! We belong together, Kit. We've always belonged together."

"You were planning to marry someone else!"

His hands dropped as if they'd suddenly become heavy weights. "Oh yes. Ronnie." The name came out almost a sigh. "Is she a problem?"

"I'm not sure. Maybe you should tell me about her. And don't say, 'There isn't much to tell,'" she added warningly.

He leaned against the opposite side of the raft, eyes unfocused as he looked into the past. "I met her at college that fall after you and I broke up. Actually, she sought me out. She said she was fascinated by white-water rafting and had heard I was a 'top gun' at it."

"How flattering," Kit murmured.

"Yeah, it was flattering," Tyler admitted. "I was also lonely and angry and ripe for a big mistake, I suppose. Anyway, we started dating and at Thanksgiving she invited me back to Boston to visit her family. I also met her ex-boyfriend there, a lawyer type going to Harvard. If I hadn't been so dumb or naive…" He paused and smiled wryly. "And *naive* is not an easy thing for a man to admit, you know. Makes me feel like some backwoods, country clodhopper."

Tyler might be *country*, Kit thought silently, but he'd never been a clodhopper.

"Anyway, if I hadn't been so naive," he repeated, "I'd have realized she was just playing games with old-boyfriend Corwin, flaunting me as this macho, white-water river guide, this he-man of the west, to prove something to him. Anyway, during the visit she produced a ring that had been in her family for generations and somehow—I swear, I never was sure quite how it happened—by the end of Thanksgiving break we were announcing our engagement."

He ran his hand through the curly blond hair that still tended toward an unruly independence. Kit just stood there, arms crossed. One part of her scoffed, *Oh, c'mon, you expect me to believe you just blinked and suddenly found yourself engaged?*

Yet when she tilted her head and surveyed him, that suddenly didn't seem so unlikely. Lean, rugged body, tousled blond hair, expressive blue eyes, strong mouth, clean-cut jaw. Yes, if a woman was looking for a spectacular guy with whom to stir up another man's jealousy, Tyler was definitely an appropriate candidate.

And another part of her felt an unexpected twinge of tenderness. She was the only girlfriend Tyler had ever had before Ronnie; he was straightforward and moral and knew nothing about the manipulative games some couples played.

"So then you broke it off with her?"

"No. We were engaged for several months. Until her scheme worked, and she got ol' Corwin whipped into shape. Then she broke the engagement with me and went back to him."

"I see," Kit said, the twinge of tenderness turning to dismay. "So, if she hadn't dumped you, you'd be married to her right now."

He considered that, his expression in the fading canyon light half troubled, half embarrassed. "I don't think so. I think I'd have had better sense than that. But…" He lifted his shoulders, and his uncertainty drifted into the song of the river.

Kit swallowed, hating to ask the question yet unable not to ask it. "Were you in love with her?"

"I didn't feel about her the way I'd felt about you, but I thought I loved her. I thought I *would* feel about her as I'd once felt about you after she and I had been together as long as you and I had." He shook his head and smiled ruefully, apparently sensing that was not what Kit would have preferred to hear. "I'm not coming off looking very good in this, am I?"

"No, but you're honest. You didn't tell me some phony story

trying to make yourself look good."

"I have something else honest to tell you. After the dust cleared around the breakup with Ronnie and I got past the wounded-ego stage of outrage that I'd been dumped for another guy, I realized I was more relieved than heartbroken. And I still love you, Kit. I've pushed my feelings for you into the background for a long time. I had to or my heart would have ripped apart like that raft we lost on a river in Russia. But I can't pretend I don't love you when you're right here beside me, when I can reach out and touch you."

He reached for her, voice and gaze suddenly urgent.

"Marry me, Kit. We'll do the big ceremony, just the way we once planned, if you want. Or we can just go off by ourselves and do it. I still have the ring."

She was still trying to absorb all he'd told her about his relationship with Ronnie, but she stopped short when he mentioned the ring. "You kept it? Why?"

"I don't know." He smiled, fingertips of one hand hungrily tracing her temple, ear, jaw, as the other arm locked around her. "Sentiment? Foolishness? Hope? Love," he finished with husky certainty.

His head dipped toward her, and Kit knew he was going to kiss her again. Instinctively her face lifted, wanting his kiss, aching for it.

Then, heart whispering one thing but head frantically shouting contradictions, she scrambled backward. She stumbled over a tool kit, floundering against the motor. She got on the far side of it, so it was a lumpy metal barrier between them.

"I still love you," he repeated. "I think you still love me."

She'd tried for so long not to love him that now she wasn't certain herself what was behind the walled-off place in her heart. But she knew kissing him again could only be a mistake that might explode into the even larger and more disastrous mistake of jumping headlong into what he offered.

"Tyler, I—I still have feelings for you. I can't deny that. We can talk and laugh—and kiss—and it almost seems like old times. But if Dad and Rella hadn't died, their marriage would still be like an enormous canyon between us. I've forgiven them for the way they hurt and betrayed Mom." She paused and took a breath, sensing a certain doubt in him. "I know you probably don't think that's true, but it is. But forgiveness and love don't mean *acceptance* of wrong-doing. I could never, even if they'd come back and I'd had the chance to tell them I still loved them, have made them a part of my life."

"I didn't *accept* what they'd done, Kit." She could hear the frustration in his voice. "I just didn't think the Lord wanted me to cut them out of my life. I didn't think he wanted me to abandon them."

"Maybe they needed abandoning." She shook her head. "See? We're still on opposite sides of the canyon, yelling across it with the same old arguments."

He rubbed the back of his neck in an uncharacteristic gesture of frustration and helplessness. "It's always seemed so strange and puzzling that we both studied the Lord's Word, both wanted to do his will in this, both sincerely thought we were right. And yet we came up with totally different paths to follow."

Kit nodded. "I remember mentioning that to Mom once."

"Yet at this point, I don't see what difference any of it makes!" he exclaimed with a sudden storm of passion. "It's over, Kit. They're dead. Maybe at the last minute they turned to the Lord. Maybe they didn't. There's nothing we can do about it either way now. Let's get on with our lives. *Together.*"

"I'm not sure that's possible," Kit said softly.

He gave her an odd look. "You don't trust me, do you? That's really what's going on here. You think that because I didn't cut Ben and Mom out of my life, didn't rush to paint a scarlet *A* on their foreheads, that I might do something like what Ben did. You think that because I was engaged to Ronnie Willoughby that there's something lacking in my love for you."

"I'm not sure what I think, Tyler," Kit confessed. "I just know I'm not ready to jump into anything."

They stood there in silence, the dusk deepening around them while a narrow line of sunset gold lingered at the top of the canyon wall. Was he right? Kit wondered as that last glow faded from the canyon. Was it a matter of trust, an inner fear that he was a different man than she'd always believed before Ben and Rella ripped their lives apart? Was this lack of trust another canyon between them that couldn't be crossed or closed?

"Well," he said finally, "it looks as if this means we're going to have to figure out who buys whose half of Canyon Cowboys."

TWENTY-TWO

S ummer storm clouds covered the sky by midmorning the next day, but the air didn't cool. It clung like a warm sponge, thick and oppressive, with an occasional muffled growl of thunder.

They had planned to take the passengers on a hike up the Havasu Creek canyon, where the turquoise water of the creek pooled into fun swimming holes in several places. However, at a rest stop before reaching the creek, they decided against that plan. They couldn't see beyond the canyon rim to the sky over the head of the canyon on the Havasupai Indian Reservation, but the clouds appeared to be massing more heavily in that direction. Kit and Tyler both remembered a time when there wasn't even a sprinkle of rain in the main canyon, but a flash-flood wall of muddy water carried two hikers down the creek and into the river, where the Canyon Cowboys' rafts had helped fish them out safely. Havasu Creek was, in fact, one of the more notorious sites for dangerous flash flooding, not a place to be caught in a downpour.

They instead made an early lunch stop and explored some unusual rock formations near the river. The threat of storm still hanging in the air had Kit feeling uncharacteristically jittery. Or, more likely, she had to admit, holdover nerves from last night's clash with Tyler.

After lunch, as they were floating a stretch of calm water, she also didn't welcome the sight of Les clambering across the other passengers' feet to get back to her position in the motorwell. Now what? she wondered warily.

She expected a complaint, but he started out with congenial small talk. "Great lunch today. You people really know how to put on a feed."

"I'm glad you enjoyed it." She noted the straps of his life jacket were loose, and it hung open over the team logo emblazoned on the front of his red T-shirt. "Would you fasten the straps on your life jacket, please? Falls into the water can happen at the most unlikely times." She half expected an argument, but he was in a cooperative mood and immediately fastened the straps securely.

"I was wondering how far it is to Lava Falls."

"Several miles yet. Lava is a mile or so below Vulcan's Anvil, which is an old volcanic cone in the middle of the river where we always stop for a few minutes."

"There are probably at least five or six of us who want to ride the horn through Lava Falls." Les was still sounding casual, but Kit realized he was now getting around to the point of this pseudo-friendly chat. "Since there are only two horns on each raft, we're wondering how we'll decide who gets to do it."

So that was it. The Three Toads had unexpectedly split up that morning, two taking Kit's raft, the other one going to Tyler's. Kit had wondered at the time if there had been some rift in the tight little trio. Now she realized they were working on a sly agenda. Les and his buddy wanted to grab the horns on this raft; the third Toad planned to snag a horn on Tyler's raft.

"We figure drawing straws, or toothpicks actually," Les said, holding up a half dozen of assorted lengths, "would be the fairest way."

Even if she and Tyler had planned to let anyone ride the horn through Lava, Kit knew she wouldn't trust Les's little scheme any further than she could throw both him and his toothpicks.

"I'm sorry, but no one will be riding the horns through Lava."

The mask of congeniality collapsed. "How come?" Les demanded angrily. "I know a guy who made this trip last year, and he did it!"

"Occasionally we do allow riders on the horn through Lava," Kit conceded carefully, "but the guides discussed it last night and decided conditions were not right this time."

"Yeah? What conditions?"

Les's dangerously inflated opinion about his own horn-riding abilities was one "condition," but Kit didn't blurt that out. "It's simply a safety decision."

"I don't like getting cheated out of what I paid for!"

"I'm sorry you feel that way. But no one will be riding the horns through Lava."

Les, heating Kit's ears with a mutter of invectives, clambered back to his place near the front of the raft. His buddy was on the horn now, and Les leaned over to yell something at him, no doubt the unhappy news Kit had just given him.

She called the riders off the horns just before the raft reached Vulcan's Anvil and announced that there would be no horn riding from this point on. The green water didn't look rough here, but the raft bounced and twisted from the treacherous underwater currents and upsurges as she maneuvered alongside the looming rock. When they pulled away from the Anvil, after the passengers had laughingly touched it or tossed a penny, Tyler's raft was already a hundred yards ahead. It looked oddly tiny and vulnerable against the raw power of the river and the immensity of the canyon looming over it.

A mile downstream, she called a few last-minute reminders and encouragements to the passengers, then braced herself for this rendezvous with the biggest challenge on the river. And, as always, said a quick prayer for guidance and safety.

Tyler's raft was already out of sight, vanished over the edge of the drop into the white-water storm. Kit was concentrating so intensely on entering the savage rapids at the right point that she wasn't really seeing the people in the raft until JoJo yelled, "Hey, you can't...!"

Then she saw what was happening. Against all her orders and warnings, Les had scrambled from his position with the other passengers on the central part of the raft to the right horn.

"Get off there!" she yelled. She slacked the engine power, frantically trying to give him an extra moment to obey. He'd never make it through Lava! *Now!*

Les didn't budge, didn't even look back, just leaned forward like a jockey urging his mount to the finish line. There was no stopping the raft now to make him comply, no braking or turning back, and the distraction had cost Kit precious concentration. The raft swept into the rapids not head-on as it should but angled, leading with the side pontoon into the gaping hole with standing waves looming like a silver-white flame. The side of the raft surged downward on the green slick, then a mountain of water crashed over the raft, inundating everyone. Beneath it the raft rocked and bucked like some roller-coaster car turned into a suicidal submarine.

Lava was a water-terror monster under the best of conditions, and now it had them trapped and helpless. Kit fought to turn the raft, but the little motor, out of the water more than in it, whined like a mosquito helplessly trying to control a downhill locomotive.

She didn't know where they were in the maelstrom, but she knew it was all wrong. There shouldn't be this crazy, kaleidoscope of white water and sky and rocky cliffs, all in upside-down places where they shouldn't be. She knew they were far off course, bumping rocks, whipping from side to side, rearing vertically, like a bronc about to go over backwards, careening out of control.

But the Lord was always *in* control, and even as she battled river and motor and savage white water lifting and smashing them as if playing with a bathtub toy, she called on him for help.

They swept out of the rapids backwards, motor end of the raft leading—and the horn was empty!

"Look for him!" Kit yelled to JoJo. She had her hands full getting the raft straightened around and headed right. Dripping strands of hair streamed water in her eyes, and her feet sloshed in a wash of river water. "See if you can spot him!"

Tyler had taken his raft to shore so he and his passengers could watch them come through, and Kit nosed her raft in beside his. She felt weak and shaky as she pushed wet hair out of her eyes with her wrist, but she knew this was no time to panic. Swiftly she counted heads and found everyone else accounted for.

"What happened?" Tyler yelled. "What went wrong?"

"Les Anderson jumped on the horn at the last minute. He went off somewhere." Her gaze scanned the river below the rapids, searching for a bobbing head.

Tyler leaped from his raft to hers, his arms wrapping around her for a long moment before he leaned back to look at her. "Are you okay?"

She'd just made the worst run of her life through Lava, but she still seemed to be in one piece. "I think so."

"I'll take my raft out to the middle of the river where we can pick Les up. You let JoJo take over as pilot and go downriver about a hundred feet so you can rescue Les in case I miss him."

Kit and JoJo followed his orders. JoJo, with a fine show of river expertise, used the power of the motor to hold the raft against the current while they searched the water rushing by. After five minutes of watching, Tyler guided his raft down to Kit's.

"What do you think?" she called.

"He could have washed by before we started looking for him, I suppose." His gaze swept the river below, then returned to the crashing rapids above them. Even here they had to yell to hear each other over the roar. "But I don't think so."

They both knew the strange tricks the treacherous river could play. There was a raft that had accidentally gotten loose and blithely zipped undamaged through several big rapids on its own, with cargo of wetbags and ammo cans intact when it was recovered. But they also knew that on a less generous occasion the river had held a body hidden underwater for days before finally giving it up.

"If he hasn't come through," Kit said, voicing their mutual fear, "he must be hung up on a rock somewhere."

Tyler nodded grim agreement. The rafts couldn't power upriver through Lava, so Kit knew they would have to try to locate Les from shore. Tyler swiftly issued orders.

"Passengers, everybody out and on shore here," he yelled. "Ryan, you get on the radio and call for a medical helicopter. Whatever's happened, I think Les is going to need it. Then you and JoJo take the raft to the far side and start upriver on foot. It's hard going over there, but do the best you can. Kit and I will search from this side."

The passengers piled out. Les's two buddies offered to help, but Tyler told them that, for now anyway, he wanted all the passengers safely in one place where he didn't have to keep track of them. Kit suspected the two men, who both looked nervous and shaken, were glad they hadn't pulled Les's foolish stunt.

Ryan got on the radio, adjusting dials over a clatter of static. The other guides quickly assembled rescue equipment. Tyler looped a rope and a ring-shaped life preserver over his shoulder. Kit carried another stout rope. The guides were still wearing their life jackets, and Tyler draped binoculars on a strap around his neck.

Tyler led as he and Kit jumped out of the raft and worked their way upriver. It was rough going, the river sometimes nibbling greedily at their feet, sometimes leaping high as if trying to snatch them off the rocks they had to maneuver over and around. The bulky life jacket was an awkward encumbrance as they scrambled over the rocks, but Kit didn't even consider tossing it off. She wouldn't have a chance if she accidentally fell into these crashing rapids without a life jacket.

Even with a life jacket, she knew that Les's chances, if he hadn't been swept on through the rapids, were not good. He could be hung up on the surface, which was disastrous enough. Or he could be trapped underwater, where he hadn't a chance.

Across the river, JoJo and Ryan were just now tying up their raft. She saw JoJo toss the life preserver to shore, then leap out after it.

Kit's athletic body was in good condition, but she still couldn't match Tyler's speed and strength. He stopped on a rocky ledge, reached down to give her a helping hand, and they both rested a few moments as their eyes searched the wild melee of rocks and water. Kit listened, too, but she doubted any scream could be heard above the guttural roar of surging water. And Les might be beyond the screaming stage.

Overhead, the sky was still an ominous mass of clouds, but any rumble of thunder above was now obscured by thunder of the river below.

They struggled on, slipping and sliding on spray-slicked rocks. Kit saw blood seeping from a raw scratch on her hand, more blood on a scraped knee, but she felt no pain. She paused to catch her breath, then yelled, "There, caught on that rock!"

About a third of the way across the river something red clung to a rock, surges of white water battering it as if trying to demolish or punish it.

"He was wearing a red T-shirt!" she panted.

Tyler lifted the binoculars to his eyes, then silently handed them to Kit. Les wasn't wearing the red T-shirt now, she knew as she gazed at the tattered scrap of fabric whipping against the rock. The river had ripped it off him. And what had it done with Les himself?

For long moments their gazes searched the wild stretch of river. Across from them, on a rough outcropping of rock, Ryan and JoJo were doing the same. Determinedly, Tyler started off again, and Kit followed.

Water surged beside them, and misty spray kept filling Kit's eyes, but her mouth felt desert parched and her heart jackhammered in her chest. She had to rest. She stopped, head down, damp hair straggling in her eyes, hands resting on her knees as she panted for breath.

She would never have seen him if she hadn't stopped at just that moment, at just that angle, because he was almost invisible, caught behind a pair of rocks a dozen feet from shore. His head lolled limply, surges of water sloshing over it. "Tyler!" she screamed. "Tyler!"

He scrambled back to her, kneeling beside her to see where she pointed. He scanned the limp form through the binoculars, then voiced what Kit already suspected.

"There's no point in throwing him the life preserver. He's in no shape to grab it." Even with his mouth only inches from her ear, he had to yell over the roar of the rapids. "I'll have to go in after him."

"Tyler, you can't do that!" she gasped. The distance from shore might be only a dozen feet, but those dozen feet were like running a gauntlet of hungry sharks. "You'll just be swept downstream yourself."

"I think I can work my way out to him." Tyler's eyes scanned the jumbled rocks between the shoreline and the limp body. "I'll tie a rope around myself. You can hold it and keep me from washing downstream." He ducked out from under the strap of the binoculars, handed them to her, and grabbed the rope she carried.

She stood motionless, her gaze trying to pick out a possible route through crashing water and jumbled rocks. She shivered. A route or a death trap? Maybe it could be done, but…

"Tyler, look at us!" She flung out her arms, palms upward, feeling helpless and insignificant. "I can't hold you!"

"You're strong and tough…"

But when his eyes swept her slim frame, they both knew what she said was true. He outweighed her by a good seventy-five pounds. Strong as she was, she'd never be able to hold his weight against the treacherous whirls and surges of white water multiplied by the relentless force of the current. He glanced around, searching for something to anchor the rope to, but no trees grew close enough to tie to, and the rocks were too large to encircle with a rope or too unstable looking.

Kit put a hand on his arm. "We'll have to call in a rescue helicopter."

"There isn't time. But we can get some passengers or JoJo and Ryan here to help."

Their glances snapped to the limp body precariously caught between the rocks. Even as they watched, it rose and fell, shifting ominously, its position no more secure than a bit of driftwood bobbing in an eddy. His life jacket appeared intact, the collar holding his head up, but it was all too obvious that if he wasn't already dead, he would be soon. The river could smash him against the rocks or drag him under at any moment. They both knew there was no time to seek or wait for help.

"I'll just have to do it by myself." Without hesitation, Tyler looped a coil of rope around his body.

"No." Kit held out a hand to stop him. "I'll go after him. You're strong enough to hold me with a rope."

"You? That's impossible!"

"No, I can do it." Her size and strength might not be sufficient to hold Tyler's heavier weight, but she could do this. "I'm going after him."

She already had the other end of the rope around her own

waist. "Are you going to hold the rope for me or not?" she challenged when he just stood there staring at her in dismay.

Tyler glanced again at Les's lolling head, at the rise of his feet to the surface as the surging waves tugged to claim him as a victim. He nodded grimly, then turned swiftly efficient.

"Okay, you rest for a minute. Relax as best you can. You can't go into the water winded and worn out. I'll do this."

She nodded, knowing she needed to gather every ounce of strength that was in her. With efficient silence he looped the rope around her, running it down between her legs, making a rough harness of it rather than a single loop, checking and tightening knots. She took deep breaths, willing herself not to tighten up and risk muscle cramping, keeping her gaze targeted on Les's limp form except for brief moments when it flicked to Tyler's blond hair as he bent over her. She resisted a strange and foolish urge to run her fingers through the mist-damp curls.

"Is he still there?" Tyler asked when he finally straightened.

It felt to Kit as if she had been trapped there in the cold mist of the spray, caught in the endless roar of the rapids, surrounded by an alien landscape of dark rocks, for hours, although she knew it couldn't have been more than bare minutes. "He's still there."

But maybe not for long. The current played with the helpless form, a white-water cat toying with its prey.

"Okay, here's what you do when you reach him." Tyler's eyes locked on hers and his hands clamped her shoulders, only their pressure betraying that the calm instructions he issued were not some simple coaching on one of their childhood schemes. He showed her how the extra rope was tied and how to release it. "There won't be time to do a Girl Scout job of tying it around him. You don't dare be in the water more than a few minutes. Just do the best you can *fast*."

She nodded.

"Ready?" he asked.

She nodded again, the taste of fear a burn of cold acid in her mouth. She'd been a swimmer all her life, blithely cannonballing into creeks or rivers from heights that would have made her mother faint if she knew. She'd water raced with Tyler and played king-of-the-rock games with him, recklessly pushing and shoving each other, splashing and climbing to fight again. But this, this wasn't swimming. This was descent into watery jaws ridged with snapping white teeth, a surging trap that almost seemed to have a malevolent, violent will of its own.

"Kit, you don't have to do this."

A wry thought slammed across her mind. Les Anderson had gotten himself into this jam with his own stubborn recklessness, and there were people she'd much rather risk her life for than this man. But the Lord wasn't offering that choice. She didn't answer what had almost sounded like a plea from Tyler, just crawled and scrambled over the rocks, ropes trailing behind her, until water licked hungrily at her feet.

She hesitated, and Tyler wrapped his arms around her, the embrace passionate in spite of the bulky life jackets and harness of rope between them. "I won't let go of you," he vowed. "Not now, not ever!"

Kit had no time to think what that meant. They stood a moment longer in a union of fervent prayer, and words from the Psalms, more fierce than her fear, rose within her. "*When I am afraid, I will trust in you.*"

Then, trusting the Lord, trusting Tyler, she plunged into the water.

TWENTY-THREE

E ven at the edge of the water the swift current instantly caught her, the cold an icy threat against her skin. But as she struggled along the route they had set out, not so much swimming as floundering, she could feel the solid anchor of the rope harnessed around her body. Feel it holding her back when the water tried to snatch her away, feel it releasing to give her freedom to struggle onward. Feel Tyler and the Lord holding her tightly.

She had to snatch desperate gasps of air between the white-water surges rolling over her. They filled her eyes and nose and mouth and ears. But she wasn't conscious of the cold now. Several times the ominous suck and pull of the undertow threatened to drag her under, but the steady pressure of the rope sustaining her never faltered. Like an unbreakable bond, it held her, gave her a solid holding point from which to forge ahead.

There, there he was! A sly twist of the current flung her against him. She tried not to recoil from the strange feel of his leaden body giving imitation life by the tug and swirl of the water. She couldn't tell if he was dead or alive, and she didn't waste time try-ing to find out.

Following Tyler's instructions, but working with hands that now felt clumsy and unwieldy, she got the extra rope around him. She couldn't construct a harness as Tyler had done for her, but she worked the rope under one arm, then the other. Sometimes it felt as if he were fighting her, trying to keep her from helping him as he twisted and turned, but she knew it was only the water, fiercely battling her for control of this intended victim. Finally she knotted the rope, then shoved herself to one side and lifted her arm to sig-nal Tyler to start pulling.

The rope tightened. Kit could almost see it stretching! Les's limp form moved, causing a ripple in the surging water. And then it stopped! Desperately she yanked on him, but nothing happened. Sluggishly, knowing she could be coming close to hypothermia in the cold water, Kit maneuvered around the rocks. She held to a slick rock with one hand and desperately fumbled underwater with the other.

There, his hand! Caught between the rocks. Using all the strength she still possessed, she yanked upward. Knowing she wasn't doing his hand any good scraping it through the rocks, knowing she had to do it to set him free before the water dragged him under.

He was loose! Kit glanced toward shore and saw that Tyler wasn't where she had left him. He'd moved downstream. Her sluggish mind took a moment to comprehend, but then she realized that rather than try to pull both her and Les upstream, he was using the current to help bring them into shore.

She followed behind the limp form, guiding it between rocks, whipping the rope over one when it became entangled, frantically keeping herself disentangled from his drifting legs. Through water-blurred eyes she caught glimpses of Tyler braced behind a rock, muscles straining as he fought to bring both Kit and Les in. At a couple of feet from shore her knees struck an underwater ledge, a blow hard enough to make her numbed mind reel, but she scrambled onto it gratefully.

Tyler used one hand to help her out of the water, the other still locked on the rope looped around Les. Rock scraped her skin as he pulled her out of the water, but the pain didn't penetrate her numbed flesh. Together, though Kit knew she was little help, they dragged Les out. Then she collapsed on a rock, shivering violently, too little strength remaining to help further, only now truly conscious of the closeness of her own brush with death.

Tyler didn't look up as he stripped the life jacket off Les and stretched him out so he could do CPR. Les's skin looked bloodless, the vicious gash in his head pale and ragged. Only a tattered ring of red around his neck remained of the T-shirt now, and abrasions and cuts disfigured his body everywhere. His ride on the horn in Lava Falls had not come cheaply.

"Is he alive?"

"I don't know yet. Get back to the raft. Send someone up here with a sleeping bag or something to wrap around him." Tyler's tone was curtly decisive, but Kit wasn't offended. She appreciated his take-charge leadership. Her own mind felt as if it were filled with icy slush, trapped in slow motion. "Tell Ryan to get on the radio again and find out how soon we can expect help and where we should meet the helicopter. Send JoJo with a first-aid kit."

He glanced up, saw her weak and shivering. His hands, already poised to start the CPR, paused, and she saw the conflict flare in his eyes, saw that he wanted to drop everything and wrap her in his arms. He stretched out a hand to grasp hers.

"I'm okay," she gasped, taking strength from his grip. "I'll get help."

He nodded, and she stumbled back toward the raft, even in her dazed state desperately aware of the dangers of the slick rocks and narrow places where she had to edge close to the water. The other raft was churning across the rough water below the rapid now. JoJo and Ryan must have seen what was going on over here.

People from the raft ran to meet her, and she gasped out Tyler's orders. Someone wrapped a sleeping bag around her shoulders, and she was dimly aware of a hum of excited conversation, a clatter of radio static, and then someone cleansing and treating her wounds.

A few minutes later, using the sleeping bag as a makeshift stretcher, the men returned to the rafts with Les.

"He's alive. Barely." Tyler gently pushed her back to the raft when she struggled to stand. "We're to meet the helicopter about a mile downriver, where there's a better landing spot. You just take it easy. JoJo can handle the raft."

They put Les on Tyler's raft, where his two buddies braced and held him. The helicopter arrived within fifteen minutes after they put in at the meeting point downstream. The medical team didn't offer any opinion on Les's condition other than terse agreement that he was alive.

This wasn't one of their usual camping spots, but Tyler decided it would do for tonight, and the rather somber passengers seemed to agree.

By mealtime, however, spirits were lifting. The storm clouds, after a minor sprinkle, had passed on, leaving blue sky and a fresh-washed canyon heat that Kit's chilled body welcomed. The men wouldn't let her help with dinner preparations. She teased them, saying she'd remember that whenever she wanted to get out of cooking all she had to do was take a dunking in the river. But she was grateful for their concern. She no longer felt as if her blood were stalled motionlessly in her veins, but all her scrapes and bruises were now making themselves known. Little Lisa solicitously Band-Aided scratches that had been missed earlier.

Kit thanked Tyler when he personally brought her a plate of spaghetti and salad and grilled French bread. She wasn't sure where things stood between them now. Tyler's statement, when he handed her the plate, did nothing to clear the situation.

"We have something to talk about, but we'll do it later. I want you rested and thinking clearly, not brain-numb from cold water."

Kit indignantly started to protest that she wasn't brain-numb, but because her brain did feel as if it were still operating on low voltage, she simply nodded.

He hadn't said anything momentous by the time the passengers loaded out on the helicopter at Whitmore Wash the following morning, Kit and Lisa sharing a final hug. Neither was he conversational on the overnight float down to Pierce Ferry, and the quiet trip gave Kit time to think. Time to look within herself, to thank the Lord for watching over her there in the cold river, time to think about Ben and Rella, about forgiveness and trust and the paths of their lives. Time to surreptitiously watch Tyler and ponder his terse statement that he wanted to discuss something with her. Ownership of Canyon Cowboys, of course. But had he decided to sell out to her? Or try to browbeat her into selling out to him?

Red Sizemore met them with the truck at Pierce Ferry, and, hours later, Kit wearily retrieved her pickup at the Canyon Cowboys' office. At the motel she luxuriated in a hot shower and shampoo, then collapsed on the bed for a nap. A hard knocking on the door woke her. Shaking the sleep out of her head, she padded barefoot to the door.

Tyler stood there, freshly shaved, hair with that rowdy, just-showered look. He inspected the scrapes and bruises visible around her clean shorts and blue T-shirt. For a moment, from the look in his eyes, she thought he was recklessly going to wrap his arms around her. But, shoving back unexpected disappointment, she realized she'd apparently misread the look because all he said was, "How are you?"

"A little worse for wear, but okay. At least I don't think I'm brain-numb now," she added defensively. Actually, she thought wryly, there was nothing like a brush with death to clear your mind.

"I didn't mean that the way it sounded," he muttered. "I just didn't want to take advantage of you in a weak moment."

"Business is business," she murmured.

He gave her a blank look but didn't ask what that meant. "May I come in?"

She hesitated, then opened the door wider and stepped back to scoop a damp towel off the floor and retrieve some discarded clothes. "It's kind of a mess in here." But Tyler already knew she wasn't the world's greatest housekeeper, of course.

"First, I called and checked on Les Anderson. He got water in his lungs, of course, and hypothermia from being in the cold water so long. He'll be in the hospital a while, but apparently he's tough—if a little short on good judgment—and will recover."

Kit nodded, relieved to hear the news about Les. "Look, before we get into an argument about ownership of Canyon Cowboys..."

"You think I came over here to talk business about Canyon Cowboys?" He stared down at her, amazement in his look, anger in his voice.

She took a wary step backward. "Our last discussion suggested a rather sharp difference of opinion about who should own the company."

"Kit, forget the company!" His arm slashed the air in angry impatience. "Let's sell it. Give it away. Disband it. Whatever it takes!"

"Whatever it takes to do what?"

"To close this canyon between us. If Canyon Cowboys is somehow standing between us, let's get rid of it. Kit, I love you. I've loved you even when we were arguing and condemning each other. I've loved you even when I was denying it to myself or doing my best to beat it down."

Kit blinked. She had the strangest mental picture of him standing on a rocky shore, desperately flailing away at *love* with a battered oar.

"Canyon Cowboys has always been important to me, but out there on the river, when you were on the end of that rope and I knew I held your life in my hands..." His hands fisted, opening and closing. "It went a long ways toward getting priorities straight in my head. And Canyon Cowboys isn't at the top of the list."

"What is?"

"You. Us. Kit, we can't always agree on everything, not even on Christian matters. We're human. But you trusted me with your life there on the river." His hands enclosed her shoulders in a rough grip, but his eyes were tender, almost pleading. "Can't you also trust me with your heart?"

Trust me with your heart. Another vision came to mind, a photo of a big dog and a fuzzy yellow duck, and the sweet, playful words that accompanied it: *"We may have our differences, but I really wuv you."*

"Kit, I don't think we can understand what the Lord was doing in everything that's happened, but I think he's given us a second chance. Let's not ruin our lives with mistakes Ben and Mom made. Or mistakes you and I have made in the past. Let's grab this second chance the Lord has offered us."

"You're willing to trust me with your heart after what I did?" She shook her head as she gathered the thoughts that had churned through her mind ever since her encounter with the river. "I've finally realized that I'm not necessarily the innocent party that I've made myself out to be in all this."

"We both did what we believed was right."

She nodded. "And I guess I still don't see how I could have responded any differently to what Dad and Rella did. But..."

Tyler picked up her thought. "It's possible the Lord truly led us down different paths, that this was his way of bringing his message home to Ben and my mother at the end."

Kit frowned. "But now I also wonder if I didn't look to God's

Word to back up what I'd already decided. If I wasn't so much searching for the Lord's guidance as I was looking for validation and support for my own decision."

Tyler nodded slowly. "There could have been some of that in my search, too," he admitted.

"What I do know is that I shouldn't have condemned you for taking the path you did or tried to force you to take the path I thought was right. It was between you and the Lord even more than between you and me, and I ask for your forgiveness."

"If you want it, it's there," he said simply. "I love you."

Words came to her then, words not sought but offered from the Lord's Word. "Love is patient, love is kind…it keeps no record of wrongs." She felt the fountain of love that she had so long kept under powerful restraint burst through the artificial barriers. Felt the warm waters of love cascade through her.

"Out there on the river, you said you weren't letting me go, not now, not ever."

He nodded, but his gaze searched hers. "I wish that could be true. But I can't hold you if you don't want to be held, so the decision is up to you, Kit."

"Then dig out that old ring, Tyler McCord," she said fiercely. "Because I love you, and we're going to use it."

And they reached across the canyon, crossed it on a bridge of love, and stepped into each other's arms.

Dear Reader,

My husband and I had been thinking for several years about taking a raft trip through the Grand Canyon, but I had strong misgivings when we actually stepped into the raft at the river's edge. I'm a person who can't swim more than a few feet, a person who always edges tentatively into the water rather than gleefully diving in, a person who loves the outdoors but whose athletic abilities are nonexistent. And when the avalanche of water hit us at the first big rapids, my panicky thought was, *Seven days of this? No way. I'll never make it.*

But I did make it, and the trip turned out to be exciting and fun, and most of all, awe-inspiring to see the beauty of what the Lord had created. There seems to be something very special about communing with the Lord when you're surrounded by the breathtaking wonder of creation.

Yet his wonders are all around us, even if we can't be out in the midst of some magnificent wilderness setting. They're with us every day, in the tiny perfection of a baby's hand, the flight of a bird outside the window while we're doing dishes, the anticipation of a flower when we plant a few seeds in a pot on the patio. These are times to give thanks for what the Lord has given us, wherever we are.

And I give special thanks to you, my readers, for your encouraging letters and cards.

Lorena Mc Courtney

Jude 2.

Write to Lorena McCourtney
c/o Palisades
P.O. Box 1720
Sisters, Oregon 97759

THE PALISADES LINE

Look for these new releases at your local bookstore. If the title you seek is not in stock, the store may order you a copy using the ISBN listed.

Dalton's Dilemma, Lynn Bulock
ISBN 1-57673-238-X
Lacey Robbins, single mother of her sister's four children, is seeking adventure. But she never expected to find it by running into—literally!—handsome Jack Dalton at the roller rink. And she never expected the attraction between them to change her life forever....

Heartland Skies, Melody Carlson
ISBN 1-57673-264-9
Jayne Morgan moves to the small town of Paradise with the prospect of marriage, a new job, and plenty of horses to ride. But when her fiancé dumps her, she's left with loose ends. Then she wins a horse in a raffle, and the handsome rancher who boards her horse makes things look decidedly better.

Shades of Light, Melody Carlson
ISBN 1-57673-283-5
When widow Gwen Sullivan's daughter leaves for college, she discovers she can't bear her empty nest and takes a job at an interior decorating firm. But tedious work and a fussy boss leave her wondering if she's made the right move. Then Oliver Black, a prominent businessman, solicits her services and changes her mind....

Memories, Peggy Darty
ISBN 1-57673-171-5
In this sequel to *Promises,* Elizabeth Calloway is left with amnesia after witnessing a hit-and-run accident. Her husband, Michael, takes her on a vacation to Cancún so that she can relax and recover her memory. What they don't realize is that a killer is following them, hoping to wipe out Elizabeth's memory permanently....

Spirits, Peggy Darty (October 1998)
ISBN 1-57673-304-1
Picking up where *Memories* left off, the Calloways take a vacation to Angel Valley to find a missing woman. They enlist the help of a local writer who is an expert in Smoky Mountain legend and uncover a strange web of folklore and spirits.

Remembering the Roses, Marion Duckworth
ISBN 1-57673-236-3
Sammie Sternberg is trying to escape her memories of the man who betrayed her and ends up in a small town on the Olympic Peninsula in Washington. There she opens her dream business—an antique shop in an old Victorian—and meets a reclusive watercolor artist who helps to heal her broken heart.

Waterfalls, Robin Jones Gunn
ISBN 1-57673-221-5
In a visit to Glenbrooke, Oregon, Meredith Graham meets movie star Jacob Wilde and is sure he's the one. But when Meri puts her foot in her mouth, things fall apart. Is isn't until the two of them get thrown together working on a book-and-movie project that Jacob realizes his true feelings, and this time he's the one who's starstruck.

China Doll, Barbara Jean Hicks
ISBN 1-57673-262-2
Bronson Bailey is having a mid-life crisis: after years of globe-trotting in his journalism career, he's feeling restless. Georgine Nichols has also reached a turning point: after years of longing for a child, she's decided to adopt. The problem is, now she's fallen in love with Bronson, and he doesn't want a child.

Angel in the Senate, Kristen Johnson Ingram
ISBN 1-57673-263-0
Newly elected senator Megan Likely heads to Washington with high hopes for making a difference in government. But accusations of election fraud, two shocking murders, and threats on her life make the Senate take a back seat. She needs to find answers, but she's not sure who she can trust anymore.

Irish Rogue, Annie Jones
ISBN 1-57673-189-8
Michael Shaughnessy has paid the price for stealing a pot of gold, and now he's ready to make amends to the people he's hurt. Fiona O'Dea is number one on his list. The problem is, Fiona doesn't want to let Michael near enough to hurt her again. But before she knows it, he's taken his Irish charm and worked his way back into her life…and her heart.

Beloved, Debra Kastner
ISBN 1-57673-331-9
Wanted: A part-time pastor with a full-time heart for a wedding ministry. When wedding coordinator Kate Logan places the ad for a pastor, she doesn't expect a man like Todd Jensen to apply. But she quickly learns that he's perfect for the job—and perfect for her heart.

On Assignment, Marilyn Kok

ISBN 1-57673-279-7

When photographer Tessa Brooks arrives in Singapore for an assignment, she's both excited and nervous about seeing her ex-fiancé, banker Michael Lawton. Michael has mixed feelings, too: he knows he still loves Tessa, but will he ever convince her that they can get past the obstacle of their careers and make their relationship work?

Forgotten, Lorena McCourtney

ISBN 1-57673-222-3

A woman wakes up in an Oregon hospital with no memory of who she is. When she's identified as Kat Cavanaugh, she returns to her home in California. As Kat struggles to recover her memory, she meets a fiancé she doesn't trust and an attractive neighbor who can't believe how she's changed. She begins to wonder if she's really Kat Cavanaugh, but if she isn't, what happened to the real Kat?

Canyon, Lorena McCourtney

ISBN 1-57673-287-8

Kit Holloway and Tyler McCord are wildly in love, planning their wedding, and looking forward to a summer of whitewater rafting through the Grand Canyon. Then the actions of two people they love rip apart their relationship. Can their love survive, or will their differences prove to be too much?

Rustlers, Karen Rispin

ISBN 1-57673-292-4

Amber Lacey is on the run—from her home, from her career, and from God. She ends up working on a ranch in western

Alberta and trying to keep the secrets of her past from the man she's falling in love with. But then sinister dealings on the ranch force Amber to confront the mistakes she's made—and turn back to the God who never gave up on her.

The Key, Gayle Roper
ISBN 1-57673-223-1
On Kristie Matthews's first day living on an Amish farm, she gets bitten by a dog and is rushed to the emergency room by a handsome stranger. In the ER, an elderly man in the throes of a heart attack hands her a key and tells her to keep it safe. Suddenly odd accidents begin to happen to her, but no one's giving her any answers.

The Document, Gayle Roper (October 1998)
ISBN 1-57673-295-9
While Cara Bentley is sorting through things after the death of her grandfather, she stumbles upon evidence that he was adopted. Determined to find her roots, she heads to Lancaster County and settles in at an Amish farm. She wants to find out who she is, but she can't help wondering: if it weren't for the money in John Bentley's will, would anyone else care about her identity?

ANTHOLOGIES

Fools for Love, Ball, Brooks, Jones
ISBN 1-57673-235-5
By Karen Ball: Kitty starts pet-sitting, but when her clients turn out to be more than she can handle, she enlists help from a handsome handyman.

By Jennifer Brooks: Caleb Murphy tries to acquire a book collection from a widow, but she has one condition: he must marry her granddaughter first.

By Annie Jones: A college professor who has been burned by love vows not to be fooled twice, until her ex-fiancé shows up and ruins her plans!

Heart's Delight, Ball, Hicks, Noble
ISBN 1-57673-220-7

By Karen Ball: Corie receives a Valentine's Day date from her sisters and thinks she's finally found the one...until she learns she went out with the wrong man.

By Barbara Jean Hicks: Carina and Reid are determined to break up their parents' romance, but when it looks like things are working, they have a change of heart.

By Diane Noble: Two elderly bird-watchers set aside their differences to try to save a park from disaster, but learn they've bitten off more than they can chew.

Be sure to look for any of the 1997 titles you may have missed:

Surrender, Lynn Bulock (ISBN 1-57673-104-9)
Single mom Cassie Neel accepts a blind date from her children for her birthday.

Wise Man's House, Melody Carlson (ISBN 1-57673-070-0)
A young widow buys her childhood dream house, and a mysterious stranger moves into her caretaker's cottage.

Moonglow, Peggy Darty (ISBN 1-57673-112-X)
Tracy Kosell comes back to Moonglow, Georgia, and investigates a case with a former schoolmate, who's now a detective.

Promises, **Peggy Darty** (ISBN 1-57673-149-9)
A Christian psychologist asks her detective husband to help her find a dangerous woman.

Texas Tender, **Sharon Gillenwater** (ISBN 1-57673-111-1)
Shelby Nolan inherits a watermelon farm and asks the sheriff for help when two elderly men begin digging holes in her fields.

Clouds, **Robin Jones Gunn** (ISBN 1-57673-113-8)
Flight attendant Shelly Graham runs into her old boyfriend, Jonathan Renfield, and learns he's engaged.

Sunsets, **Robin Jones Gunn** (ISBN 1-57673-103-0)
Alissa Benson has a run-in at work with Brad Phillips, and is more than a little upset when she finds out he's her neighbor!

Snow Swan, **Barbara Jean Hicks** (ISBN 1-57673-107-3)
Toni, an unwed mother and a recovering alcoholic, falls in love for the first time. But if Clark finds out the truth about her past, will he still love her?

Irish Eyes, **Annie Jones** (ISBN 1-57673-108-1)
Julia Reed gets drawn into a crime involving a pot of gold and has her life turned upside-down by Interpol agent Cameron O'Dea.

Father by Faith, **Annie Jones** (ISBN 1-57673-117-0)
Nina Jackson buys a dude ranch and hires cowboy Clint Cooper as her foreman, but her son, Alex, thinks Clint is his new daddy!

Stardust, **Shari MacDonald** (ISBN 1-57673-109-X)
Gillian Spencer gets her dream assignment but is shocked to learn she must work with Maxwell Bishop, who once broke her heart.

Kingdom Come, **Amanda MacLean** (ISBN 1-57673-120-0)
Ivy Rose Clayborne, M.D., pairs up with the grandson of the coal baron to fight the mining company that is ravaging her town.

Dear Silver, **Lorena McCourtney** (ISBN 1-57673-110-3)
When Silver Sinclair receives a letter from Chris Bentley ending their relationship, she's shocked, since she's never met the man!

Enough! **Gayle Roper** (ISBN 1-57673-185-5)
When Molly Gregory gets fed up with her three teenaged children, she announces that she's going on strike.

A Mother's Love, **Bergren, Colson, MacLean**
(ISBN 1-57673-106-5)
Three heartwarming stories share the joy of a mother's love.

Silver Bells, **Bergren, Krause, MacDonald**
(ISBN 1-57673-119-7)
Three novellas focus on romance during Christmastime.